The
Good Time
Gospel
Boys

The
Good Time
Gospel
Boys

BILLY BITTINGER

St. Martin's Press/New York

This is a work of fiction, and any resemblance to persons living or dead is strictly coincidental, although, of course, D.W. Griffith was a very real person and a great pioneer in filmmaking. It is in this context that his name is used, but the situation and the actions are creations of the author's imagination and never happened.

THE GOOD TIME GOSPEL BOYS.
Copyright © 1987 by Billy Bittinger.
All rights reserved.
Printed in the United States of America.
No part of this book may be used or reproduced
in any manner whatsoever without written permission
except in the case of brief quotations
embodied in critical articles or reviews.
For information, address St. Martin's Press,
175 Fifth Avenue, New York, N.Y. 10010.

Design by M. Paul

Typeset by Fisher Composition, Inc.

Library of Congress Cataloging-in-Publication Data

Bittinger, Billy.
    The Good Time Gospel Boys.

    I. Title.
PS3552.I7738G6   1987   813'.54   86-26306
ISBN 0-312-00013-8

First Edition

10 9 8 7 6 5 4 3 2 1

To
L.F., who does not approve of this book,
and
Maggie, who says that she doesn't

ACKNOWLEDGMENTS

My thanks to Dale, who forced me into writing this book and then spent hours happily red-penciling the manuscript.

My gratitude to Meg, Laurie, Brad, Mark, Larry, and Gary, who thought this book was a masterpiece just because they are related to me.

A special thank-you to Pat Spears, who used her typing skills to correct mistakes made by a berserk computer printer.

PART ONE

1940

1

Every time the Good Time Gospel Quartet came to town, Lucille Byrd got laid. Since Lucille was six feet tall and weighed three hundred pounds buck naked, and since the Good Time Gospel Quartet only came once a year, a sultry weekend in August, once a year was plenty and at that it took all four of the Gospel Boys to take care of her. She gave in return, however. Each year, when the quartet rolled in, they parked their bus behind the Holy Roller church and went directly into the sanctuary to make sure the piano was halfway in tune. As soon as she spotted the bus from where she was waiting at the general store across the street, Lucille would run right over to the church to greet them, and then that night she'd perform with them. She would sing, Lord, how she would sing.

She'd stand there, monolithic, tight black curls framing her white moon face, wide chocolate-brown eyes scrunched ecstatically closed, open red mouth pointed straight up to heaven, and the rich, molasses contralto sounds would soar up to the roof, down the aisles and out the open windows. The Good Timers and Lucille really rocked on "Church in the Wildwood," and every year Brother Zack Hayes got the glory when they would move into the chorus and start booming out, "Come, come-come to the Church in the Wildwood." Once, Zack had the spirit come down on him so bad that he moved out in the aisle and started dancing and speaking in tongues.

Of course, Brother Zack was a true Pentecostal, but the Holy Rollers weren't the only denomination that attended when the quartet sang. For a fact, everybody in town was there, the Southern Methodist Episcopals, the Baptists, the backsliders and the unsaved, even the colored people were bound to be there sitting in the back pews. When Lucille did her solo of "Amazing grace, how sweet the sound, that saved a wretch like me" all the coloreds clapped along, humming and swaying. Even Miss Ora and Miss Nora Philpot, the only two left of the family that founded the town, who lived out a little ways on what was still called the Philpot Plantation and who always wore white gloves and veiled hats and corsets to the gospel sing even though it was the dog days of August, sometimes clapped discreetly along with the coloreds.

When the last of the piano keys were pounded, the paper fans courtesy of McAfee's Funeral Home put back in the racks on the pews, and sleeping young ones slung up on their mamas' shoulders, everybody passed out to the churchyard and stood in the heavy, laced-with-heat-lightning air, and visited for a spell. The men would talk about the tobacco crop and either too much or too little rain, the women about canning tomatoes, and the older children would race around to the back of the church to run and push and shove each other in the excitement of being up so late at a special event.

The Good Time Gospel bus was always parked out back too, and every year the children approached it with awe. Even though the Good Time Gospel Quartet had been coming to town for the past ten years in the same blue bus with their name written right on the outside in bold red and yellow script, it was always a topic of conversation that the same bus had traveled through Tennessee and Georgia and Alabama and West Virginia. All those places had been studied in geography class, but nobody in town had ever been to any of them. The furthest anyone got was over to Boonetown to go to the moving picture show, and that didn't happen very often because it took a quarter to get in and in 1940 the Great Depression was still happening. Besides, it was an everlasting source of amazement to consider that the Gospel Boys truly slept on a bus so that they'd have a place to stay wherever they rolled. Of course, they didn't have to do any cooking on the bus because every woman in town considered it a real honor to get the boys for a meal. It was told that last year Myna Norberta Smoot had served the Gospel Boys two kinds of chicken—fried and baked with dressing—and made a Lord Baltimore cake and a lemon meringue pie, which certainly gave the other ladies in town room for thought in figuring out how they could top that.

Too soon the children's mothers' shrill voices would come circling around to the back of the church calling for Ben and Alice and Norma and all the rest. The children came slowly back to the front of the church, dragging their feet through the puddles of darkness, reluctant to let go of the excitement. The Clay twins and Thelma Taylor begged their mamas to let the twins spend the night over to the Taylors, and finally both women said all right if they promised to be good and not give any trouble. And because Lizzie Clay and Alice Taylor agreed to humor the girls in this seemingly innocent request, the town finally discovered that Lucille Byrd got laid every year by the Good Time Gospel Quartet. And the night of that discovery became the time for retribution, an accounting that dated from the year when three men rode over the great buffalo trails down into the valley and founded this town by a sulphur springs.

PART TWO

1930

2

Lizzie LeCompte was the most luscious piece of ass to ever come out of LeCompte Bottoms, or at least that's what all the boys in Taylor Springs said. Lizzie was small, with a generous bosom and a heart-shaped behind, and had a face graced with a bee-stung mouth, a *retroussé* nose, and enormous hazel eyes fringed with thick black lashes, all of it framed by a short cap of golden brown curls. She knew all the latest songs that were crooned on her tinny-sounding radio, painted her fingernails and her toenails bright red, and got all the latest movie magazines the minute they arrived by mail truck at McAfee's General Store.

She'd sashay right in and drawl, "Howdy, Mr. Bob." Every male head would turn in her direction and she'd look around, hungry like, and then turn on her dazzling smile. Oh, she knew what she was doing all right.

"Well, hello there, Lizzie." Bob McAfee winked at her. "How's your mama today?"

"She's feeling right pert today, thank you. Seems like she's getting over that sinking spell she had last week. She's improving a lot, least that's what Doc Smoot said."

Ruth Taylor was over at the piece goods counter trying
to decide whether dotted swiss or organdy would make up
prettier in that new Butterick pattern. When she heard
Lizzie's drawl, she frowned, but then forced a smile on her
face as she walked over toward the girl.

"I'm real glad to hear that about your mama, Lizzie.
Do you think she'll be able to get to the Sewing Circle this
Wednesday? We surely have missed her."

"I declare I don't know, Mrs. Taylor. She hasn't said
anything about it. But I'll ask her, and when Bucky comes
to pick me up tonight to go to the picture show, why, I'll
tell him and then he can let you know."

Ruth grimaced. She would just as soon that her son
Bucky had nothing to do with Lizzie LeCompte, but knew
she couldn't stop him from chasing that girl any more than
you could stop a tomcat that sniffs a female in heat. Why,
her own daughter Becky had told her that all the girls at the
high school knew that Lizzie LeCompte was loose and had
already done it with two boys on the football team. Ruth
just told her, "Now, you just hush your mouth because I
don't want to hear words like that come out of you. Even if
there is some truth in them, ladies don't talk that way. Besides, it isn't Christian to repeat something like that."

And now Bucky—who was one of the most popular
boys at the high school even if it was her saying it and a
football star to boot and had a chance to get a football scholarship to college, at least that's what the new coach was
saying, and since it was the Depression the good Lord
knows it was the only way he'd get there—was flitting
around that same LeCompte girl.

What made it even worse was that not only was Bucky
carrying on with the girl, so was his best friend, Junie
Hayes. Why, they'd been little tads together, and now they
played football together, and the coach said Junie had a

chance at a scholarship, too. Ruth knew that Lizzie could sure stir up a hornet's nest between those two boys.

Ruth purred, "Why, I didn't know Bucky was carrying you to the picture show tonight. I thought him and Junie said something about filling out papers with the coach for that football scholarship."

"Well, Junie might just come along with us, Mrs. Taylor. You know how those two boys are. They just stick tighter than glue. Maybe they're going to fill out those old papers before they come over to my house."

Ruth felt even more pained when she considered the LeCompte house. It wasn't even a house, more like a shack sitting down there at the end of the graveled road in the Bottoms. Why, right at that house the road turned to dirt and not twenty-five feet away colored town began. To think that her Bucky was calling at a place that had not seen a coat of paint in Lord knows how long, didn't even have any screens on the windows, and had a front porch that was sagging pert near to the ground.

Of course, all the houses down in LeCompte Bottoms were nothing but shacks, a far cry from what the place once had been, or at least what Ruth had been told about it. The Bottoms had been settled by a French family that had come in to work the salt lick just after the town was founded. And Bullet Taylor, her own Bucky's ancestor and founder of the town, had taken one of the LeCompte daughters for his wife. Her portrait was still hanging up in the very house where the Taylors lived to this day. The portrait showed a young girl with flashing black eyes whose glossy chestnut hair curled down to reach an incredibly tiny waist. Incredible because Georgette had borne Bullet Taylor thirteen children in as many years, seven of whom had lived.

For a fact it was Georgette LeCompte Taylor who had built the house after old Bullet had fallen in the springs one night and drowned. Just took all the money the old man had made from the salt lick and built a big stone mansion up on the hill so she could look down at the springs and the Bottoms. So it was a LeCompte that had left succeeding Taylors their legacy of red hair plus the big stone house on the hill. Ruth frowned as she thought that that meant the Taylors were remotely kin to the LeComptes, but consoled herself that it was just barely kin since, my goodness, that all happened back in the seventeen hundreds.

"That reminds me, honey, did your daddy ever get that old wringer washer fixed up for your mama or is it still sitting on the porch? Seems as she's feeling so poorly, she could certainly use it now. It sure beats scrubbing on a washboard and with her not having any colored help . . ."

"Bet I know what you come for, Lizzie," Mr. Bob interjected, "and here it is, the latest from Hollywood, *Photoplay*. Why someday I wouldn't be the least bit surprised if you was to end up in Hollywood, Cal-i-for-ne-ay, yourself, a good looker like you."

Lizzie pouted, "Now, you just quit your teasing, Mr. Bob. All I aim to do is get married and have me some children and lead a decent life."

Hearing that, Ruth Taylor forgot Butterick pattern number 398 and left, letting the screen door slam behind her. She also forgot to pick up the pound of baloney and the loaf of light bread, which was why she'd come to the store in the first place.

What Becky Taylor told her mama was true. Lizzie LeCompte did do it. And Lizzie LeCompte just loved to do it. Besides being luscious looking, Lizzie was right smart and figured out that if she liked it and the boys liked it and if she always made them wear a rubber, there was nothing wrong about feeling so good. In fact, Lizzie was so smart that she'd figured out by the time she was around nine years old that all those tales she was hearing in Sunday school were simply trying to make her think that she had to be miserable here on earth in order to get to Heaven. Since she couldn't feel Heaven, but certainly could feel the here and now, she decided to go with the sure thing.

The thing of it was she particularly liked doing it with both Bucky Taylor and Junie Hayes. With them being best friends and both football stars, it gave her a feeling of glory and power to know they both wanted her, and in order to get her would even put up with maybe having to share her, though neither one of them knew yet that she was doing it with both of them. She told them what she told her mama and the preacher and anyone else who asked her about the stories being whispered around. She'd toss her head and sigh. "Everybody in this town just loves to talk. It's the rest of the girls, they're just jealous because the boys like me and I get lots of dates. Besides that, I'm a cheerleader and got to be runner-up in the Miss County Fair Contest this past summer. I can't help it if they're jealous and like to be catty."

Her ma replied, "Take a look at me, missy. I wasn't always like I am today. I come from quality folks over in West Virginia. Why, my daddy even owned a coal mine. Your daddy, he always was the restless type, come over to work in that mine and he was the handsomest thing I ever spied. You get those looks of yours from him. I know he don't look that way now, but he used to. Pretty soon he had his way with me and before I knew it, I was in the family way with you. I wasn't but fourteen years old, just a baby a having a baby. We run away, and we had nowhere to run but back here. I ain't never seen my family since, too ashamed. Your Uncle Jack let us move in this house and your daddy started sharecropping. No money in that. Now, you just keep your legs together and you go to church and

you pray to Jesus that you are saving it for a man who can
do a lot better by you than what I ended up with."

Although she'd decided religion was ridiculous, Lizzie
knew enough about the town to know that it was intelligent
to take her ma's advice about going to church. It certainly
could do nothing but help her reputation. She attended Sunday morning service and Sunday evening service and
Wednesday night prayer meeting and the Epworth League.
When the preacher asked her to teach the Little Angels Sunday school class, the three- and four-year-olds, she dimpled
and said she'd be proud to do it.

Lizzie liked the preacher; he was young, good looking,
and unmarried. Sometimes when he really got into a hellfire
and brimstone sermon and the amens got loud, she'd get a
tingling feeling all over, almost like doing it. Of course, he
was even more interesting because he was a Clay and had
been born and grown up right here in Taylor Springs.
Somehow he got the call to preach and had gone off to college and seminary and had come right back here to pastor
the Southern Methodist Episcopal church. His spinster aunt,
Bertha Hayes, had moved into the big white parsonage with
him to keep his house and keep appearances respectable.

Bucky and Junie both came to take her to the picture show
at Boonetown that night. They'd ridden over in Junie's
daddy's old Ford, rattling through the darkness, laughing
and singing. After the show, they'd gone over to Mary D's
Cafe and each had a chocolate soda, even if they did cost
fifteen cents apiece. When they got back in the Ford, Lizzie
sat squeezed between them in the darkness of the front seat
with one hand on Junie's knee and the other on Bucky's.
She wished that the three of them could stay that way forever, just frozen like that in time.

Lizzie squeezed Junie's knee a little harder. "Junie, you know something? You are the best-looking thing. All the girls tell it. What they can't figure out, though, is how you are kin to all them dark Hayes. Course your hair is the slightest bit curly, but then Lucille Byrd declares she likes it that way and said she'd adore to kiss your thick lips."

Bucky snorted with laughter and Junie said, "Oh, go on with you, Lizzie. You got a smart mouth."

Bucky put his arm around her shoulders and gave her a little hug. "You know good and well that the white Hayes tell that the colored Hayes used to be their slaves and when the slaves were freed, why, they just took their former masters' names. Now, ain't that the way it was, Junie? Besides, Lucille would adore you even if your hair was yellow and straight and your a-dor-a-ble lips were thin. It's the reputed size of your pecker she's interested in."

"Bucky Taylor, you just quit that dirty talk," Lizzie squealed. Bucky's hand dropped off her shoulder and brushed her nipples. This made Lizzie feel so good that she, in turn, squeezed Junie's knee even harder. She wondered what it would be like if both of them did it to her at the same time.

"Now, I'm sorry that I started this whole thing about Lucille. It was mean of me and she can't help it that she's so big. Besides, she does have a pretty face and she can sing like an angel. If one of you was to do the Christian thing, why you'd ask her to the dance after the first football game."

"Shoot," Junie responded, "Old Bucky ain't got the nerve to walk into the gymnasium with Lucille Byrd on his arm. He thinks he's number one at school, but even he couldn't get away with that. Think you could, Bucky? You'd get laughed right out of town."

Lizzie's hand moved up Junie's thigh as he was talking,

and Junie could feel himself getting hard. Oh Lord, how he
wanted just to bury himself in that girl. She'd told him that
she was bound to go out with a lot of boys; that way nobody could ever suspect about him and her. She only would
do it with him, though, and that was because they were
truly in love and going to get married after he got through
with his football at college.

He reckoned she was right, but it made it awful rough
when he knew that Bucky was dating her, too. He and
Bucky had always been closer than brothers and did everything together ever since they was in the first grade. They
told each other everything, too. But now he couldn't tell
Bucky the best thing that ever happened to him in all his
eighteen years, that he was the one and only getting it from
Lizzie LeCompte.

"Oh, yeah." Bucky snarled. "Well, you can bet your
bottom dollar I'll do it, June boy, and I'll come out of it
looking like a hero. You know I never backed down on a
dare in my life."

Junie laughed. "You can just consider that a double dog
dare, Mr. Taylor." Now, for sure, Lizzie would be going to
the dance with him and everybody could see once and for
all that Junie Hayes was the one she really favored.

Bucky wondered, right afterward, why he'd said it.
Not that he didn't think he couldn't do it. Lord knows he'd
always liked the idea of people noticing him, and they'd for
certain do just that when he showed up at the dance with
Lucille Byrd. Just like when he played football and the
crowd hollered his name and the cheerleaders yelled Bucky,
Bucky, he's our man, if he can't do it, nobody can. Especially when he would look over and see Lizzie jumping up
and down with her short little cheerleader's skirt flipping up
and showing that glorious ass.

And it was all his, she'd told him that. It kind of made

him feel sorry for old June Bug. Junie was crazy about her, anybody could see that, but the one thing Bucky couldn't tell his best buddy was that Bucky Taylor had her all wrapped up and was screwing the best-looking girl ever to come out of LeCompte Bottoms. Bucky knew his mother didn't like the fact that he was courting Lizzie, because Ruth Taylor kept reminding him that the girls he dated should be a credit to the Taylor name. He could hardly wait to see how she'd act when he told her that he was asking big fat Lucille Byrd to the football dance. Probably throw a hissy fit, Bucky thought. He grinned to think of the ruckus he was going to cause tomorrow morning.

It was early the next morning when Ruth Taylor opened the kitchen door and stepped onto the back porch hoping for a sweet-smelling breath of air, but heat still hung over the valley, pressing the sulphur smell of the springs down to the ground. There'd been no rain for three weeks now. The corn and tobacco were stunted and she'd never had such a bad year for her hollyhocks. Everything looked dry, dusty. It was beginning to look like those pictures of the great dust bowl that was happening out west. No crops, no money, seems as if the world was turned all upside down. Oh, well, she thought, the Lord chastens those he loveth. That's what young Preacher Clay was always saying, or something like that.

She turned back into her kitchen, wondering why it was her kitchen. Ruth wondered about a lot of things, like the reason she was born herself and not somebody else or what was really the purpose of being born. Was it just to grow up and get married and have babies and then die? Wasn't there any more to it than that? She just wondered, though, and never asked aloud. Nobody would ever have the chance to accuse Ruth Taylor of being foolish or not seriously bearing her responsibilities as a wife and mother.

Elvira came into the kitchen, softly closing the screen door behind her. She sat down, her toting bag in the corner by the pie safe, and removed her large white apron from a hook by the door. "Morning, Miss Ruth, Bucky ain't up yet? With it being the first morning for his whole team to do the football practice, I figured he'd be down here hollering for his breakfast."

Elvira moved her puffy bulk over to the new kerosene stove, turned up the wick under one of the burners, struck a big kitchen match, and jumped back apprehensively as orange flame shot up. "Miss Ruth," she grumbled, "I surely don't like this stove at all, it don't cook right, it makes the biscuits soggy, and I don't see no reason why we didn't keep the old wood-burner we done always had."

"Elvira, you will dearly love this stove just as soon as you get used to it. Hot as it's been, look at how cool the kitchen has stayed, and you can't believe those stories about how kerosene ranges is always blowing up."

The new stove was a joy for Ruth Taylor. She knew it was prideful of her, but it was certainly a nice bragging point, especially since there wasn't another one in the whole town. At the last Missionary Society Meeting, she'd just said, so very offhand, "Why, yes, I do agreed with you that Elvira did herself proud on this jam cake. Of course, with the new kerosene stove . . ." leaving the idea delicately hanging there.

Ruth poured herself some coffee and watched Elvira mix the buttermilk biscuits. She would have started the ham to frying, but had learned long ago not to mess in Elvira's cooking.

"Bucky ain't down yet because he didn't come home 'til the early hours this morning. Him and Junie Hayes took that LeCompte girl over to the picture show at Boonetown. Elvira, in all my born days, I never heard of two boys taking one girl between them on a date. Some things are just not proper, but Bucky just grins at me and says, 'Now Mama.' You know he sweettalks me, Elvira, 'don't be so old-fashioned, we are living in modern times.'"

Elvira gave the biscuit dough a mighty thump and shifted her weight, trying to rest her always aching feet. The only shoes she ever wore were hand-me-down carpet slippers with holes cut in the sides to ease the pressure on her bunions.

"Don't tell me about no modern times, Miss Ruth, modern times is just like olden times. That little girl gonna get herself a big belly, only thing is that she ain't gonna know for sure who helped her make it big. Sure don't like Bucky fooling around with no trash like that, no, sir. Seems like that boy ought to remember who we is."

Ruth nodded her head in agreement. To be a Taylor of Taylor Springs was certainly a position of pride and responsibility. Of that Ruth was convinced. She had certainly preached it to both Becky and Bucky, but it appeared as if Bucky wasn't attending her words lately. Lord knows she's worked hard enough herself to become a Taylor. It seemed as if she had climbed to the top of the mountain instead of just to the big stone house at the top of the hill, when she finally had finagled Bubba Taylor into marrying her.

Ruth Taylor's children never knew the truth of her childhood. She had arrived in Taylor Springs with her father, when he was called to pastor the newly built Pentecostal church that stood starkly on Main Street, right across from McAfee's General Store. There were just the two of them, Ruth and her pa, Ruth's mother dead so long ago that Ruth only remembered her smile and a sweet, sudden phrase of song, "Oh the moon shines tonight on pretty Redwing."

They came out of the eastern mountains of the state, where her daddy had founded the Church of the Avenging Jesus. With his church securely hidden back in the hollow, he had taken on the handling of snakes, the pouring on of the burning oil, and the speaking of tongues when the Holy Ghost descended upon him. He served a vengeful God.

The images still burned bright in Ruth's mind. The church was only a small cabin, tucked down in a ravine, and accessible only by a teetery swinging bridge. Inside, there was an odd collection of old cane-backed chairs, bentwood rockers, and four pews picked up from Lord knows where. Right up front, where regular churches had an altar, there was an old potbellied wood-burning stove. She could still see that stove, stoked full of hickory wood, glowing red hot, with the iron kettle of holy anointing oil sitting on the top. The stench of the smoking, rancid oil still filled her nostrils.

Then her daddy would call out for the sanctified, for them what were ready to prove their faith in the Lord Jesus Christ to step forward and be blessed with the boiling oil. This was after he had already handled the rattlesnakes to show that their pastor was without sin and that the Lord God Jehovah stayed the fangs of the serpents for those who believed in Him. Only Ruth and her pa knew that he had already defanged the rattlers.

And they came swaying and glassy-eyed up to the potbellied stove. Men and women with pinched, pasty faces and bodies like gnarled sticks came to be blessed with the boiling oil and prove their righteousness. Those whose skin turned bright red and who screamed in pain were obviously not right with the Lord.

To leave those mountains and come down into the rolling hills of Taylor Springs seemed an almost miracle to the thirteen-year-old Ruth. She and pa had a real house, built by the side of the new church, and there were no more snakes or boiling oil. But there was still a great deal of speaking in tongues, which Ruth found at least tolerable even though she knew that the folks in town poked fun at the Holy Rollers.

Pa evidently found the laughter frustrating, too, as the beatings he had always administered to his girl child in order to drive out the demons of evil increased in frequency, and his eyes became even more glittery and jumpy. He would roar as he took the razor strop to her back and bottom, Lord God—whack—look upon this blossoming female and drive—whack—all thoughts of carnal doings from her flesh—whack—and deliver her from the desires and devilment of the daughters of Eve—whack—and let her body not tempt the loyal servants—whack—of Jesus Christ amen.

Pa never whipped her where the marks showed, for which Ruth was grateful. She was also grateful that Pa let her go to school, for Taylor Springs had a real school. That school was a revelation for Ruth, not for the reading and ciphering and all the other knowledge she rapidly absorbed, but because of the others who were there with her. She carefully monitored those who were of consequence in this town and patterned her behavior on theirs. Ruth Banta was going to become someone respectable.

For five years, she watched and copied mannerisms, dress, and the proper way of doing things. She twisted her cornsilk hair in a demure chignon, cinched her waist in a corset, and reached her goal of respectability when, with eyes downcast and cheeks blushing, she told Bubba Taylor that she could never consent to kissing any man who was

not her husband or at least her intended. He then dropped
to his knees and proposed marriage.

Ever since she came to the valley, she had coveted the
big stone house that crowned the hill overlooking the whole
town. Bubba Taylor was just her way of getting there, but
she determined to do him and his name proud. To be a part
of the Taylor family of Taylor Springs was surely the highest honor to which she could aspire, and she vowed that no
one would ever be more respectable than Ruth Banta Taylor.

Oh, she knew that the Philpot sisters, Miss Ora and
Miss Nora, laid claim to being the true nobility of Taylor
Springs. Asa Philpot had ridden into the valley as a Virginia
gentleman with two slaves and a chamois pouch of gold and
a companion named Robert McAfee, who claimed to be a
nobleman from England, and that old Bullet Taylor, who,
the Philpots asserted, had only been their hired guide. But it
was Bullet Taylor who had left Philpot and McAfee behind
when an Indian told him about a great salt lick and pointed
out the buffalo trails that led to the valley. So it was a Taylor who got to the springs and the salt lick first and the
town was named after him. Never mind that Philpot and
McAfee caught up with him and forced him to give them
their fair share of the claim. The town was named Taylor
Springs.

However, she was a little surprised to find out that her
duties in bed as Bubba's wife were reminiscent of the tin-
glings she felt when Pa beat her in the name of Jesus; but, of
course, she certainly didn't talk about that. Fortunately, her
pa died of the pleurisy two weeks after she moved with
Bubba into the big house on the top of the hill, so that
Ruth, without impediment, could hold her course of attain-
ing to be the first lady of Taylor Springs. The Philpots
might rule the valley, but the town was named for the Tay-

lors. She just had to get that fixed real firm in Bucky Taylor's mind.

By the time Bubba Taylor came from the barn into the kitchen, Elvira had breakfast ready. Thin slices of country-cured ham, pink with crisp, golden-fried edges, and mounds of scrambled eggs were piled on platters. Bowls of butter-puddled grits with cinnamon and brown sugar–drenched fried apples were carried to the dining room table. The much maligned oven of the new kerosene stove belched out a batch of thin, crusty buttermilk biscuits, which were immediately wrapped in a white linen napkin.

As Elvira transported the biscuits and a crystal bowl of water-beaded, fresh-churned butter to the table, she proclaimed, "If Bucky ask me again today why they ain't no light bread on the table, I'm going to tell him surely about that store-bought trash, 'cause he might surely be able to know all about trash right now."

"Elvira, what in the world are you complaining about now?" Bubba pulled out his chair and plopped down in his place at the head of the table. "What in the world does store-bought bread have to do with Bucky and trash?" He reached for the ham with one hand and grabbed three biscuits with the other.

Ruth, standing at the bottom of the long, spiraling stairway, yelled up, "Bucky Taylor, breakfast is on the table. You better get on down here or else you are gonna be late. Do you hear me? You better answer me. You, too, Becky, get on down here. Your daddy is in from the barn and waiting at the table."

Bucky appeared at the top of the staircase and grinned down at his mother. As he jumped three steps at a time down the stairs, he said, "Guess what, Mama? I'm taking Lucille Byrd to the first football dance."

3

While Bucky Taylor was wolfing down his last biscuit on his way to the door, the new football coach was on his way to the first team practice. 1930 was a year when it was hard to find a job in any field, but teaching jobs seemed to be nonexistent. That's why Tony Dagostino considered himself lucky to be living in this godforsaken, minuscule town named Taylor Springs. Sweet Jesus, he thought, three churches, one general store, one filling station, and a population that seemed Neanderthal in intelligence. What the hell is a smart dago boy from Chicago doing in a place like this?

He moved up the graveled road that led from LeCompte Bottoms to the main street, sweat from his armpits already darkening his blue cotton shirt. The dusty heat was choking even this early in the morning, and he wondered how long his first football practice would last. Those boys who showed up last week when he called his organizational meeting were surprised enough at the unheard-of idea of practicing before school began, much less holding practice in the early morning. Not all of last year's players had shown up. As the other boys had explained to him in their colorful, cadenced, and ofttimes illiterate speech, "Some of the boys what don't live in town but are farming might find it right tight to get here."

"Yoo-hoo, Mr. Dagostino, Mr. Dagostino." He turned around to see the dumpling shape of Myna Smoot scooting across her front porch. As she hurried down the brick walk, she waved a white-covered basket at him. As he walked back toward her, she puffed, "I do declare, I almost let you get away without your dinner. You was out the door before I knew it, and I saw that basket a-sitting on the kitchen table and I thought, why, Myna Smoot, that young man will be over there training those young'uns with nothing for his stomach at dinnertime. Cora done fixed you some nice ham sandwiches and some of my own bread and butter pickles and a chunk of rat cheese and a piece of last night's peach pie."

She paused, perspiration running down her plump cheeks and causing her gray hair to lie in wet curls around her face. She handed him the basket, wiped her moist face on her blue-checked apron, and smiled back at him as she turned to go back down the road. "Don't forget now, suppertime is at five o'clock, so don't get so tied up over there at the school that you go forgetting the time. And remember what I told you about the Sheely's house. When you pass it, don't be getting agitated if Mary William jumps out of the bushes at you and starts a-waving her arms and making woo-woo sounds. She just ain't all there, even if she is forty years old, but she wouldn't harm a soul."

"Thank you, Mrs. Smoot, I certainly do appreciate this, and thank Cora for me, too." He stood there, a bulky, muscled man with curling black hair and a prominent Roman nose, wondering how the hell he was supposed to walk down main street all the way to the school carrying a silly little basket in his hand.

When Dr. Roger Byrd had visited the state university in June and hired a grateful Tony Dagostino to come to Taylor Springs to teach high school science and math and be the football coach, he had thrown in the fringe benefit of the school board's paying full room and board at Myna Smoot's house.

"Myna sets a fine table, her colored girl Cora is renowned for her cooking, and you'll have a bedroom and a sitting room for your use. The Smoot place is a big old house and Myna lives there alone now. There's a fine library, too. Myna's father, Adolphus Smoot, was a scholar, a graduate of Harvard who became a professor at the old Springs Military Academy, which was located on the Philpot Plantation. I'm certain you'll enjoy meeting the Misses Ora and Nora Philpot, also. They are quite cultured, educated ladies."

Hearing this, Tony visualized a place of old families with old money, and he salivated at the thought that he was going to make it away from the stench of the Chicago stockyards and his large, brawling, poor immigrant family to a world of gentility, culture, and wealth. And he had done it by using his brain to market his body for a football scholarship to a university far enough from Chicago that being Italian was considered exotic rather than inferior. Tony further fantasized for Dr. Byrd a beautiful, delicate daughter who was just waiting for his arrival to melt in his arms, marry him, and bring him into the family of land and wealth. Dr. Byrd had told him that his only child, Lucille, attended the high school and that he and his daughter had lived alone on the Byrd Farm since his wife died when Lucille was quite young.

"I would like to phrase this courteously," said Dr. Byrd, looking over his pince-nez, "however, it is probably best to be direct in this matter. If you are of the Roman

Catholic persuasion, I must tell you that the nearest church is thirty miles away in Nelsonville, where a group of French immigrants settled in the early 1800s. If this would be an impediment to your accepting the position . . ."

Quickly interrupting, Tony replied in what he hoped was suitably earnest, pious tone, "Oh, no sir, although my family is Roman, I have come to believe that God can be found where the heart seeks Him. I have been attending the Methodist church while here on campus." Seeing Byrd's half-smile, Tony thought, Got you, you old bastard. No way would I tell you that I don't believe in anything, especially anything that's not going to get Tony Dagostino where he wants to go.

And now here he stood, in the middle of a podunk town that had neither culture nor wealth nor any normal inhabitants, holding a stupid basket in one hand. He had certainly made the acquaintance of Myna Smoot, and had met the Misses Philpot, who turned out to be ancient relics decaying as rapidly as their plantation. He had visited the school, a sagging two-story white frame building that housed all students in all grades, first through high school seniors. He had surveyed his football field, a pasture adjacent to the school, where roaming cows left cowflops, which he had had to remove prior to this first practice. And he had also dined with Dr. Roger Byrd at Byrd Farm where he had met his daughter, Lucille.

He moved on down toward the end of the graveled road, where it merged into the asphalt of the main street. The last house on the left was a yellow gingerbread Victorian, turreted and verandaed on all four sides, surrounded by hedges grown wild and honeysuckle grown rampant. Arms flapping wildly, a tall stick of humanity with chopped-off hair, vacant eyes, and drooling mouth came charging from the hedges, placed itself directly in his path, and began cawing, "Woo-woo."

Tony stopped dead. "Could it be, why, it must be, the notorious Miss Mary William Sheely. Allow me to be so bold as to introduce myself, madam. I am Anthony Xavier Dagostino, at your service."

The figure started a jerky, grotesque dance, and gave a parody of a smile, spittle running down the chin. "Woo-woo, woo-you-two-new."

"Miss Mary William, woo-woo to you, too." As Tony bowed, Mary William's hand snaked out to grab the basket. Just as her clawing fingers wrapped around the handle, they were clamped by another hand, gnarled and liver-spotted. Tony looked up into fierce black eyes surrounded by shocks of white hair.

"Young man, please forgive my daughter. As you can see, she is what the natives here, in their picturesque speech, describe as 'tetched in the head.' However, she is a good girl and means no harm. Allow me to introduce myself. I am Professor Eliot Sheely, really Professor Emeritus Sheely of the School of Divinity of the University of Louisville. I now live here in my retirement. My late wife was a Hayes of Taylor Springs and we came back here to her homeplace. Mary William is our last child, a child of our old age. Our other child, Eliot, lives in New York City, where he acts in the theater. Perhaps you have heard of his work? Of course, he uses the stage name of Eliot Mansfield. He seems to feel than Mansfield is more euphonious than Sheely."

"*The* Eliot Mansfield . . ." Tony stumbled. "The Shakespearian Mansfield? Why, of course, he came to the university two years ago and was marvelous. By the way, sir, my name is—"

"I know who you are, young man. In Taylor Springs, it is impossible not to know about any stranger who comes

here. You are so rare, you understand. Good day to you,
Mr. Dagostino, and good luck with the football team. Such
a fine sport. Builds character, don't you think?" And he led
Mary William back into the yellow house.

Well, Tony old boy, you have yourself a choice here.
You can either pursue Miss Mary William Sheely, daughter
of Professor Emeritus Sheely and sister of Shakespearian ac-
tor Eliot Mansfield, or you can get hot after the large Miss
Lucille Byrd, daughter of Dr. Roger Byrd, principal of the
esteemed Taylor Springs School. Tony, you are up to your
neck in lunatics, your dreams are nightmares. Let us not
forget, however, that you are employed, you have a roof
over your head and food in your belly, not to mention in
your basket. You are far removed from your embarrass-
ment of a family, you can also get your ass out of here in a
year when your contract is up. With these positive
thoughts, he turned onto the main road, wheeled into
McAfee's store, bought a Nehi grape soda, quenched his
thirst, and started on down the road still thinking about Dr.
Roger Byrd's daughter.

The first time Tony Dagostino saw Lucille Byrd, he was
speechless. He had anticipated his first dinner at Byrd Farm
with fervor, and finally decided to dress for dinner by wearing his only suit. Gray flannel was a bit warm for August,
but, still, it was a suit, and the blue polka-dotted bow tie
was spiffy. He admired himself for some time in Miss
Myna's pier glass, and decided that Lucille Byrd was going
to see one hunk of a man.

The Byrd touring car was to pick him up at six o'clock,
which caused Myna Smoot to snort, "Ever since Roger
come back here, he acts so uppity. Dinner at seven, indeed,
acts like he never grew up here where he always had supper

at five like the rest of us. I declare, you'll be starved to death
afore you get a bite out there. Why don't I have Cora just
bring you a little something to tide you over. Maybe just a
couple of biscuits with some of that ham that was left over
from breakfast and a glass of buttermilk?"

"No, now please don't bother, Miss Smoot. I wouldn't
want to spoil my appetite with your good cooking and not
show my proper appreciation for Dr. Byrd's table. That
would not create a good impression on my new boss."
Tony winked and Myna's plump face melted with pleasure.

"Well, I can surely see that, but still Roger had better
be getting back to home folk ways. He left, you know, to
go up north to the university, and never came back here
until three years ago. Why, he didn't even come back to his
own mother's funeral, and considering her being French and
not having no natural family here, of course all the Byrds
considered her just like family, still and all he should've
come back, and he didn't come back either for his step-
daddy's funeral. Bud Byrd treated that boy like his own,
why even legal adopted him and give him his name and left
him everything. And Bud accumulated quite a bit and of
course the Byrd Farm ain't nothing to be sneezed at."

Tony interrupted the flow, "I'm just a little confused,
Mrs. Smoot. I'm not sure I'm following exactly what
you're saying. Now you're saying that Dr. Byrd is not
really a Byrd, but was adopted and his mother came from
France?"

Myna tittered, "Mercy, naturally you're confused. I
just forgot that you just got here and don't know nothing
about who belongs to what around this place. Now, let's
see if I can set this straight for you. Roger's mother was a
French woman named Edmee Delamare. Now, when Ora
and Nora Philpot went on the grand tour of Europe, oh that
musta been way back in the early eighties, they was over

there for about two years and when they come back to Taylor Springs they brought Edmee and her baby, Roger, with them. Edmee was their personal maid that they hired in Paris, France, at least that's what Ora and Nora told. Oh, Roger must have been about a year or eighteen months old, then. So you see, his name was really Roger Delamare. Ora and Nora said his daddy, Edmee's husband, had been kicked to death by a horse.

"Roger was just the cutest thing you ever saw, babbled in French, with those reddish-gold curls. Listen, Ora and Nora was just crazy about him and treated him like their own child. Edmee was housekeeper for them until Roger was about ten years old and then she up and married Bud Byrd and took Roger with her to Byrd Farm. Bud adopted him, he was just crazy about him, too. Particularly because Bud and his first wife, she was a Smoot, a distant cousin of mine, never had no children, and when Christina died, why, Bud just didn't have nobody.

"It like to broke Ora and Nora's heart when that boy left, but he visited them real often, in fact spent a great deal of time at the plantation. Ora and Nora was the ones who sent him up to Ohio to that Methodist university. After he graduated, he just stayed and taught there. He was real late in life getting married, and never did bring his wife back here for a visit—none of us ever seen her. Then, three years ago, Roger come back to Byrd Farm with Lucille, settled in, and started principaling the school."

A discreet tap on the front screen door, a soft, growly voice, "Khaki here, Miss Smoot. Come to pick up the young gentleman." Myna led Tony to the door and escorted him onto the front porch. "How're you, Khaki, and how's Eula and the young'uns?"

Khaki replied that everyone was doing just fine and that young Ben was already over to Lincoln Institute for his first year of school and that Eula surely hoped he'd stay and finish high school.

"This here is Mr. Dagostino, Khaki, our new school teacher. And this is Khaki Hayes, who is Dr. Byrd's man." Tony extended his hand, but Khaki only bowed slightly and said, "Pleasure to serve you, sir," and pointed the way to the gleaming Packard touring car sitting in front of the house.

Khaki opened the back door for Tony. "I think I'll just sit up in the front, thank you, Khaki." The black man gave him a sardonic look and then opened the front passenger door. "Yes, sir, Mr. Dagostino, whatever pleases you." Still standing on the porch, Myna gasped, "Well, I never. Roger Byrd is just going to die when he sees that!"

As they drove north on the main road, Tony turned and looked at Dr. Byrd's chauffeur. He could plainly see how he got his name. His skin was a very light tan and his hair the same tan. The nose, in profile, was aquiline and the mouth thin. "You always lived in Taylor Springs?" he asked.

"Yes sir, I was born here and always stayed right here except during the war. I joined up and was right proud to do so. I ended up serving in France. Got some gas in the trenches though, and can't do no heavy work since that time. Sure was nice when Dr. Roger done come back here and hired me to do his driving and errand running."

Just then they pulled in the oak-lined lane that led to the main house at Byrd Farm. The old white farmhouse looked inviting in the fading light, and waiting on the wide front porch stood Dr. Byrd ready to greet his guest. Standing by his side was his daughter, Lucille.

As the car neared the house, Tony eagerly looked out the window, trying to distinguish the woman who was to be his fairy princess and lead him into a new life. When the

Packard finally came to a halt in front of the porch, Khaki jumped out and trotted around to open the door, and Tony descended from the car and stood at the bottom of the broad steps. He looked up and saw the most massive female he had ever seen in his life. Considering that Tony came from a background that included a passel of pasta-devouring females who ran to fat the minute they delivered the first child, his astonishment at Lucille's girth was significant. He stood there, speechless, with a stunned look in his eyes, his dream shattered.

He could never totally recall that evening, only fragments of it. Blackberry wine in the cool front parlor that was furnished with antique cherry pieces placed on a creamy, faded Aubusson carpet. Snatches of conversation about the school. Lucille, elephantine, sitting on a rose velvet sofa, daintily holding her wineglass in sausage fingers. Dinner served by thin, cream-colored Eula, Khaki's wife. Dr. Byrd at the head of a shining mahogany table. Lucille sitting across from him, rapidly shoving food into her mouth, her jowls constantly in motion. Thick slices of red-juiced beef, steaming mounds of mashed potatoes, green beans shiny with ham fat, kernels of golden corn glistening with butter and heavy cream, crusty, yeasty light rolls, slabs of ripe red tomatoes, wedges of caramel-iced fudge cake. Words about Tony's football career at the university. Comments from Dr. Byrd about his career at Bishop University. Lucille did not talk. She ate.

After dinner into the back parlor. Hot black coffee in Sevres demitasses served by Eula. Lucille taking her place on the bench before a rosewood piano, her massive haunches dripping over the sides of the bench, accompanying herself as she sang German lieder in the most magnificent contralto voice that Tony Dagostino had ever heard.

As he continued walking down the main road toward

the school, Tony thought about that voice. He could almost hear it still ringing in his imagination. Boy, would my old man love to hear her, he mused. Hell, he'd tell me to grab her and say, by God, she's got plenty to grab on to, she's full of juice, a mountain to be climbed. Well, forget it, old man, I want one that's tall, thin, blond, Protestant, and rich. Lost in thought, he looked up, startled, when he heard, "Hey, Mr. Dagostino, where you going? You going to walk on past the field?"

Bucky Taylor and Junie Hayes stood in front of him grinning. "Here, let me take that basket for you, Coach." Junie grabbed the handle. "Figure if I help carry it you just might give me some of what's in it. Knowing Miss Myna and Cora's cooking, surely must be something worth having in there. You might as well know now, afore you're invited over to supper to my house, that my mama can't cook worth a diddly-ot-squat and she ain't never been able to find no colored help who can cook either. Just ask Bucky, he'll tell it's the truth.

Bucky danced in front of them, throwing imaginary passes. "Oh, sure, Mr. Dagostino, Junie is telling the simple truth. You can tell by looking at him that he hardly gets any decent food at his house. Dainty little thing, ain't he?"

"All right, Mr. Hayes and Mr. Taylor, forget the basket. We are here to start building a football team. Gather up the rest of those gorillas while I unlock the school, and we'll get into some practice clothes."

The boys shoved and pushed their way into the old building. In the combination boiler-locker room, they shucked their clothes, hooting and commenting on each other's genital attributes.

Homer LeCompte tried to goose Airy Clay while Bud

Smoot jumped up on a bench and declared that he'd challenge anyone to beat the size of his. Junie snorted, "Why, you ain't even full grown yet, bub. Take a look at this if you want to see what a man looks like." Bud snickered, "That's what you been slipping to good old Lizzie? No wonder it's taking more than you to keep that girl happy." Junie and Bucky both jumped him, knocking him to the concrete floor. The rest of the boys gleefully piled on, joining in the scuffle.

Tony walked into the shambles, yelling, "All right, gentlemen, knock it off." He waded in, pulling bodies apart, finally hoisting Bud out of the center of the pile. "Let's get one thing clear, men. We will expend this type of energy in training to beat shit out of our opposing teams, not out of each other. Now, get out of here onto the field and we'll begin our first session by doing ten laps around that field."

He stopped Bucky as the boys filed out of the room sheepishly. "What was that all about, Mr. Taylor?" Bucky mumbled, "Oh, nothing much, just some foolishness."

"Listen, Taylor, you're the captain of this team, you're the quarterback, and I'm holding you responsible as the leader of this team to see that it is a team. So let's see that this type of foolishness doesn't happen again. Now get out there and lead those laps." Tony looked up to see Junie coming back into the boiler room.

"What are you doing back in here, Hayes?"

"Just come back to tell you that all the cheerleaders is here, Coach. Reckon since this here is the first time we ever had any practice afore school started, they wanted to see it and show their support or something. Anyways, they are there and so is Mr. Bob McAfee and Brother Randall Clay and," turning around to grin at Bucky, "Dr. Byrd and Lucille."

The boys ran laps, did calisthenics, leaped through worn-out tires donated by Coleman LeCompte's filling station, and ran plays while Tony blew his whistle. Lizzie LeCompte flipped around the sidelines, earnestly smiling up at Preacher Clay and Dr. Byrd, dimpling at Mr. Bob McAfee, moving over to talk with Lucille Byrd from time to time, and leading the cheerleaders in some sporadic cheers when the occasion seemed to call for it.

The morning sun burned hotter; the sulphury air became more stifling. Sweat poured off the boys and Tony. Finally, Tony whistled practice to a close and motioned the boys back into the school building. Walking over to speak to Dr. Byrd, he glanced at Lucille, collapsed on the grass, oozing greasy perspiration, and at Lizzie, who stretched beside her, arms extended behind her supporting her weight, ripe bosom extended in an invitation.

Tony stopped. My God, what do we have here. He turned toward the girls and Lizzie jumped up, shaking her brown curls and running her tongue over her incredible mouth.

"Mr. Dagostino, I'm Lizzie LeCompte and it surely is a pleasure to meet you. I am your head cheerleader and I just wanted to bring the other girls down here today so's you and the boys know we are supporting the team." She slowly looked up at him. "I do declare I can't hardly believe that you are a coach and teacher. You don't hardly look old enough. Not that I'm meaning any disrespect, 'cause my mama wouldn't stand for that." Lizzie felt that little tingle and just knew that she was going to have to do it with the coach. When Tony Dagostino looked back at her, she knew that he knew it, too.

"I was just wondering, and I know you're busy what with this practicing and all, but could I come over to school some day soon to talk with you about some courses I was aiming to take this year? I purely need some advice, 'cause I'm just thinking about going over to Nelsonville to that business school after I graduate this year. Mama says no need to stay here in Taylor Springs the rest of my life and no telling where I could go if I learned to type."

Oh, Jesus, sweetheart, Tony thought, there's no doubt about where you're going. He wanted to throw that sassy ass on the grass and tear into her right here and now. "Why, of course, Miss LeCompte, why don't you come by the school tomorrow afternoon. I think it's admirable that you're thinking about your future and have such ambitions. It's my job to help you plan for what you want to do."

"I'll be over, Coach . . . after dinner, oh, around one o'clock. I really do thank you."

Tony stopped and said good morning to Lucille Byrd. "Thank you again for such a pleasant dinner, Lucille. But most of all thank you for the music. You have a truly magnificent voice." Lucille smiled shyly and reached into her pocketbook for another Moon Pie.

Dr. Byrd, Preacher Clay, and Bob McAfee came up and started talking about the practice. Tony had a feeling that he was not going to be coaching his team alone. "You see, young feller," McAfee harrumphed, "most important thing you are bound to do is to get these boys up and out for blood for the Boonetown game. Reckon it's been ten years since we whipped Boonetown, ain't that right, Randall?"

"Most certainly is . . . it was my last year here in high school, fact that's probably the last time we won any ballgame. I was thinking," the preacher turned to Tony, "probably wouldn't do any harm if we were to get a little Jesus on our side. I certainly wouldn't mind coming out on the field before the game and leading the boys in a prayer. Sure couldn't hurt any."

Dr. Byrd interjected, "I think that's a splendid idea, Randall. We could make you the team chaplain, so to speak, and you could certainly pray loudly enough so that it could be like an invocation for the team and the crowd. Of course, we would be sure to make the prayer ecumenical so that it could be appreciated by all the doctrines."

Tony thanked them for coming and turned back into the school to consume the food from Myna Smoot's basket and think about exactly how he was going to advise Lizzie LeCompte tomorrow afternoon.

4

As soon as Bucky Taylor got home after practice, his mama made him take the wash basin and soap and clean himself up. "I don't care if you did wash this morning. Another spit bath never hurt anybody and I swear you smell worse than any field hand." Ruth shooed him up the stairs. "Now you're not sitting down to my dinner table until you wash and change those clothes. We ain't trash from down in the Bottom, you know."

"Well, Mama, Daddy's gonna come in from overseeing the fields and he ain't gonna smell like roses," Bucky teased. "You gonna make him strip, too?"

Ruth flicked his behind with her tea towel. "Get on up there. Elvira's 'bout got it ready for the table and you know she doesn't hold with her fried chicken getting cold. Besides, your daddy has gone over to Boonetown to the bank and is eating at Mary D's Cafe with Mr. Haucom. There's just you and me and Becky."

Becky, small and rounded, had a carrot version of the Taylor red hair and freckles sprinkled over her pert face. She bit into a crunchy drumstick, chewing decorously with her mouth shut. Becky was prim and prissy and fully believed

in what her mama told about the responsibility and respectability of being a Taylor. It was something nobody could
make light of.

"You really aiming to ask Lucille Byrd to that dance
like you said at breakfast?" she purred at her brother.

Bucky forked a huge load of creamed butterbeans into
his mouth. "What makes you think I was funning? Truly,
Lucille is a large girl; however, she comes from the Byrd
family and I feel an obligation as the son of the first family
of Taylor Springs to take out the only daughter of the Byrd
family."

Elvira waddled in carrying a plate of hot corncakes,
which she thumped down on the table.

"Bucky, it ain't fitten for you to be talking like that.
You been flitting around with trash. I knows it, your ma
knows it, Becky knows it, every soul in town done know
it. It be a fine thing if you really gonna ask Miss Lucille to
that dance. You laugh, but you do have a cause to honor
your name and your ma and pa. You jus' remind me of my
Tweenie. We begged her not to carry on with that black
nigger boy. I prayed night after night 'cause we never had
no dark skins in our family, we is apart from that. Well, she
done it anyway, you know that. It's a good thing the two of
them done left here and went up to Ohio, but it sho' don't
ease the shame."

Ruth nodded her head in agreement. "Bucky, I am
most proud that you are going to escort Lucille Byrd to the
dance." Bucky looked up, startled, as Ruth and Elvira exchanged triumphant smiles.

Lizzie LeCompte was having her dinner at the Methodist
parsonage with Randall Clay and his Aunt Bertha. Brother
Clay had offered her a ride with him back from the football

field since the LeCompte house was just down the road from him. He'd been wanting to talk to her about her Little Angels Sunday school class anyway, and as they were in full discussion about the propriety of ordering the Baby Jesus coloring books because, well, somehow it just didn't seem quite serious enough, Randall suggested that Lizzie stop and have dinner at the parsonage.

"I'll just swing on down by your house and you can run in and ask your mama if it'll be all right. Now, tell her not to worry. Aunt Bertha always fixes plenty."

"No need to do that, Brother Clay. Mama don't worry none about any of us showing up at mealtimes; we're all busy going a dozen different ways. Usually, we just piece anyway with Mama being sick."

After Randall blessed the food and especially called down God's blessing on Lizzie's work with the Little Angels and God's healing on her sick mama, Bertha Hayes rang a little silver bell, and Colored Bertha came into the dining room to serve the cold roast chicken and a leaf lettuce salad, studded with bits of bacon and green onion, glistening with vinegar and bacon grease. Colored Bertha was always called Colored Bertha because she bore exactly the same name as Randall's Aunt Bertha; both were Bertha Hayes.

"I declare, Lizzie, it has been so hot that a body hardly wants any heavy food. Randall and I have been eating real light and I just feel badly that this isn't company food. Now, I just hope you'll excuse us this time. Why, we don't even have any hot bread for you. I've just told Colored Bertha not to bother to bake right now as the stove just heats up the kitchen intolerable. I would certainly admire to have one of those new kerosene stoves like Mrs. Taylor. They do say, however, that they can blow up right in your face, least someone told me that happened over at Nelsonville. I believe they said it happened to one of the Finches, can't recollect if it was supposed to be Gladdy or Roberta."

Lizzie had never eaten food like this before. She was enchanted at its elegance, for it was a far cry from the fat-back, milk gravy, beans, and baloney that was served at home. Her fingers caressed the heft of the sterling silver-ware, and her mouth liked the feel of the crystal as she drank the iced tea with a slice of lemon floating on top. She dabbed her mouth with the white damask napkin, imitating the way that Brother Clay and Aunt Bertha did it.

Aunt Bertha pushed back her chair. "Now, I do hope you'll excuse me, children. I have the Literary Guild meeting out at the Philpot's this afternoon and Miss Ora is going to read her paper on *The Scarlet Letter*. I know that some feel the novel is not quite proper, but I do feel it has a moral message. It will be most interesting to hear Ora's viewpoint. It is a wonder that Ora and Nora are seventy years old and still as feisty as they can be.

"Now, Colored Bertha will be right in to serve you peach ice cream. I swear she had Aaron cranking all morning. Course, he did get to lick the dasher. That was a sight, cream smeared all over that little colored face. I dasn't eat any, not with the refreshments I know will be served this afternoon." She rose, running her hands down her stiffly girdled hips, and left the room, reminding Lizzie to tell her mama how much she was missed at the Sewing Circle and how they were all praying for her full recovery.

Randall Clay looked over at Lizzie and felt the heat spread in his groin. His palms began to sweat and his mouth felt dry. She was running the point of her pink tongue over her mouth, licking off the little drops of melted ice cream. She leaned over to spoon up another bite, and he could see the cleavage of those two perfect breasts. Oh God help him, he wanted to lick them just like she was licking her mouth.

Any minute, he knew he was going to come, just sitting there watching her. And he had taken a vow, a solemn vow of celibacy, and it was right that he had done so, for it was in reparation for a terrible wrong. It was penance, and God help him now.

He'd known when he came back to Taylor Springs to pastor his first church, that same church where he'd received his call to preach, that he should stay away from Lizzie. When he'd gone off to Peavine College, Lizzie had just been one of the skinny, snot-nosed LeCompte kids who lived at the end of LeCompte Bottoms, practically in colored town, and had nothing to do with the life the Clay family led in their brick house on the eastern side of town. The only time the two families encountered one another was at services at the Southern Methodist Episcopal church, which was itself surprising as Lizzie's family seemed to be a lot more Holy Roller than Methodist.

Two years ago, when he returned, he had found Lizzie in his congregation, a Lilith, a wench who had every male in Taylor Springs panting with lust, sometimes concealed, but always there. He could not keep his eyes off her ripe body, the swish of her walk that proclaimed her sensuality, the mouth that looked perpetually swollen from kissing . . . even when he was preaching the Gospel and hearing the amens. When he heard the gossip about her, he decided he must discreetly question her, convincing himself that it was his pastoral duty. Of course, he knew, in fact, it was only from curiosity and jealousy. He knew better than to put her in his car today; he knew better than to bring her here. He also knew that Aunt Bertha thought he was trying to save the little hussy's soul. Right now she was probably regaling the old biddies of the Literary Guild about dear Randall's attempts to do something about the LeCompte girl.

Randall Clay had two problems: one, that he was a

good boy and two, that he was always horny. He was born beautiful and his mother adored him. He was her own little doll baby and she spent hours making sure that he never had a speck of dirt on him and twisting his blond hair in finger curls. His pa, Dr. Burton Clay, never seemed to pay much attention because he was busy with his practice. He was always in his buggy, on house calls day and night, but he figured the boy was still a baby. When Randall got old enough to talk to, Burton planned on sending him away to boarding school and then making a doctor out of him so's he could take over his practice.

Burton knew that he was never going to have any more children. Ramona had carried on so when Randall was born, in labor for three days and screaming the whole time. Two hours after she had delivered, she announced flatly, "I have done my duty by you, Burton Clay, and suffered the curse of Eve, just like it says in the Good Book. Even the Lord himself couldn't fault me. You being a doctor should know that it would kill me to go through this again." And she had had his belongings moved into the spare bedroom and devoted herself to her only child and other good works.

Burton knew that he had to rescue Randall. He planned to wait and then send the boy away from Ramona. She spent hours in praying for and with Randall, and held Bible readings with the boy every morning and afternoon. She particularly held with those passages that decried the evils of the flesh, and also delighted in reciting the terrible suffering she endured to bring him into the world. She was determined that Randall would grow into a pure, noble creature who would never feel carnal desire. "Randall, my son," she would repeat often, "I do not pray that you will be a great man. I only ask the Lord Jesus that you remain pure in body and spirit."

When Burton Clay died of a heart attack one night during a house call at Philpot Plantation where Miss Nora was suffering one of her migraines, Ramona buried him properly and put on the widow's weeds, which she wore the rest of her life. She invited her spinster sister, Bertha, to move into the Clay house with her and Randall, and was very content with her household. When Randall received the call to the ministry at a revival service being led by Brother Hayden of Lake Junaluska, North Carolina, Ramona knew that her life's work was complete. Randall was only sixteen, but Ramona knew that God had answered her prayers: Randall was on his way to follow the path of Jesus.

By the time he received the call to preach, Randall had been horny for about four years. How he fought the siren calls of the flesh and how he anguished, no one knew. While the other boys sniggered and told jokes and bragged about pulling down Geneva Hayes' drawers, Randall fought and prayed to remain pure in heart, to be a good boy like his mama wanted him to. He was embarrassed to wake in the mornings and find his bed linens damp with spilled seed and didn't know what else to do but act like it had never happened. He certainly hoped that it wasn't as much a sin as the Bible said about spilling your seed on the ground.

By the time he got into high school, he heard the other boys talking about doing things with some of the girls around town. He knew what they were doing and he knew that the Devil was tempting him, because all he ever thought about was doing the same things they talked about. He felt better when the football coach told them that thinking about females or engaging in certain practices could sap their strength and endanger their health, so's they should devote themselves to work and sports, taking a bath in cold water when necessary.

He figured that the only way he was going to remain a good boy was by becoming a preacher. Surely that would remove all temptation. So he publicly proclaimed his intention at Brother Hayden's revival service. His mother and Aunt Bertha rejoiced and, wearing the cloak of his new calling, he managed to walk in purity for his last two years at Taylor Springs High School and his first year at Peavine College.

Randall's downfall came during his second year at Peavine in the form of a bubbly girl nicknamed "Boopsie." Around the campus she was called a jazz-baby, but she always managed to display decorous behavior around the teachers who were their keepers. Peavine was as fervent in guarding against the lures of the flesh as Randall's mother had been. There were constant, compulsory Bible readings, dormitory prayer meetings, church services, and chapel attendance. Strict separation of the sexes was enforced, and all students were locked in their dormitories before nightfall. Boopsie Duncan just laughed at all this and told him, "It's just as easy to do a little loving in the daytime as it is at night, and a hell of a lot more fun."

Randall had never heard a woman say hell before, and he was fascinated by everything the insouciant Boopsie said and did. "Listen, sweetie-pie," she whispered in his ear, "This is the year 1922, the world is wild, don't be such an old fogey." They were sitting side by side in chapel, Professor James was praying, and Randall was sweating. "As soon as chapel is over, light out of here and meet me over by the back of the cafeteria."

He did, and she showed him that the window into one of the storerooms was unlocked. He boosted her in, followed her, and lost his virginity and his purity plunging into the wiggling, squealing Boopsie, who lay cushioned on several fifty-pound sacks of flour. It was the most marvelous experience of Randall's twenty years, and he repeated it as often as he and Boopsie could sneak away and go to the storeroom.

When they were finished, Boopsie would lie there and talk to him while he traced the erect pink nipple of her breast or stroked her rounded hips. He could not get enough of looking at her or touching her. He found the female form to be truly a marvel and pondered how anything that felt so good could be said to be so bad.

"Randall, you know my mama and daddy sent me here to Peavine because they thought it was so strict. They were always worrying about me. They just knew I was wild and they just didn't know what to do with me. Oh, I just love to have fun. I just love to dance. Do you know how to Charleston? Bet you don't, you've been such a good little boy. The minute I can get out of here, you know where I'm going, don't you? New York City. I just know I can get a job dancing in one of those speakeasies or just do a million exciting things. Oh, Randall, I am going to live Mmmm. Do that again, just like that."

"No, you aren't going to New York City. You know why? Because you like that and that too much, and I'm the one you like to do that and that to you. You're going to stay right here and you're going to marry me. You know we couldn't be doing this if we weren't going to get married. It's bad enough that we're doing it before we're married, but God knows that I could never stop it."

She squirmed as he kissed her slightly rounded belly. "You have to be funning me, Randall Clay. You think I'm going to be a preacher's wife? Can't you just see that now. Boopsie doing good works and singing in the choir and saving the heathen. Oh, kiss me there again."

When she got pregnant six months later, Randall wanted them to elope right away. She laughed at him. "I told you from the beginning what I was going to do with my life. I'm going to live it fast and furious, and that just doesn't include having any squalling babies right now. Besides, I don't know for sure if you're the daddy, sweetie. You surely didn't think that Boopsie was going to limit herself to knowing just one piddly man, did you? I told you that I'm going to live to the hilt. I am a bohemian, Randall. It could be you, but it could be Jake Bonner or Jim Blakemore or several others. No, I'm going home this weekend. It's all arranged, there's this place down by the river with somebody who'll just get rid of it for me."

So Boopsie left and never came back. It was announced at school that when she was horseback riding at home, the horse spooked and threw her headfirst into a tree, killing her. Some of the students went down to the funeral, but Randall didn't go. He was kneeling before the altar in the chapel, begging God's forgiveness for his sins of the flesh, and vowing eternal celibacy.

And he had kept the vow. Even when Ramona passed away while he was at the seminary and wasn't around anymore to call him Mama's good boy, he knew that he would be eternally damned to hell if he ever gave in to the demands of the flesh again. After he finished at the seminary, he was overjoyed that the Presiding Elder of the Methodist Conference had appointed him to serve Taylor Springs. It would be a lot easier to remain good in a place that was permeated with his Mama's spirit and where Aunt Bertha was watching him in the flesh.

However, he realized as he looked across the table at Lizzie LeCompte that he was going to risk hellfire for her. Rising, he said, "Let's us go over to the church and look at those Baby Jesus coloring books again. 'Bout time we made up our minds to do something, one way or another."

*   *   *

As the Reverend Randall Clay and Lizzie LeCompte were crossing the road over to the church, Nora Philpot was checking her dining room, just to make sure that things were in order before the ladies of the Literary Guild arrived.

Ora had said, "Sister, would you please make sure that Ludie has put on the Army and Navy tablecloth and that the silver tea service is properly shined. And would you mind checking in the kitchen. I'm just not sure that Ludie will ever learn to do a proper crème brûlée."

I mean, for God's sake, the thoughts tumbled through Nora's mind, who the hello that's coming here today would know whether or not the crème brûlée is proper or not, much less even know what crème brûlée is. She puffed on the small, black, twisted cigarillo that she held in the corner of her mouth.

Nora moved around the table, squinting down at the appointments. Although she and Ora were twins, they were not identical twins; the only thing they had shared was their glorious reddish-blond, thick, curly hair, which they had inherited from their mother who had been a Taylor. Ora was tall and thin, with a regal bearing; of course, now Ora was stooped and wiry, though she still thought she had a regal bearing. Ora's nose, however, had remained straight and her big green eyes were still dramatic. Nora had always been short and plump with a faint dusting of freckles across her pug nose. Her brown eyes, at age seventy, still reflected curiosity and amusement at the goings on of the world. The table, of course, was perfect. What else could it be, since Ora had arranged for it to be so.

Ora, she thought, you are full of *merde*. The Literary Guild of Taylor Springs, indeed. A gathering of Myna

Smoot, Bertha Hayes, Mary McAfee, Lucinda Clay, Annette LeCompte, Armilda Taylor, Jessie LeCompte, and Ruth Taylor. The elite, the intelligentsia, well, all excepting Ruth Banta Taylor, who was the byblow of that horrible Pentecostal preacher, but Ora decided that since she was Bubba Taylor's wife and lived in the Taylor house on the hill, she'd have to be invited to join. Which just showed you what a real ass old Ora was and had always been. She really seemed to believe that the last remaining Philpots were some kind of sacred guardians of some special culture. God, if she were a Druid, she'd probably be humping an oak tree. Ah, but I'm no one to judge—how many years have I been playing the charade?

Nora propelled her plump body back into the drawing room. "Everything is in perfect order, Ora. Is your paper all ready? I can hardly wait to hear your opinions on *The Scarlet Letter,* the big A. You should really have something to say."

"Of course I have something to say, Nora. Your flippancy is hardly becoming to a woman of your age. Please remove that filthy cigar from this room before our guests arrive. There is no reason for you to disgrace the Philpot name by behaving vulgarly. There are certain reasons why we have always been looked up to in this town."

Nora removed the cigar from her mouth and chucked it out the open window into the rose bushes. "Well, here come Myna and Bertha charging right up the drive in Randall's coupe. I swear, Ora, that boy was always weird, and he's definitely weirder since he got ordained. Of course, if Burton Clay had ever slapped some sense into Ramona and insisted on his marital rights, maybe she'd have had something better to do than lollygag over that boy."

"I hardly think you would care to discuss Burton Clay and his marital rights, Nora. Considering that he died right in this house while he was attending to you . . . well, your migraine headache."

"Funny," Nora cackled, "I haven't had one since then. Maybe it's something you outgrow with age. Oh, shit, Ora, your damned dogs are loose again. Brutus just jumped up on Myna."

Ora moved in a stately manner out into the immense entry hall, through the front door, down the steps, and out onto the circular driveway. "Brutus, Anthony, down. Down I say. Come here. Come." Two Great Danes the size of small ponies jumped down from a disheveled Myna Smoot and loped over to Ora.

"Myna, my dear, please accept my apologies. Ever since Khaki went to work for Roger Byrd, well, he's hardly ever here, and Brutus and Anthony just get out."

Myna smoothed her dress and patted the marcelled waves of her hair. "Ora, it's not like me to be criticizing, after all it was my own daddy, Adolphus Smoot, who tutored you and Nora right here in this house, and taught for your own pa here at the academy, and we are distant kin, but those dogs do not belong out in front of this house. Why, they could be a real menace if they ever really got loose. I was just reading in the paper the other day about this dog, now I forget if it was one like yours or a German shepherd, but it was definitely one of them big dogs like that, well, this dog what was a family pet and had always been gentle and lovinglike just all of a sudden went berserk and attacked the little baby in the family and ripped out its throat and killed it. I think it might have eaten up part of the poor child."

Taking her arm, Bertha Hayes propelled Myna up the steps and into the house. "Now, Myna, just calm yourself down and consider your nerves. Ora is taking care of those dogs and you know that no Philpot is going to harbor any killer dogs. Besides, you've been knowing those old dogs for years. They were just being friendly, so there is no need to carry on so and spoil the Literary Guild."

"Afternoon Myna, Bertha," Nora greeted them. "Please have a seat. It has been so unbearably hot. Why don't I just ring for Ludie to bring you a nice cold glass of lemonade while we're waiting for the others. Really, we're just going to have to make sure that Brutus and Anthony are penned up. But you know how Ora is about those dogs. They're her babies."

"I reckon I just got flustered," Myna panted. "You know, Nora, none of us ain't that young anymore and things tend to bother you as you get older."

"I certainly do understand that, Myna, much to my chagrin. Why, look, here's the rest." Nora rose in greeting as Ludie ushered in the ladies of the Literary Guild.

5

While Myna Smoot was describing the bed and board habits of the new schoolteacher and football coach, Mr. Dagostino, and Bertha Hayes was telling of the Reverend Randall Clay's noble efforts to bring Lizzie LeCompte into the fold and Ruth Banta Taylor was announcing that Bucky was right now on his way to ask Lucille Byrd if he could escort her to the football dance, and Miss Ora Philpot was attempting to dam this torrent of talk and bring the Literary Guild meeting to order, Dr. Roger Byrd and his man, Khaki Hayes, were sitting in Sukie Bee's cabin down in colored town drinking Sukie's homebrew.

The walls in Sukie's one-room shack were covered with pasted-up sheets of yellowed newspaper, which made interesting reading since they dated from 1916 to 1918. One corner held an old tarnished brass bedstead with a saggy mattress covered by a tattered patchwork quilt. Another corner held a big black wood-burning stove, a table, and an odd assortment of wooden chairs. Roger Byrd and Khaki sat on an old horsehair Victorian sofa, given to Sukie by Bubba Taylor's mother.

The rest of the room was a jumble of piles of junk,

clothes, magazines, papers. A sweet-sour smell permeated everything, a musty combination of old body juices, steam escaping from the kettle of soup beans simmering on the stove, and smoke from the ever-present Camel cigarette hanging from Sukie Bee's mouth.

Sukie stood by a long, narrow table placed in front of the cook stove, pulling pieces of ironing from a wicker basket. The flesh on her upper arm hung down and jiggled in rhythm with the strokes of the flat iron across the cloth. Three more irons sat heating on the stove, and as the one she was using cooled down, she'd whomp it back on the stove, pick up another, spit on it to make sure it sizzled hot enough, and attack again.

As she ironed, she sang "Swing Low, Sweet Chariot" and moved her huge body in cadence with her song. Sweat drenched her body. "If it gets any hotter, the whole world gonna catch on fire. No rain, everything dried up, not gonna have no garden truck to can . . . 'coming for to carry me home' . . . sure Lord wish it would rain, can't hardly sleep nights . . . 'I looked over Jordan and what did I see, coming for to carry me home' . . . got all this white folks' ironing to do, just pay enough to keep a little food in my mouth."

Dr. Byrd and Khaki ignored Sukie's liturgy, knowing that it wasn't intended for them. Their purpose was to sit there and drink, just making sure that they left a little love offering on the kitchen table, not to pay for the homebrew, which was offered to a select few of Sukie's guests, but "Just a little something for your trouble, Sukie, and we certainly enjoyed our visit."

"Khaki, it is impossible to tell lies in a small town. There just isn't anything to lie about since everybody knows everything about everybody else, even back unto the seventh generation. Now, the only lies that can exist in a small town are the collective lies, the ones that we have all agreed upon either to mask the truth or ignore the truth. Now, I am passing no moral judgment because these collective lies serve a purpose in our small society; we decide on our collective lies because it makes all our lives bearable."

Roger hiccuped, took another swig of the clear liquid from his jelly jar, and continued. "For example, right now you and I are sitting here in Sukie's, drinking homebrew and engaging in several collective lies. First, that white men and colored men do not associate in a purely social setting. Two, that white gentlemen do not visit domiciles in colored town. Three, that honorable men do not violate the law, which we are certainly doing by drinking this homebrew."

"But what you're saying, Mr. Roger, is just that that's the way things has always been. We talk one way and do the way we always done. That just keeps things smooth on the surface and more tolerable. Just 'cause you knows something, don't mean it needs to be talked about or have something done about it. When I served in France during the war, well, the ways them frogs done things were surely not the ways we do things. You're a man of the world, you're educated, Mr. Roger. I'm not going to be shocking you any when I say that being a colored man over there made no difference with them mam'zelles. For a fact, they made over us more than they made over the white boys."

Khaki carried his jelly jar over to the stove, reached into Sukie's woodbox, pulled out the jug, and poured a refill.

"Fetch me just a little more, if you please, Khaki. Why did you leave, why did you come back? You know I was born in France. My mother and father were French. Of course, I don't remember it, came here as a baby. But my mother always spoke French to me, and I can still even think in French, but I've always felt like I was Taylor Springs, not foreign."

Khaki filled Roger's jelly jar to the brim. "Guess I came back 'cause, well, I got the mustard gas and felt poorly and figured I ought to get on home. I don't know. Why'd you come back, Mr. Roger?"

When Roger Byrd left Taylor Springs in September of 1898, he had every intention of coming back as soon as he had completed his education. His stepfather, his mother, Miss Ora, and Miss Nora had driven him over to the depot at Nelsonville to catch the train that was to take him to Girty, Ohio, and Bishop University. The memory was yet vivid in Roger's mind. The matched team of bays, smartly pulling the carriage . . . old Uncle Clay Hayes, Khaki's grandfather, driving proudly and wearing his special driver's hat, the tall one with the big plume tucked in the hatband . . . his mother and Miss Ora and Miss Nora arrayed in their best bustled taffetas and silks and wide, veiled hats . . . Turk behind them driving the wagon with his luggage, the big steamer trunk and gladstone bags . . . the locomotive steaming into the station . . . the excitement of the good-byes . . . standing on the steps of the railroad car and waving until they all became tiny dots and faded into the horizon. He had felt so special, but then he had always felt that he was special.

His first memories were of Philpot Plantation. The entire place belonged to him; he was a ruler secure in his kingdom. His mother, Miss Ora, Miss Nora, and all the colored help cosseted and spoiled him. He spent as much time in the colored quarters as he did in the big house. Ludie, who was to become Khaki's mother, and her brothers, Turk and Captain, were his earliest companions. Even when he was old enough to start going to the Taylor Springs School, he always came home to share everything with them.

His life wasn't at all disrupted when his mother, Edmee, rather suddenly married Charles Byrd when Roger was ten years old. Mr. Bud Byrd had been visiting Philpot Plantation for as long as Roger could recollect. He took care of the Philpot accounts for Miss Ora, as financial matters were not the proper province of a female. Mr. Bud always played with Roger and took him fishing, talking with him about important town and world affairs. So, when Mr. Bud's wife, who had been poorly for a long time and had not left her bed for fifteen years, died and Roger moved with Edmee to Byrd Farm, he was right happy to be adopted and change his name to Byrd. Of course, he visited the plantation two or three times a week and every Sunday, after services at the Southern Methodist Episcopal church, the Byrd family always dined with the Philpot sisters.

And it seemed that every Sunday Miss Ora discussed the history of Taylor Springs and the Philpot family. "Of course, Roger," she always began, "There is no use in trying to cover up the fact that Asa Philpot was cashiered out of the Army, he was at the fort at West Point, and then banished from his ancestral home in Virginia. We do not know the reason. All we know is that in 1773 Asa Philpot, accompanied by two slaves named Hayes and Fanny and an Englishman named Robert McAfee, came to White Bone Lick, where they met a man named Bullet Taylor whom they hired as a guide."

Then Miss Nora would always say, "Really, Ora, I'm sure that everyone at this table could recite from memory what you're going to say next. You've told the same story every Sunday for Lord knows how many years. Yes, we all know that Bullet Taylor found out about a great salt lick from a drunken old Indian and that the old scoundrel gave the Indian a bottle of whiskey to guide him over the great buffalo roads down to the great salt lick. And we all know that Asa Philpot and Robert McAfee caught up with him and claimed their share of the land because the great salt lick

equaled great wealth, but since Bullet Taylor got there first
he insisted the place be named Taylor Springs."

Roger would invariably giggle at this point and be
given a stern look by Miss Ora and a wink by Miss Nora.
"It is important that we all remember our origins, Nora,"
Ora would continue. "The boy needs to know that the
Smoots and the LeComptes and the Clays were brought
here to begin the salt works. Now the Byrds, your family
now, Roger, came in the 1830s. Dr. William Byrd came
here from Louisville when the healing properties of the
spring waters were discovered. Soon he was joined by a Dr.
Esau Hayes from Cincinnati and by 1840 Taylor Springs
was known throughout the South and the East Coast as a
spa and resort. It was then the Taylors added the two big
wings to the stone house and it became a Grand Hotel. And
then in 1850 my father established the Springs Military
Academy, right here in this house." Then Miss Ora would
sigh. "Of course, it all began to deteriorate after the War
Between the States. But Papa did keep the academy open
until 1878, or was it '79, Nora?"

And Miss Nora would reply, "It was whatever year
you say it was, Ora," and then they would all laugh, even
Miss Ora.

Bishop University was the choice of Miss Ora Philpot.
Miss Nora thought they should seriously consider sending
Roger abroad for a year, "to visit France, you know. After
all, it is the boy's heritage and he should get to know his
family. Then, when he returns, he can take up his higher
education." Miss Ora glared. "Nora, Roger is much too
young to be going abroad." Nora smiled. "Why, we went
abroad when we were eighteen, Sister."

"That was entirely a different matter, and besides, there
were two of us. No, it will be Bishop. It is a small, ex-
clusive school with an excellent academic reputation and it

is church related. And with Jordan Nash being the president, after all he was one of Papa's students here at the military academy, he will take a personal interest in Roger and make sure that he gets a proper education and introduce him into the proper society."

So Roger arrived at Bishop, and became a part of the world that attended daily chapel, strolled by Girty Spring, and took classes in McKinley Hall. He also dined often with President Nash and his family and was introduced by them to the proper people. He visited young women in the parlor of the female dormitory and paid them suit in a gentlemanly manner.

What he could not find at the university was a place to satisfy his need for sexual gratification. Evidently, gentlemen at Bishop did not have such needs or speak of such matters, and, unfortunately, there were no colored quarters to visit here. Roger had been visiting the quarters at Philpot Plantation since he could remember. First, it was to play with Ludie and Turk and Captain, then it was just to bed Ludie. He was fourteen when he first wrestled the willing twelve-year-old Ludie to the ground and pulled her legs apart. She was his to fuck whenever he felt the desire, just as everything at Philpot Plantation was his to use. When Ludie had given birth to a light-skinned baby boy the previous year, he laughed when she named the baby Khaki.

Finally, after he joined the Sigma Chi Fraternity, the older Brothers took him down to Girty's one whorehouse, located out of the city limits on the south bank of the river. Although he relieved his needs with the whores, he found the experience unsatisfying. The women were all sagging flesh and empty eyes, and did not recognize that he was special. He felt that instead of using them, he was being used. Roger didn't begin to feel special again until the day he first saw Bridget O'Neil.

She couldn't have been more than twelve or thirteen years old, not a woman yet, with a tiny bosom just beginning to bud and no hips at all. Her black hair hung to her shoulders, she wasn't old enough to put it up yet. Her blue eyes were still round and childlike in her heart-shaped face. Her skinny form was enveloped in a huge apron and she clutched a feather duster in one small hand. She stood frozen in shyness when she realized that someone had entered the parlor. This was her first day of hire as help in this big, grand house, and she still wasn't sure as to what she should be doing. All she knew was that her ma had told her she'd be working for Mrs. Casey and it was a grand opportunity to bring in some money and make a place for herself if she done good. She'd never been in such a place before; it was a far cry from the two rooms that her ma and pa and her seven brothers and sisters lived in out on the Brucker farm where Pa was a handyman.

Roger looked at her and smiled. "Good morning. And just who might you be, young lady?" She looked up and saw a handsome gentleman with reddish hair and a curling mustache who was dressed just like a real swell. And he was smiling and looking at her so kind like. So she just spoke right up and told him that her name was Bridget and she was the new day help.

Then he started telling her all about the house, how it was a fraternity house and a lot of young gentlemen lived here and all about the college and what a college was. She stood there, all eyes and all attention, marveling to be talked to so by a man of his class. "What time do you finish your work, Bridget?" She replied that she finished at seven o'clock and then she had to walk the five miles back to the Brucker farm to go home, but she didn't mind that because she walked along the river and it was so pretty. He said, "Well, good luck with your work. I enjoyed talking with you, young lady, but I'm afraid it's time for me to go to my next class." He went out the parlor door and she stared after him in awe.

She was walking home that evening and hurrying some because it was almost dark. She was thinking of the money she'd be carrying home at the end of the week, because Mrs. Casey had told her she was a willing worker and learned quick, and about the good dinner she'd had in the fraternity house kitchen. Wait until she told at home about the brown-crusted roast pork and the thing called chocolate mousse, which was like clouds dissolving on your tongue. Just then she felt a hand on her shoulder, and gasped in surprise and fright. But the hand quickly turned her around, and she was relieved to see it was only the young gentleman with the reddish hair and mustache. He was smiling at her again.

"It's only me, Bridget, don't be frightened. I thought about you walking alone here by the river and I thought I'd better come and walk with you for your safety. It's almost dark." He stroked her shoulder and then ran his hands up and down her arms. "You're such a pretty little girl. Come on over here with me. Let's go sit under that big tree. I can tell you're tired and this is a long way for a little girl to walk." He scooped her up in his arms, carried her over to the tree, and sat down, placing the girl in his lap, still cradled in his arms. She had never been treated with so much kindness and looked up at him adoringly.

He fondled her, kissing her eyelids and then her mouth. He undid the buttons on her dress and caressed her skinny chest and her childlike nipples. His hand found her hairless pubes and he moaned as he fingered her. Bridget made no protest, but lay motionless, confused but happy that he liked her so much. When he entered her very slowly, it hurt, but she still said nothing because he was crooning in her ear, "Oh, you beautiful baby, yes, real slow and easy, it won't hurt much, ah, now," and she was glad that she was being singled out by someone so special. Suddenly, he began to thrust and pump himself frantically and she screamed, inadvertently, from the tearing pain. Roger clamped his hand over her face and kept it there until he shuddered with a release that he had not had since he had left Taylor Springs. When he was finished, he looked down at the lifeless body and walked away.

The murder of Bridget O'Neil was never solved, but it was the consensus of opinion that she must have been set upon by some tramp or vagrant wandering through the area. Young girls were warned time and again not to dare go down by the river because remember what happened to poor Bridget O'Neil. Of course, Roger Byrd was never suspect, for what connection could a gentleman of the university possibly have with a servant child?

Roger Byrd did find out what he needed, though, to make him satisfied and special; Roger needed pubescent girls. And he became sophisticated enough to find them in special whorehouses in Columbus and Cincinnati and Dayton. But he knew that he could never return to Taylor Springs, for there were no special places in that area where he could go for relief, and then he just might have to do something like he had done to Bridget O'Neil. So he graduated from Bishop and remained there to teach. He married one of the Nash daughters, the youngest, childlike one. They had one child, a baby named Lucille, with whom he finally returned to Taylor Springs, thirty years after he had left.

Dr. Byrd scratched his balding head, gazed around Sukie's shack, and gulped the rest of the liquid in the jar. "Why did I come back, Khaki? Same as you, I had nowhere else to go . . . nowhere else to take Lucille. I guess it was time to get on home."

Khaki helped Dr. Byrd out to the Packard, shooing Sukie's roosting hens out of the way as he guided Roger across the swept-dirt yard. Sukie stood in the doorway, her girth filling it, and laughed as the car weaved up the dirt road. "There they goes, one white gentleman and one nigger, both as tight as ticks on homebrew. And acting like they don't know what they be to one another. Well, what do I care, so long as they done left enough on the table for me to buy plenty Camel cigarettes."

Khaki steered the car up on the graveled part of the road, past Lizzie LeCompte's house and the Methodist Parsonage. Colored Bertha, who was out in the side yard taking down the wash, waved in reply to Khaki's honk of the horn. Directly across the road in the church, Brother Randall Clay and Lizzie LeCompte were in the pastor's study carefully examining the Baby Jesus coloring books. Randall jumped when he heard the horn and looked out the open window.

"Oh, it's just Khaki and Dr. Byrd passing by. Now, Lizzie, we've looked carefully at every one of these books, and I am of the opinion that we should try them with the Little Angels. After all, we must use every means available to bring the message, and although there might be some criticism from the older members of the congregation, I feel we ought to go ahead."

"Brother Clay, I am perfectly willing to go ahead with anything that you want to. However, if we're going to have the children coloring in these books, we are going to have to get us some tables down in the Sunday school room. All I got now down there is them rows of little chairs."

"I never thought of that, Lizzie." Randall moved toward the door, taking Lizzie's smooth arm, and began walking to the steps that led to the basement. "Let's just go right down to the basement and check out that room."

Lizzie walked closely beside him, her rounded hip bumping into him as they went down the steps. He let go of her arm, and put his arm around her shoulders, pulling her even more tightly next to him. "Careful now, wouldn't want you to fall."

Practically stuck together, they moved into the Little Angels Sunday school room. Lizzie turned her body into his and began rubbing against him. "Oh, sweet Jesus Christ, Lizzie, what are you doing to me?" She threw back her head and laughed, "Brother Clay, I can feel what I'm doing to you, you're just as hard as a rock." She moved in close again, her mouth partly opened. "Now kiss me, like you know you been wanting to for the longest time."

He put his mouth on hers and began to suck on those lips. Backing her to the wall, he rubbed her breasts, and she quickly undid the buttons of her dress and removed it. She stood there naked, for she wore nothing underneath. He looked at her, stunned by those fantastic tits, the tiny waist, that perfect ass. She unbuttoned his trousers, and he moaned at the feel of her fingers. She leaned against the wall, and, as he impaled her, she wrapped her arms around his shoulders and her legs around his waist, and crooned, "Do it to me, Brother Clay, I just love to do it."

He banged her against the wall as she arched her back, riding Randall Clay until he exploded, calling out, "Glory to God, glory!" He collapsed on the cement floor, Lizzie all in a tangle on top of him, breathing hard. "I meant that . . . it was glory. Lizzie, that was what God meant for a man to do, never mind what my mama told me." And he turned her over on her back, and started kissing her all over. Lizzie just wiggled, because this was far beyond anything Bucky

Taylor or Junie Hayes was capable of even thinking about doing, and whispered, "Brother Clay, I reckon I better come back tomorrow so's we can look for them tables."

Bucky Taylor and Junie Hayes were riding out to the Byrd farm in the Taylor pickup truck. Bucky figured he'd stop and pick up his friend because Junie wasn't never going to believe he'd invited Lucille Byrd to the dance unless old Junie witnessed it in person. Bucky halfway had the feeling Lucille was going to turn him down, and then for sure Junie, unless he was there, wasn't going to believe it. Junie yelled over the rattle of the truck, "Hey, Buck, what say we go after some rabbits soon."

"Sounds like a good idea, Junie. Can't go tomorrow morning, though, 'cause we've got football practice. Ain't that Dagostino something, though. We could go early Saturday morning. Let's see if Lizzie wants to go along. She ain't half bad with a shotgun."

The truck bumped up the driveway. "I'll go down and visit her tonight, see if she wants to go," Junie replied. "Look there, isn't that Lucille sitting out in the side yard?" He shaded his eyes with one hand and leaned out the open truck window. Turning back around, he exclaimed, "Lawsy me, no, I mistook Eula's big copper wash pot for Lucille. Must be this hot, dusty air is affecting my sight."

The truck swerved and screeched to a halt as Bucky, laughing, started pummeling him on the arm and back. "Cut it out, Junie. Now we are going to get out of this truck and walk real nice up to the door and politelike ask to see Miss Lucille Byrd. I should of known better than to bring you along."

Eula answered their knock on the front screen door. "Howdy, Mr. Bucky, Mr. Junie. Sorry to say but the doctor ain't to home right now. Him and Khaki have gone to do some business. Don't rightly know when to expect them back. What was you wanting, anyhow?"

"Well, Junie and me didn't exactly come to see Dr. Byrd, Eula. We was wondering if Lucille was at home." Eula raised one eyebrow. "Why, she surely is. You young gentlemens just step in the door here, and I'll go let her know you is calling." Eula moved sedately down the long hall toward the kitchen, behaving as if Miss Lucille received gentlemen callers all the time and silently praising the Lord that this miracle had occurred.

She pushed open the swinging door that led into the kitchen, where Lucille was standing at the big wooden work table rolling out the pie dough. Lucille did have a light hand with pastry, Eula couldn't deny that. Beside the circle of dough that she was delicately expanding with a marble rolling pin stood a soup tureen half-full of banana pudding, golden nutmeg-sprinkled custard laced with pale yellow banana slices and layered with vanilla wafers. The other half of the pudding had disappeared into Lucille's busy mouth during the time it took Eula to answer the knock on the door.

"Lucille, Bucky Taylor and Junie Hayes are standing in the front hall and are waiting to see you. Now let's just get this apron off, here, let me look at you. Well, I guess you is acceptable enough." Eula fluffed back Lucille's black curls with busy hands. "You sure has sweated up that dress, but, as hot as it is, everybody is done sweated up. Here," she grabbed a bottle from the table, "just let me put a little dab of this vanilla extract behind your ears, that'll make you smell sure enough sweet. Now, you just march right out there and invite those boys into the front parlor, and I'll be in directly with some refreshments." She pushed Lucille through the swinging door and out into the hallway.

She walked ponderously down the hall toward the waiting boys, eyes fixed firmly on the floor. When she saw their feet, she still didn't look up but mumbled, "Hello, Junie, hello, Bucky, won't you come and sit in the parlor?" Leading the way in, Lucille landed with a whoosh on the rose velvet sofa. "Have a seat. It surely is hot today, isn't it?"

"It sure is," Bucky replied. "Why, it was so hot at football practice that I thought we was all going to pass out. That new coach is really something. What did you think of the practice, Lucille?"

"It was very nice, but it was awfully hot. I just thought I'd come down with Papa to see how the team was going to be."

"What do you think of Mr. Dagostino? Funny name, ain't it? Course he's Eyetalian and all. He seems like he is really serious about his football, I mean when you consider beginning to practice even before school starts."

Eula marched into the room carrying a big silver tray with a crystal pitcher of iced tea and the flowered Limoges plate piled high with her famous sugar cookies. Yes, sir, just show these boys they are visiting real quality folks. They should be happy to be let in the front door. She placed the tray on the table in front of the sofa. "Just let me serve you some refreshments, Miss Lucille, gentlemen. I tell you it's been so unbearable hot that a body can hardly breathe. If it don't rain soon . . . How is your folks, Mr. Bucky?" She handed him a glass of the tea.

"Everybody is right fine, thank you, Eula. Mama says that her new kerosene stove surely does keep the kitchen cool, even in this heat, but Elvira don't like it at all."

"Elvira is just a-scared that it's going to blow up." Junie laughed. "Thank you, Eula, these cookies look mighty good."

"Oh, go on with you, Mr. Junie, you always was a sight, ever since you were just a little bit of a thing. You know these is just some of my own baking, not even store bought."

Lucille stuffed three cookies in her mouth and took a great gulp of tea. Eula looked at the empty plate. "I'll just go out to the kitchen and fill this plate up since you young folks seems to enjoy them.

"Well, speaking of football, Lucille," Bucky started, "the reason I dropped by was to say that I would be mighty proud to have you go to the dance with me, you know the dance after the first football game." Eula, standing in the doorway, dropped the plate, which ended up in slivers of flowered Limoges. Startled, Bucky and Junie jumped to their feet. Lucille swallowed her cookies, belched, and said, "All right."

6

The next morning Mary William Sheely was out on the road before the first light. She danced stiffly along, bare feet ignoring the gravel, raising her stick arms up and down in a windmill motion, and softly singing her woo-woo song. A sliver of light began to edge the horizon, roosters began crowing, and Mary William's song got faster and she pounded her skinny thighs excitedly.

She wandered into Randall Clay's barn, which sat just beyond the parsonage garden. She sniffed the warm, milky smell that meant food and followed it to the cow. She rubbed her hands over the hairy warmth, but could find nothing to put in her mouth. Her stomach was empty and her woo-woo became a scream of rage. She frantically twisted the material of her long white nightgown. Soon, she forgot her hunger and left the barn, crossed the road, and entered the church. Doors were never locked in Taylor Springs. She squatted down by the altar and relieved herself. Crowing delightedly at what she had produced, she dipped her fingers in the feces, and, with the happy innocence of a baby, began finger painting the altar rail and the pulpit.

Quickly losing interest, she lurched from the church and ran down the rest of the road, zigzagging from side to side in her jerky gait. The sun was coming up hot on the horizon, and the still, dusty air was filled with the sulphur scent from the nearby springs. She stopped at Lizzie LeCompte's house, stood rigidly at attention, and then crept up on the sagging front porch. Softly she sang, "Woo-new-two-woo," as she stuck her arms inside the rusty washing machine that was sitting there and softly drummed on its sides. Suddenly, she raised her head, her nostrils flared, and spittle ran out of the corners of her mouth. She had caught an odor that she recognized as food, and she excitedly left the porch and followed the scent onto the dirt road that led to colored town.

When the first light came through the kitchen window, Eula Hayes turned out the kerosene lamp. Every morning, she was up before the roosters crowed and got herself ready for the day. She stood by the cook stove, dressed in the starched gray cotton uniform and white ruffled apron that Dr. Byrd provided because he certainly wanted both her and Khaki dressed right for serving in his house. Why, he'd even said, "It is very important that both of you project the proper image, the image of Byrd Farm." Eula felt all puffed up when he said that, and after all nobody else working in any of the houses had a uniform. Even her own mother-in-law, Ludie, who still lived out at Philpot Plantation and waited on Miss Ora and Nora, didn't have no uniform, only those long white cover-up aprons she had to wear over her own dresses, which were usually hand-me-downs from the Philpots.

Khaki laughed at her, saying, "Listen, girl, you think Roger Byrd doing something out of the kindness of his heart for a couple of niggers. I just as soon have the money he putting on these clothes for my own use. The only reason he doing this is to satisfy his own pride." She noticed, though, that Khaki strutted around when he was dressed up in his gray pants and tight buttoned jacket, wearing that gray cap with the shiny black bill. And he couldn't deny that Mr. Roger was paying for Ben to be over at the Lincoln Institute to get his chance to finish high school. Every night Eula prayed that the Lord would watch over Ben and fill him with great ambitions to finish this school and get a real diploma. Of course, he had to board there and they missed him bad, but this was the only colored high school in the whole state, and Ben was getting his chance.

Eula sighed and murmured, "Lordy, lordy," as she poured herself some coffee. Every night, when they left the Byrds, she carried home in mason jars the leftover coffee and the other food she was allowed as part of the job's toting privileges. The aroma of the biscuits she was heating up filled the cabin, and she figured that would roust Khaki out of bed soon as he caught a whiff. Shoot, she thought, that man born hungry. Course, every morning when we get to work, I always fix up a good breakfast for him and me long 'fore Mr. Roger and Lucille gets awake, but Khaki just got to have a little something for his stomach the minute he gets out of bed. Maybe I might have to get him up this morning, though, the way him and Mr. Roger come back to the farm yesterday afternoon, both reeking of homebrew and a-trying to walk straight.

She smiled when she thought of Khaki guiding Mr. Roger up the front steps, through the front door, and to the sofa in the front parlor. Old Khaki could hardly walk himself. Lucille was playing the piano in the back parlor and singing some of them songs they played on the radio, which Mr. Roger didn't approve of at all. "Lucille," he'd emphasized, "that kind of trash is not music. It would not surprise me if that dross will not be the ruination of Western culture, and I absolutely forbid it in my house." So Lucille just snuck and played them when her pa was out. Course, Mr. Roger was in such a condition yesterday that he didn't even know what Lucille was a-playing.

So early in the morning, and the air was stifling. Eula, blue enamel cup in hand, went over and opened the cabin's front door and stood trying to get a breath of air. She spied Elvira moving herself up the road, on her way to start her day at the Taylors' house. Don't know how she gets her body up and down that hill, Eula thought. But I reckon we all do what we has to do. That woman has surely had more than her share of the miseries. Don't think she'll ever get over Tweenie marrying that real black boy and going off up north. Course, she was real satisfied when my Jessie married up with her boy Sampson. Jessie's such a pretty girl, even lighter than Khaki. But Ben's the lightest of us all, could easy pass for white. And Sampson doing so well, too, going off to Nelsonville like that and working with Mr. Bob McAfee's boy in that funeral parlor he done started. Sampson getting to wear a black suit and drive that big hearse and even learning how to lay out the bodies. And Jessie getting to be the receiving maid, not doing no cleaning or cooking, but just opening the door for the mourners and taking care of the flowers and serving refreshments at the viewings. Yes, doing real well and if Ben just gets that high school diploma, Khaki and me can be real proud. Funny, us just having the two of them. Course, Khaki come back from being in the Army and being in France with some ideas strange to folks around here. Khaki told me that we wasn't going to have no big brood of young'uns, and that's why he was always going to use those rubber things. Course, he didn't never know about the potion I got from Sukie neither. Took a teaspoon ever day, she guaranteed it, and it worked. Trust Sukie's potions over them rubber things any day. Khaki just laughed ever' time anybody talked about Sukie and her voodoo and her spells and potions, said that was just superstitious nigger talk, but I know that some of them old ways still work. Maybe I ought to go see her about some charm to keep Ben over there at Lincoln Institute.

"Morning, Elvira," she called out as she moved out the door and down the path to the road. "How you this morning? Looks the way you moving that your feet are still a-bothering you."

Elvira puffed to a halt. "Eula, honey, I tell you that it takes me longer ever' day to get this old body up that hill. However, praise the Lord, I got enough left in me to get up there and take care of my family that is depending on me, just as I've been doing ever since afore Bubba married Miss Ruth. Now, what you think about that Bucky asking Lucille to that dance? Ain't that a caution? I just told him it was a fitten and proper thing he was doing. Sometimes, I think Miss Ruth just too soft on that boy and he needs some sitting on, the way he been running around with that LeCompte trashy girl. Course, I wouldn't say this to nobody but you, but you knows and I knows that Miss Ruth herself didn't come from no quality family, never forget when her pa came here to open up that Holy Roller church, him being so strange. Must say, though, that Miss Ruth always try to behave ladylike and has been a decent wife to Bubba."

"Surely would have to say that," Eula agreed, "and there's some here passing off as quality that purely acts like trash. Don't we both know that. Now, Lucille, she mighty shy and ain't been out much since she and her pa come back here, but I think it's a mighty fine thing that she accepted to go to that dance with Bucky. Thing is, she is got to be fixed up right and I'm just going to let it drop real gentle like to

Mr. Roger that he needs to get some woman help in taking her over to Nelsonville to get a dress and get fixed up. And he can't be letting old Miss Ora and Nora do the advising, Lord, they'd gussy her up in a bustle or some such old-fashion foolishness."

"Maybe Miss Ruth and Becky—" Elvira broke off and pointed up the road. "Good Lord a mercy, look at that. It's Mary William a-coming, that girl is loose again. Run quick and get Khaki, you know she strong like a mule and we've got to trap her and get her home." Eula ran to the door as Elvira planted her bulk and extended both arms in front of the rapidly advancing Mary William, whose cries became more rapid and louder the closer she came to the smell of coffee and biscuits.

Mary William, tied to one of Eula's kitchen chairs, sat docilely as she moistly chewed on the biscuits that Eula kept popping in her mouth. Every now and then Eula lifted the cup of coffee to the slack mouth because there was no way she wanted Mary William to start choking here in her cabin. Don't need any trouble on account of this crazy white girl, she thought. Never mind that she ain't got the mind of a two-year-old, she still white. Don't see how her pappy going to be able to keep her much longer, he too old to keep watch on her and she bound to do something harmful or be harmed herself sooner or later. Oh, well, ain't none of your concern, long as you get her out of your house, woman.

The door opened and Khaki led Professor Sheely into the room. "Here she is, Professor, all safe. Sorry we done had to tie her down, but we wanted to make sure she didn't get away again. Eula been feeding her, appeared like she was hungry."

"Good morning, Eula, I can't thank you and Khaki enough. Mary William, look at your papa." Mary William drooled half-chewed biscuit down her chin and shook her head from side to side. "Mary William, you are a bad girl to leave the house. Now I am going to take you home. Khaki, Eula, I would appreciate your discretion in not relating what has transpired this morning. I'm sure you're aware that some people in this town do not understand Mary William's unfortunate condition . . . well, that she's harmless . . . and I would prefer that there be no talk about her escapade this morning. I just want to leave these few bills here on the table for your trouble, and I'd appreciate it, Khaki, if you'd drive us home. That way we will attract less attention."

"Professor Sheely, I'll be most happy to carry you back, and we don't want no money for watching Miss Mary William for a little while, no trouble at all. And you can be assured that we not going to discuss your business with no other folks. You ever thought, though, of maybe getting someone to help you watch after her, you know, being as Miss Mary William does like to wander out now and then, and seemed like she was heading down toward the springs this morning."

Eliot Sheely untied his drooling daughter and slowly led her toward the door. "No, please accept the money. Send it over to Ben. Every boy can use a little pocket money while he's away at school. I don't know about getting someone to help with Mary William. She had only her mother and me to tend to her needs, and of course since Molly has been gone, well, there's only me. Don't know what she'd do with anyone else. Come along, child. We're going home now."

Randall Clay took the last of his hotcakes and swished them through the remaining sorghum molasses and butter puddled on his plate. He chewed sensuously, swallowed, and rubbed his stomach with gusto. "Aunt Bertha, could you ring for Colored Bertha to bring me some more coffee, please. I don't know when I've had a finer breakfast."

"My goodness, Randall, I don't know what's come over you, although I must say it does my heart good to see you all perked up and enjoying your food the way a man should. Ever since your dear mama died and you've been pastoring, I think you have been so conscientious and driven to do good works that you just never let down. Now let me tell you that is not good for a person; your own father was driven that way with his practice of medicine and died too young of a heart attack."

"Well, Aunt Bertha, just let me say that I had, well, what some might say was a divine revelation yesterday. I think the Lord let me know that a man's spirit is housed in the flesh, and that there is an obligation to take care of body needs. The spirit cannot flourish in an unsound body." Randall smiled contentedly.

"Why, that is really deep thinking, Randall, and it does make sense. It does say somewhere in the Scriptures about the body being the temple of the Lord, doesn't it?" Bertha rattled on and Randall sat nodding his head while remembering every move that Lizzie LeCompte's body had made yesterday afternoon and anticipating every move he was going to make this afternoon when she came back over to the church basement so they could consult further on the tables for the Little Angels Sunday school class.

"Randall? Randall, what are you daydreaming about? I declare I don't think you heard a word I said. I was telling you about the Literary Guild meeting yesterday. Ora's paper on *The Scarlet Letter* was just fine. But the way she tore up that poor preacher, Arthur Dimisdale, for being cowardly and craven. Well, Ora said that he was more guilty than Hester Prynne because he lusted after her and took her but never admitted to it. Ora showed him no mercy at all."

Randall looked up, startled. Seemed like Aunt Bertha might be reading his thoughts—oh, that was ridiculous. "Anyway," Bertha went on, "Nora piped up and said that both Arthur and Hester were weak fools, running around feeling sorry for themselves, but only after they were caught and had already done what they wanted to do, and Mr. Hawthorne's novel wasn't about the hypocrisy of the Puritans, but about two people whining around when they couldn't cover up anymore.

"Well, I thought she and Ora were going to get into it right there, but then Ruth Taylor remarked that she surely didn't understand why people in books couldn't do decent things, like her Bucky taking Lucille Byrd to the first football dance. Myna Smoot said she didn't see what that had to do with adultery. Yes, she came right out and said the word and I reckon it's all right to say it if you're quoting from the Bible like the 'woman taken in adultery,' but in the Philpot parlor! Well, then, Nora started laughing to beat the band, and thank goodness, Ora said she did believe that Ludie had the refreshments laid in the dining room and we should adjourn there."

"Did you say that the Taylor boy had invited Lucille to the dance?" Randall asked with a puzzled look. Just then he heard the telephone bell faintly ringing in the front hall. The telephone hung on the wall of the first stairway landing. He knew that Colored Bertha would not answer it; she thought the brown wooden box with the receiver on a hook to one side, the crank to ring the operator on the other side, and the black horn-shaped speaker tube with bells on either side located in the middle, was the work of the devil. She was afraid of the contraption, convinced it was black magic, and knew if she spoke into it, it would surely steal her soul. "I better go get that, Aunt Bertha. Might be something important; Bob McAfee's mother has been mighty sick."

He put the receiver to his ear, stood back a little, and yelled hello into the tube.

"That you, Reverend Clay? This here is Reverend Jim Jordan. Are you there?"

"Yes, I'm here, Brother Jim." Even though Jim Jordan was the pastor of the Pentecostal church, Randall didn't feel it proper to call him Reverend since the Holy Rollers were not graduates of divinity schools like real ministers. They were what they called self-ordained, not that he would be judgmental and say they weren't doing the Lord's work, but they still weren't reverends.

"Wonder if you could come up to my church in about half an hour and meet with me and Reverend Poe? I have the opportunity of having a gospel quartet come into town and was thinking we could band together and make this a community occasion for the glorification of the Lord."

So Randall, instead of going over to his church as he did most every morning, climbed in the black Ford coupe and drove up to the main road to the Pentecostal church. Normally, he would have walked, but it was already so hot that he knew he'd get all sweated up and he certainly wanted to look his dignified best at Taylor Spring's first ecumenical council. After all, everybody knew that the Southern Methodist Episcopals were socially and doctrinely superior to Pentecostals and Baptists, so that did make him the leading preacher in town.

Jim Jordan and Adam Poe were sitting on the wooden steps of the Pentecostal church when Randall pulled the Ford up into the driveway. Adam, laughing, scratched the protruding gut that slopped over his blue cotton wash pants, and then pulled a blue and white bandanna out of his pocket to wipe the sweat that streamed down his whisker-shadowed jowls.

When Adam was called to pastor the Mt. Pisgah Baptist congregation some ten years ago, he'd been fifty pounds lighter, a fine-looking figure of a man, and a very eligible bachelor. Within six months, he had been ensnared by one of the Hayes girls, the daughter of a first cousin of Randall's mother and Aunt Bertha. Bertha said that did make him kissing kin, but she did wish the man would bathe more often and develop some manners, after all, being a Baptist didn't excuse everything.

But the Poes were family and Bertha invited them several times a year down to the Methodist parsonage for supper. "At least," she said, "those four youngsters can see what a proper set table and a proper served meal looks like. Lord, they're always running around half-raggedy and with runny noses. If my cousin, Dicey, hadn't already passed over, she'd die of shame to know of her grandchildren being in such a condition. I just don't understand how Ellen could have let herself and her family go like that. Dicey certainly didn't raise her that way. I have tried my best to talk to Ellen, but she is so bent on thinking that the Lord has called her to help Adam save souls for Jesus that she just neglects her house and her children. She even said to me, 'Now, Cousin Bertha, you know how it talks in the Bible about Mary and Martha, well, the Lord wants me to be a Mary.' Bunch of plumb foolishness to get out of doing her duties to her house and children, if you ask me."

Getting to his feet, Brother Jim Jordan walked out to meet Randall. "Glad you could make it, Reverend Clay. Reverend Poe and I was just a-sitting out here waiting because of the heat. If this don't break soon, I can't begin to foretell the suffering this heat and drought could bring. Just like the seven plagues of Egypt."

This didn't make much sense to Randall, but then anything that Jim Jordan said rarely made sense. He spoke in rolling, disconnected phrases pulled at random from the Good Book. The trouble was that if you listened to him long enough, it began to sound like it might make sense. When old Preacher Banta died, Jim Jordan had come from somewhere down in Tennessee to take his place. He'd come with a mule and a wagon. The wagon was filled with his household truck, his wife, and four children. They'd all stayed; the children married and were now an entrenched part of the town and its families. Two of the girls had married into the LeCompte family and the other one had bettered herself by marrying one of Bob McAfee's boys, the one that started that funeral parlor over at Nelsonville. The only boy had married into the Smoot family and farmed with his father-in-law over beyond the Philpot Plantation. It looked like Jim, skinny and resilient as a hickory stick, was going to be speaking in tongues in this particular Holy Roller church as long as he drew breath. He had made his connections.

"Morning, Randall." Adam Poe heaved himself to his feet and followed the other two men into the church and back into Jordan's tiny office, which contained a battered rolltop desk and two decrepit cane-bottomed chairs.

"Sit yourself down, take a load off of your feet." Jordan positioned himself behind his desk and began to talk about how the Good Time Gospel Quartet was going to be visiting Taylor Springs.

"Now, these quartet boys come out of Alabama, I believe the town is Prattville, which ain't too far out of Montgomery. From what I understand, they got their start singing right there in the Light House Tabernacle Pentecostal Church, and was so good that soon they was a-singing in Montgomery and Birmingham and all over the state. They bought themselves a bus and fixed it up and been singing in Georgia and Tennessee and Louisiana, just all over the place. I have it on good authority that they bring the powerful message of the Lord on wings of song, and everywhere they go they bring a blessing. Now, Muncie Purvis, who pastors the Nelsonville church, is a-having them in next Friday night and they'd be willing to come on over here for a Saturday night gospel sing. I figure that if we was to announce it to our congregations this Sunday and also talk it up all over town, we could get most of the people in Taylor Springs in for a spiritual and uplifting experience. We could all band together in a Christian effort to glorify the Lord in song."

Randall leaned back in his chair. "Well, now, Brother Jordan, it sounds fine and like it could really bring the community together in a Christian experience. But since the three of us sitting here are the shepherds of our flocks, we know that we are not only responsible for the spiritual welfare of our churches, but also the financial well-being."

"Yes, indeedy," Adam interrupted, "do having these boys cost us anything, Jim? You know with times being the way they are . . ."

"No, sir, that is the beauty of it, men. While we are a-bringing the Christian community together in this common effort and bringing them this fine Christian entertainment, it don't cost us one red cent."

"I don't understand how that could work," Randall said. "How could these boys afford to travel and go all over the place in a bus without having any way to meet their expenses or support themselves?"

"Well, sir, this is how it works. All we do is guarantee these boys fifty dollars. Now, hold on. Between our three

churches we ain't going to have any trouble guaranteeing
that money and we ain't going to have to pay any of it
anyway. When the quartet is finished singing, they take up
a love offering from the people, and if it's over fifty dollars,
we don't pay a cent. If it's under fifty dollars, we just make
up the difference. Now, every pastor I've talked to tells me
that the love offering is always way over fifty dollars, praise
the Lord, and they ain't never had to pay a cent."

What Jim Jordan didn't bother to mention to the other
two was that any love offering over fifty dollars the Good
Time Gospel Boys collected, why, they gave ten percent of
that amount to the host church. No need to mention that.
After all, he was the one responsible for bringing the Good
Time Gospel Boys to town, and he'd just keep any money
gained for a kind of private fund to do his own good works.

"Jim," Adam wiped his face with his bandanna again,
"I'd say this is a fine opportunity what with those condi-
tions. I'm sure that we could fill the church."

Jordan chuckled, "Yes, sir, why it's just like bringing
the psalmist David before King Solomon."

"I'm not quite sure I follow you there, Brother Jordan," Randall stated, "however, it does seem like an excellent idea. If we're all in agreement, I think you should
contact Brother Purvis and arrange to have the Good Time
Gospel Quartet be here next Saturday night."

Adam Poe slapped his hand on his wide thigh. "It's
done, then. Now, Jim, I think you ought to contact Brother
Glover Hayes down at the African Methodist Episcopal
church and we should invite all the coloreds, too. After all,
they are a part of this Christian community that we are talking about and we can save them pews in the back of the
church."

Randall looked up, surprised. "That's a fine idea,
Adam. I never thought of that. What do you men say we go

on over to McAfee's store and get us a cold drink. I don't believe I've ever known it to be so hot for so long. And while we're over there we can let Mr. Bob know our plans so he can be telling everybody who comes in the store. I think this is surely going to cause a lot of excitement in town."

They crossed the street, and as they opened the screen door of the store, a bell tinkled announcing their arrival. Bob McAfee looked up. "I do declare, if it ain't the total preaching force of Taylor Springs. Have all three of you boys come in here for to pray over me, or did you have something else in mind?"

Adam laughed. "Better watch it there, Bob. You are getting dangerously close to being irreverent. We might have to bring lightning down on your head or something equally bad."

Bubba Taylor was standing over by the meat counter, chewing on a chunk of rat cheese that Bob's wife, Pearlie, had just cut for him. "Shoot, nothing you could bring down on McAfee could puncture his thick hide or his thick head. Howdy, Randall, Adam, Brother Jordan."

"No," Randall said, "We are not concerned with the precarious state of your salvation, Bob. We are thirsty and we would like real quick three bottles of Coca-Cola. And some of that rat cheese that Bubba is devouring wouldn't go down too bad, either, Pearlie." He turned to Bubba, "I went over to football practice yesterday morning and Bucky was looking mighty fine. I do think that Dagostino fellow just might be what the doctor ordered."

Bubba grinned. "He surely seems like he's going to work those boys. He seems mighty sure that he can get a football scholarship for my boy Bucky and Junie Hayes at the university. I don't know, but Ruth is all set up about it. What with times the way they are, that's the only way

Bucky is going to get to college. Course, that is if he wants to go. Not sure he needs that—he's got the farm and maybe he needs to just start working it with me."

"Well," Jordan intoned, "whatever the Lord wills will come to pass. Anyway, we got some exciting news for you all." He took a long gulp of the Coca-Cola that Bob handed him. "The Good Time Gospel Boys is coming to town."

Pearlie McAfee could hardly wait to shoo the men out the door, her husband and Bubba Taylor and Adam Poe on their way to football practice and the Reverend Clay and Brother Jordan back to their churches, so she could ring up everyone in town and pass along the news about the Good Time Gospel Boys.

Located just to the right of the store's front door, the telephone switchboard was installed in a small room that also housed the post office. Pearlie McAfee was both the postmistress and the telephone operator of Taylor Springs, and when she wasn't looking over everybody's mail, she was listening in on the telephone calls. Any time anyone turned the crank on their telephone, it rang on Pearlie's switchboard. They'd tell Pearlie the person they wanted to talk to and then she'd have to ring that telephone and put the proper plug in so they could talk. There wasn't much that went on in town that Pearlie McAfee didn't know.

"Hello, hello. Is this you, Bertha? Yes, this is Pearlie. Well, I called you so's you'd be the first to have the news!"

Randall Clay steered his coupe down the graveled road and pulled up in front of the Southern Methodist Episcopal church. He decided to go directly to the church office and not stop in the parsonage first. Pearlie McAfee for sure had already rung up Aunt Bertha to pass on the news about the gospel quartet coming to town. Aunt Bertha would be all in a tizzy and Randall didn't want to listen to her. He wanted to think about Lizzie LeCompte and his meeting with her this afternoon. Randall knew he wouldn't be bothered; he had always insisted that he must have privacy in his office so that he could meditate and write his sermons. If he was needed, Aunt Bertha could just ring him on the phone.

The stench assaulted his nostrils immediately when he opened the door into the sanctuary. Stunned, he stood immobile. His mind refused to believe what his sense of smell was relaying. Looking toward the altar, he saw the excrement smeared on the altar rail, the pulpit, the cross.

His thoughts raced frantically. Oh, my God . . . this can't be real. I'm hallucinating. The stench, the stench of hell, the desecration . . . this is punishment for the sin I commited in the temple of the Lord yesterday. . . . I broke my vow, I gloried in breaking my vow. This is the work of demons. It is a warning of my evil . . . done by witches, yes, witches.

He threw himself frantically on the excrement-covered altar and prayed for forgiveness and to be saved from witches, for God knew that Lizzie LeCompte was a witch. She was Lilith, he had known that from the beginning. And he had succumbed to her temptations. But God knew that the fault lay with her. She was the evil one; he was the victim.

He rose, knowing that he must clean and purify this place. No one must ever know about it, this indictment against him, this result of his sin of lust. Stumbling down the same stairs he had sensuously trod yesterday with Lizzie, he ran into the basement and gathered a bucket and soap and rags. Returning to the sanctuary, he fell to his knees and began to scrub.

The smell of lye soap and wet wood began to permeate the stifling stink in the sanctuary. Randall raised himself to his feet and stumbled to open the stained glass memorial windows that lined both walls of the church. He remained rigid before the last window, his body bathed in its red and gold reflections. Inscribed to the memory of Ramona Clay, it portrayed an agonized Christ being crucified, bloody and frozen in colored glass forever.

As the hot, humid air entered the church, Randall stood before his mama's memorial window with tears streaming down his face. Stooped and slow, he walked to gather his bucket of filthy water, his soap, his brush. Returning to the basement, he carried the bucket to the back door and flung its contents outside.

Sukie, gathering bird feathers for her charms in the woods behind the church, looked up and saw him. She wondered how come that preacher man was doing the cleaning when they already had them two Jones girls come in to do it twice a week.

7

Across the road, Bertha Hayes sat at her dressing table, looking into the mirror. Holding her marcelled hair between two fingers, she carefully clamped the wave clips on each ridge of gray hair. A lady can never be too careful of her appearance, she mused. That's what Mama always used to say. She peered into the silvering glass but did not recognize the aging woman who looked back at her. The plump face with slightly sagging jowls and a fine cross-hatching of lines was not her face. Her face was round and firm with a fine peaches and cream complexion. Her eyes were a sparkling blue with tiny flecks of gray, not those tired, washed-out eyes in the mirror. Her hair was not gray; it was a shining blond twisted in a thick mass on top of her head. The thick, corseted body did not belong to Bertha Hayes; her body was round and lithe and sweetly curved in an hourglass shape. How can I still feel sixteen inside, she pondered, and look like this on the outside? Is it because I never married, never was bedded by a man, never bore a child? Maybe I am trapped forever, inside, as a girl of sixteen.

She had fallen in love that summer of her sixteenth

year. Bertha remembered it as a season of blue-skied, golden-aired days when, dressed in full-skirted, ruffled gowns of white muslin and blue dotted swiss and peach and lavender organdy, she cut roses to twine in her hair and sipped lemonade while gently rocking in the wicker swing that hung on the front porch. It was the summer of at last being a grown-up lady and paying calls with Ramona and Mama and leaving her own cards, engraved in Spencerian script "Miss Bertha Hayes," at the Philpots and the Taylors, even going into Boonetown once a week, in the shiny buggy, to pay calls on selected families. It was the summer of her sensuous blooming, an unfolding that flowed through her body as slow and sweet as honey.

She looked back into the mirror and saw her face flushed with the joy and the shame of remembering. The affair began with an innocent call. She and Mama and Ramona in their sweeping skirts and huge flowered and feathered hats and long buttoned gloves and beaded reticules leaving to visit the Philpot Plantation because Thursday was Ora and Nora's at-home day.

How odd, she thought, that all these years have passed and I still recollect the day of the week. Lord, we swept up the drive and Roger Byrd was stationed there to hand the ladies out of their buggies. He was always in attendance on the Philpot at-home days. Same age as I was, sixteen, but skinny and gangling, red hair parted in the middle, slicked down, his nose already grown to man-size and too big for his still-baby face. I was already years ahead of him. Girls ripen so much quicker than the boys.

But still, I was curious about Roger. Everybody knew there was some scandal attached to Roger Byrd and the Philpots, but nobody ever came out and said so publicly. Guess if you never say out loud that something is so, then it isn't so. Guess it's easier for us all that way. But I do remember overhearing Mama talking to Miss Jenny Taylor one day. I was real little, couldn't have been more than nine years old. "Jenny, you and I both know that Roger is no more that French woman's child than my Ramona or Bertha is. And we both suspect who the daddy is. Dear Lord, every soul in Taylor Springs knew about that carrying on. You can't keep no secrets in this place, you know how the darkies talk. However, as long as appearances are kept, I reckon it doesn't matter none. Ora and Nora both treat him just like their own child and I'm sure the right thing is being done by him."

That day, Roger escorted us up to the front door. We left our cards in the silver tray on the hall table. I was so proud to have my own cards to leave, feeling so grown up and ladylike. Ramona peered in the big baroque mirror that hung over the card table and adjusted her hat. Mama said, "For heaven's sake, Ramona, quit your preening. You look just fine. Ever since Burton Clay started calling on you all you do is want to admire yourself in the mirror."

"Mama, I'm just trying to make sure that I look presentable." She smoothed back her pompadour and bit her lips, trying to make them look red. Ramona never was really pretty; her face was narrow and her nose too wide. She didn't have my pretty coloring either. She was sallow, her complexion was almost the same tint as her dishwater blond hair, and to tell the truth, she didn't have much of a bosom. Randall surely got his good looks from his daddy—that Burton was a fine figure of a man. Never could understand why he married Ramona. I used to think that maybe it was because he thought she was what the boys used to call a hot number. I'd seen her run her fingers up and down his arm and even over the back of his neck. I could have told him that all my sister wanted was a husband of good family and property. That girl was born conniving and cold as a chunk of ice.

Bertha remained transfixed in her thoughts. Course, he found that out quick enough. I'll never forget the night he died right out at the Philpot Plantation. I knew why he was there and exactly what he was doing when he had that heart attack. Not that I'm judging him, or her either, for that matter. I can't be anyone to be judging someone else. Everybody knew what was going on. In this town we just don't act like we know what's going on. Must say that it didn't bother Ramona a bit. I do believe she was relieved to be shed of him. Course I can't complain. She invited me in to live with her and Randall and gave her poor old maid sister a home. It must have given her a great deal of satisfaction that her pretty younger sister turned out to be a spinster. Oh, yes, I was pretty, so pretty.

I remember after Ramona moved away from the looking glass, I sneaked a peek into it and saw myself as fair as the rose of Sharon. I had a smile on my face as we entered the front parlor and dimpled my prettiest as we were greeted by Ora and Nora.

They must have been around thirty-six years old that year, and both of them still had that glorious red hair and were still elegant-looking women. They were twins, but the only feature they shared was their hair. Nora was short and round; folks said she took after her mother's side, the Taylors. Ora was tall, sylphlike, and had the narrow straight Philpot nose. Her complexion was the color of heavy Guernsey cream, and the bridge of her pert nose was dusted with freckles. Bold russet eyebrows framed large green eyes and her generous mouth was set firmly in her porcelain oval face. The most striking thing about Nora was that her eyes were a topaz color, a pale honey-brown. Nora and Ora were both standing there, smiling and gracious.

Then she looked at me. I'll never forget how she looked at me. I was so young then, but I had already felt that unease in my body that summer. I wasn't sure what it was or what it meant, but, oh yes, I felt it. There's no need to pretend to myself. Her glance seemed to bore right inside me, and when she took my hand, I felt her touch clear down to that warm center in my body.

"Bertha," she spoke, "all of a sudden you're so grown up and you've certainly become a beauty. You're just going to have to spend a lot of time out here this summer. Sister and I need some youth and beauty around this place. Ever since we closed Papa's academy, we rattle around here. Of course, we do have Roger visiting often, but we do need some feminine charm around here, too."

Mama was happy to have me go. To be close to the Philpots was an assurance of the highest social ranking in Taylor Springs. I was happy to go, for she soon taught me what those vague stirrings in my body were and how to gratify them. It was my summer of kisses and caresses and slow, sweet surrender. When autumn came, she sent me on my way, saying it was time for us to leave one another in that particular way, that I was now fully grown and it was time for me to think of marrying. After that I could never marry. I never wanted a man. Funny, all these years, and we see each other all the time, but neither one of us has ever spoken of it. I don't think that anybody knew what was going on between us those hot summer afternoons when I lay naked on her big four-poster bed.

"This bed was brought to this very house by my great-great-grandmother back in 1786, Bertha. Her name was America, America Tryon, and she was a great lady from a great family. In fact, she was such a great lady, she could find no one in this town with whom she could associate. Of course, I truly suspect Sister and I are the only people of breeding left in Taylor Springs."

She ran her long, slender fingers over my breast and down my flanks. "Not that I am insulting you, my beautiful child. We do share some of the same bloodlines, you know, or perhaps you don't know. My grandfather, Solomon, married your great-aunt Margaret. Do you know anything about the Hayes, child?" She laughed. "Perhaps we share more than you realize. Did anyone ever tell you where Esau Hayes came from? Maybe that's where you get this hot blood, this abandonment." She began to kiss my neck, my open mouth, and the talking ceased.

Bertha rose heavily from the stool, walking over to the open window. I remember asking her later, her thoughts continued, what she meant by the Hayes and hot blood. She tossed that red hair back and looked gravely at me. "My dear, you are certainly mature enough to know what certain people in certain families in this town have always known. When my great-great-grandfather settled this place he brought with him a light-skinned negress and a very light-skinned baby boy. That baby boy was Esau Hayes. Asa Philpot finally had four boys by that negress before he married. When America arrived here, she moved them out of this very house into the slave quarters. Esau ran away and was never found, as a slave, that is. He came back here in the 1830s as a doctor and a white man. How he must have laughed when his daughter, Margaret, married Solomon Philpot. Just think of it, Solomon and Margaret had the same grandfather, Asa Philpot."

"The whole idea is deliciously shocking, don't you think? And that's not all, because the second light-skinned son of Asa left the plantation, too. He ran away to the Taylor house, was freed from slavery, and took the name Taylor. He married a Clay and today's Taylors are his descendents. Asa's other two bastards remained as slaves here on the plantation and founded the darkie side of the Hayes family."

I was never quite sure whether or not to believe her story, Bertha thought. I reckon it could be true and if it was it didn't matter. If nobody acted like it was true, then it wasn't true. Besides, what difference did it make if the white Hayes and the colored Hayes were all mixed up. They both knew their proper place. Like what does it matter if anybody knew about that summer. If they did, they never let on and that's what really matters.

Bertha sighed and walked back to her dressing table, where she removed the wave clamps from her hair. Moistening her fingertip with spit, she smoothed her eyebrows, still not recognizing the old face that looked back from her mirror.

Just then, Colored Bertha's voice boomed up the front stairway, "Miss Bertha, dinner be ready directly. You gonna phone up Mr. Randall? His car's over there in front of the church, you better phone him up right now or the food won't be no good by the time he gets here. That boy sure never did hurry none on nobody's account, well, except for his mama when she was a-living."

When Randall finally answered his office phone— Pearlie McAfee had to ring him fifteen times—he said softly, "No, Aunt Bertha, I don't want any dinner. I have been praying and I have to continue praying. Now, please have Colored Bertha go down to the LeComptes and tell Lizzie that I cannot meet with her this afternoon. Yes, she was supposed to come over here so we could see about tables for the Little Angels Sunday school room. No, I must stay here and please don't phone me again. I'll be back across the road when I've finished what I have to do. Yes,

we'll talk about the Good Time Gospel Quartet later; I'll tell
you all about it."

Colored Bertha puffed down the road on her way to
the LeComptes. She didn't appreciate Mr. Randall sending
her down to no trashy house for to give a message to no
trashy girl. Miss Bertha was carrying on so yesterday about
how Mr. Randall was going to save that girl's soul, after
having her sit right at the table like she was quality folks.
Well, Miss Bertha got up and left, and she didn't see how
they was looking at each other and acting after that. Save
her soul indeed. Mr. Randall might be a preacher man, but
he just like any other man. He's got that thing between his
legs and it's always just a-begging to be put somewhere.
Didn't matter is they black or white, menfolk always looking for the flesh. Don't think they went over to the church
yesterday to talk about no soul saving.

Sitting on the steps of the sagging porch, Lizzie was
painting her nails with Tangee polish. She was just hoping
for a breath of fresh air, to get away from the whiny voice
of her ma and the constant screeching of the younger children. She looked hard at her nails and her hands and declared that they looked as good as Jean Harlow's. To go to
Hollywood, now that would really be something, wouldn't
it? There'd be real live palm trees, just like in the pictures in
the movie magazines, and glamorous clothes, and shiny
cars, and champagne, and handsome men who would probably just die to be able to do it to her.

Course, Brother Clay certainly wasn't ugly. She wiggled her bottom against the splintery wooden step when she
thought about what he'd done to her yesterday. It surely
passed what Bucky and Junie had ever done, course, they
were still just boys. Brother Clay had come right out and
said that doing it was a glory to God just like she had always thought. Course, she wondered if he meant that doing

it with him was a glory to God and it might be wrong to do it with somebody else. Maybe it was all right to do it with him because he was a preacher. Pretty soon, she'd go on up to the church and he'd be waiting for her. Course, Mr. Dagostino was expecting her up at the school, too, but he'd just have to wait his turn. Lizzie grinned and thought why give up something you know is so good for a pig in the poke.

"Lizzie, Lizzie," Colored Bertha yelled from down the bottom of the path to the house. None of the coloreds ever called her Miss Lizzie like they properly should, and it just made her so mad. She knew they thought her family was white trash, but at least they was higher than coloreds.

"Brother Clay done sent me down here," Colored Bertha continued, "for to tell you not to come up to his church office for he going to be busy all afternoon."

Lizzie got up from the steps and swayed down the path. "Thank you, Colored Bertha," she spoke in her most ladylike voice, "please tell Brother Clay that that's just fine with me as I'm going to be very busy myself all afternoon." She sashayed back toward the porch, wondering if she'd have time to wash and dry her hair before going down to the school to meet with Tony Dagostino.

As Colored Bertha turned back from the LeCompte shack and trudged up the road to the parsonage, Sukie Bee lumbered out of the woods and followed close behind her. Sukie didn't bother hollering hello at Bertha because there was a lot hanging heavy on her mind. She couldn't be bothered passing the time of day and chattering right now. Her thoughts were churning; she knew down deep that something troubling was in the air and something needed to be done about it. Let me see, now. I done gathered up the bird feathers, really need wild turkey feathers for to be a proper charm, but ain't no wild turkies left around these parts. Got the feathers, tied 'em up with a piece of dried bone, been down to the spring. Lord, it surely does stink down there, especially when it so hot and no rain. I do believe the plat man is loose, that's it, the plat man is free and wandering these parts.

Dumb white folks and dumb niggers. They run around and say the plat man he is just the boogeyman, something for to scare young'uns, not for real. Oh, he real, all right. He the evil one, he the devil. No cause to laugh at Sukie's voodoo. I know 'cause my mama taught me and her mama afore that. Needs charms to ward off the plat man. Something wrong with Mr. Randall and that church. I'm going back up there. Can't let no plat man loose in no church, good God, no. Why, he take over everything once he take over a church.

Sukie, immense and brooding, stalked stealthily to the back of the church and investigated the wet patch where Randall had emptied his bucket. She groaningly bent over, and sniffed. Good Lord a mercy, she keened in her mind, it's shit the preacher man was cleaning out. That is the worst, the very worst. Plat man done possess some soul to smear shit inside this church.

She quietly moved to the side of the building and raised her bulk on tiptoe to peek into one of the open windows. Spying no one inside, she quickly moved to the front and entered the sanctuary. Chanting, under her breath, she carefully laid three of her feather and bone charms on the altar, and then swayed backward down the aisle. When she left the church, she headed back to colored town, for she knew she had to find a rooster for tonight, had to cut out the heart at the stroke of midnight, had to drink the blood, had to sacrifice to keep the plat man away.

Long about dusk, Randall, convinced that he had prayed away the sins of the flesh, the temptations of Lilith, the desecration visited upon him and his church by that witch, left his office and went into the sanctuary to close the stained glass windows. He began in the back and when he arrived at the front, he glanced over at the altar and saw the three neatly tied clumps of bird feathers and bones lying there—voodoo charms. Breaking out in a cold sweat, he stood frozen, screaming silently inside his brain. Slowly, he forced himself to approach the altar, he forced his clawlike hand to grasp and gather each charm to put in his coat pocket, he forced his stiff zombie legs to walk out of the church, across the road, and into the parsonage. When he finally stood in the parsonage hall, his eyes rolled back into their lids and his mouth started to emit howling screams.

"What is it, oh, what is it?" Bertha jumped from her chair in the parlor and ran through the archway into the hall. Staring at her convulsed, howling nephew, she remained rooted. Bursting through the doorway that led from the back hall, Colored Bertha stopped suddenly, goose bumps rising on her flesh. Without a word or a glance at each other, the two women slowly, monolithically advanced on Randall and, folding him in their arms, half-carried him into the parlor, where they all three collapsed on the sofa.

Babbling, spit running down the sides of his mouth, tears running down his cheeks, he screamed and sobbed and told them of the excrement, the desecration, the witches, the voodoo charms. About Lizzie Lilith, the witch, and her evil in tempting him. But if God had forgiven him why were the clumps of bone and feathers on the altar, yes, witches and voodoo. It didn't make sense, did it . . . did it?

"Shh, be quiet now, Randall," Aunt Bertha crooned. "It's all right. None of it really happened, dear boy. You just imagined it all. It was a dream, that's what it was. It's so hot, it was so hot over in the church and you just fell into a fevered sleep and had a bad dream. You've been working too hard, that's all. You've just worn your body and soul out working so hard to bring souls to the Lord. That's what it is, why, let me feel. Yes, you're burning up with fever, you didn't eat any dinner. Hallucinations and bad dreams, that's all it was, Randall."

Pushing his hand into his pocket, Randall drew out the three clumps of feathers and bone and, extending his arm, held the charms rigidly in front of him. Then, as his body began to shake, he started moaning and sobbing for his mama.

Getting up, Colored Bertha backed away from the sofa, whimpering, "Plat man charms, they be plat man charms."

Aunt Bertha rose and pulled Randall to his feet. He freed his hands from hers and then stared at the charms. His eyes were red with weeping and glazed with madness. Words slowly spewed out of his slack, wet mouth.

"I have done evil and now there will be retribution. I have done evil and now evil will be done. Evil will be done and it will be done soon. Vengeance is mine, sayeth the Lord . . . and His sword is sharp and swift . . . swift . . . swift." Randall Clay screamed and fell to the floor, his fingers convulsing around the clumps of feathers and bone.

8

Only six people truly knew what happened the next morning, that sizzling hot Saturday morning, up in the hills beyond Philpot Plantation. The rest of Taylor Springs had their suspicions, but convention dictated that their speculations not be publicly voiced.

Saturday's heat still hadn't broken by Sunday morning. The sun rose in the brassy sky and the air still tasted of sulphur from the springs. Myna Smoot doubled over to tie her shoes and swore to the Lord she'd never be able to straighten up. She dabbed at her face with the edge of her petticoat and surely hoped that Randall didn't get too long-winded with his sermon today. Moving down the hallway, she tapped on Tony's door. "You 'bout ready, Mr. Dagostino?"

Tony, suffocating in his flannel suit, his shirt already wet and smelling from sweat, called back, "Be right with you, Miss Smoot."

She waited for him out on the porch, sitting in the rocker, trying to move the air in front of her face with a paper fan. There came the Professor and Mary William down the road. Sure did beat all how that man took care of

that poor creature. He had her all scrubbed up, the lank
gray hair parted neatly on one side, skinned back with a
blue barrette on the other, the gawky body tented in a
yellow flowered dress, her stick legs ending in white bobby
socks and brown tie oxfords. And Myna did admit it was
amazing how Mary William did behave in church. She'd sit
there, just as good as gold, humming her little song quietly,
just staring from one colored window to the other. Something about those windows surely did quieten down Mary
William.

The screen door slammed and Tony walked out on the
porch. "Good morning, Professor Sheely, Miss Mary William." Tony helped Myna up out of the rocker and took her
arm as they started down the walk to the road.

"Professor," Myna began, "I reckon you already heard
the news, not about the gospel quartet, but the bad news. I
can't hardly believe that the good Lord would let something
like that happen."

Mary William drooled and started blowing spit bubbles. Her father withdrew his handkerchief and gently
wiped her mouth. "Yes, Miss Smoot, a real tragedy, and
I'm sure it hit you extra hard, too, Mr. Dagostino." Tony
nodded solemnly as they continued walking toward the
Southern Methodist Episcopal church.

Putting on her best white straw hat with the wide brim and
the clever cluster of deep red cherries attached to the white
grosgrain band, Bertha took a last look in the hall mirror.
Sighing, she pushed the white gloves over her sweaty fingers, took up her shiny white pocketbook, and left for the
church.

Lord, she prayed, let Randall be all right. Nobody will
ever know what he said, what happened between him and

that girl, what happened later in the church. Soon he'll believe it never happened, because I'm insisting it didn't. But this latest thing, this thing that took place yesterday, can't deny that. But we don't have to admit as to why we suspicion it happened. It'll just be a bad accident, because that's all we'll let it be.

She entered the churchyard, nodding to the groups who stood in small clumps discussing the tragedy, their solemn expressions befitting the occasion.

Just as he did every Sunday morning, Roger Byrd drove the Packard touring car out to Philpot Plantation to pick up Miss Ora and Nora to carry them to church. After all, Khaki and Eula did deserve Sunday morning off to go to their own church, so Roger did his own chauffeuring, and since he and Lucille took Sunday dinner at the plantation it was no hardship not to have Eula at the farm.

"Lucille, will you please stop that sniffling? And blow your nose. Your red eyes and runny nose will not change anything."

Raising the pink veil that dropped from her rose Princess Eugenie hat with one hand, and searching for a handkerchief in her pink pocketbook with the other, Lucille continued blubbering. While rummaging through her purse, she found a Hershey bar, tore off the wrapping, and crammed the whole block of melting chocolate in her mouth.

Coming to a dignified stop in front of the Philpot veranda, Roger descended from the car to fetch the ladies who, along with Ludie, were waiting there. Gallantly handing Ora and Nora into the back seat where they squeezed on either side of Lucille, he placed Ludie in the front beside him. He delivered her every Sunday to the African Methodist Episcopal church before turning the car around to drive back to his place of worship. He always hopped out and opened the car door for her. She would descend regally, aware of the admiring eyes on her, saying, "Thank you, Mr. Roger. Please don't bother picking me up. Khaki will be proud to fetch me back."

"Roger, I cannot tell you how dreadfully Sister and I feel about the distressing news." Ora leaned forward to make certain that she could be heard. "It seems as if the whole world has gone awry lately. Of course, we did try to telephone, but Pearlie said they'd asked her not to ring through, and one can understand their need for privacy during this time."

"Lucille, turn around here and look at me." Nora looked searchingly at the moon face. "For heaven's sake, child, you have chocolate all over your mouth. Do wipe it off. And I can tell you've been crying, too. Remember, my dear, noblesse oblige."

Outside the Pentecostal church, Lizzie LeCompte stood with her mother, her passel of bratty little sisters and brothers, and the preacher's wife. Murmuring bands of the Holy Roller congregation approached and then receded from Lizzie like slow, curling waves.

Lizzie maintained an appropriately solemn expression on her face. She stood, ripe and bursting, in her white piqué dress, but felt that the big black picture hat she wore indicated the graveness of the occasion. She graciously extended a black-gloved hand to all who approached her and from time to time delicately dabbed at her eyes with the black-bordered handkerchief she had found buried in the bottom of the trunk her ma had brought with her from West Virginia.

"Yes, ma'am, I cannot tell you what a terrible thing it was. It still purely seems like a bad dream." Lizzie felt almost like a movie star. Why, this whole scene could be a picture like in *Photoplay* magazine. Just like she was a movie star who was surrounded by her adoring fans. "I felt like I just had to come to church today, well, like the Lord was calling me here. It would have been easier to stay at home, being private in my grief, but I knew my place was in Jesus' house today of all days."

The surrounding crowd murmured approval.

"And I knew I just had to be with my mama. I know that Brother Randall Clay understands why I wasn't able to be with my Little Angel Sunday school class down at the Methodist church this morning."

Patting Lizzie on the arm, Belle Jordan interjected, "And we are mighty happy to have this girl here with us today. Her mama has become a pillar of this congregation ever since she transferred her membership to us two years ago, and we are here to support and succor her and Lizzie in their time of need. I know that Jim is going to bring a mighty message to all of us this morning. Why, he said to me at the breakfast table, 'Belle, I feel out of this terrible thing is going to come a blessing and I feel the spirit coming on me so's I can bring that blessing.'"

Lizzie smiled demurely at the preacher's wife and then undulated up the steps and into the church.

Dressed up in his Sunday black suit that Dr. Burton Clay had passed down to him years ago, Khaki stood sweating outside the colored church, watching all the women clucking and scratching like a bunch of hens taking a dust bath. They did like to talk, he laughed to himself. They never shut up from sunrise to sunset, and not just colored women, white women, too. Never did come out and say anything direct, just talked around everything. Like if you don't say it direct, it ain't so, but if you just hint around it, you can

enjoy the possibilities. Like what Mr. Roger said when we
was drinking down at Sukie Bee's.

He glanced up to see Roger Byrd opening the car door
to help Ludie out. Walking over to the Packard, Khaki saw
Miss Ora and Miss Nora squashed up in the back seat on
either side of Lucille. They was smiling and nodding and
waving at the crowd just like they was royalty or something, while Lucille was cramming her mouth with a candy
bar. Khaki doffed his hat in greeting and took his mama's
arm.

"Surely was sorry for to hear the bad news. Elvira
done come by last night and the way she was a-carrying on,
we done figured that that coal oil stove blowed up."

Sukie, Elvira, and Eula broke away from the women-
folk and pounced around the car like a pride of lionesses. "I
tell you strange, bad things going on around here, Mr.
Roger," Sukie moaned. "I knew two days ago something
bad was loose in this town. Oh, I done seen the sights and
the signs. Saw the plat eye. Tried to ward it off, but now I
know the plat man is loose and wandering. He was wandering the old buffalo trails yesterday morning when this bad
thing done happened."

Saturday morning had dawned choking hot and bone dry.
Before the sun was full up, Bucky, Junie, and Lizzie were
bouncing along in the old pickup on their way to go rabbit
hunting. Lizzie, stuffed into a pair of her younger brother's
cotton wash pants, sat in the middle of the boys yelling
football cheers, "Strawberry shortcake, huckleberry pie,
V-I-C-T-O-R-Y."

Bucky clamped his hand over her open mouth. "Lord,
Lizzie, you're yelling loud enough to wake the dead." She
ran the tip of her tongue over his palm. "Lizzie," he

warned, "you're about to bite off more than you can chew."

Junie took his eyes off the road to glance over at them. "What are you talking about? What are you two up to over there?"

"What I mean is," Bucky replied, "is that if Miss LeCompte here don't quiet down, she is going to wake up everybody in this town. Plus, soon we are going to be passing the historic and famous Philpot Plantation and if she wakes up the historic and famous Philpot sisters, they might insist that we stop in for a spot of tea and a visit, and we will never get to the ridge."

"Shoot," Junie snorted, "old Lizzie would never get inside Miss Ora and Miss Nora's front door in them britches she has on. They'd make her go home and get dressed proper first."

Lizzie replied that so far as she was concerned she was dressed proper, at least proper for rabbit hunting. Besides, in the movie magazines, women movie stars were pictured all the time wearing trousers, even Lillian Gish. And they weren't men's pants, either. They were made for women and some were real loose and floppy and called pajamas, spelled p-y-j-a-m-a-s.

The truck jolted by the Philpot house, and then Junie took a sharp right up the dirt road that led back into the hills. The road was narrow, packed-down ruts shadowed on either side by tall stands of oak and maple trees. The tree leaves hung limp in the compacted, sulphurous air; the only sound was the complaining whine of the truck's engine as it climbed the grade up into the hills.

Junie took one hand off the steering wheel and reached over to tousle Lizzie's curls and ask, "What you been up to, Lizzie? Bucky and me ain't seen you for three-four days. You ain't been stepping out on the two of us, have you?"

She wiggled around on the seat and opened her big eyes wider, glancing from one boy to the other. "Why, Junie Hayes, I've been meeting with Reverend Clay about my Little Angels Sunday school class. We have decided to buy the Baby Jesus coloring books, and you better believe me that it took a lot of thought. However, me and Brother Clay thought we needed to be modern so our little children could be brought to Jesus in any way we could reach them. And then yesterday, I went over to the school to talk to Mr. Dagostino. I needed his advice about what courses I should be taking this year just in case I decided to go on over to secretarial school in Nelsonville next year. You can never tell how far a girl will go when she knows how to type."

Bucky allowed that he surely hoped she'd gotten good advice from Mr. Dagostino. Lizzie assured both of them that it was some of the best she had ever had.

"Anyways," Lizzie continued, "a body hasn't even had time to think what with all the excitement going on about the Good Time Gospel Boys coming to town. I can't hardly wait until next Saturday night to see them. It's just like real live movie stars are coming to Taylor Springs. I've been wondering which of you two gentlemen would like to carry me to the performance? Been thinking you're probably going to escort Lucille Byrd, ain't you, Bucky? I mean since she's done accepted your invitation to the dance."

Junie patted her on the knee. "Don't you worry your pretty head. Since old Bucky boy has got his self obligated to court Miss Byrd, I reckon the two of us will just have to carry on. I'll escort you to the gospel sing. Maybe Bucky'll save us a seat by him and Lucille. Course with Lucille, maybe he better save us a whole pew."

Bucky scowled. Damn that Junie. He sure was ready to move right in on Lizzie. Course, to be fair, Junie didn't know how things really were between Lizzie and him, else he wouldn't be acting this way. "You two just lighten up now. You know the reason I'm taking Lucille to that dance is because you told me it was the Christian thing to do, Lizzie. And then you double dog dared me, June Bug. Fine friends, you are. And I'll be sure to save a whole pew, Hayes, 'cause I'll need a whole pew to lay you out in after I clobber you one." The three of them laughed.

Junie pulled the truck to a stop in a small clearing near the summit of the hill. "Here we are, Rabbit Ridge. Let's go hunting." They piled joyously out of the cab of the truck, running back to pick up the shotguns that the boys had stowed in the truck bed. Lizzie expertly checked out her firearm and declared she was ready to go.

Bucky looked at her, that ass crammed into those tight pants, and determined that she was going off into those woods with him. By God, if he was going to lay it all on the line by taking Lucille to the football dance, he was entitled to sweeten the pot beforehand. Junie looked at her, those tits straining against the tight-buttoned blouse, and decided that since she was secretly really all his, he was ready to openly claim her.

Lizzie stood in the hot, still air, gun held erect, licking her lips. Both boys stood before her, ready to begin the steps of an atavistic mating dance. She slowly lowered her shotgun. "Listen, I think we should all three split up . . . have a better chance that way. I'll go on up the ridge, and Bucky, you work your way over to the clearing. Junie, you go back in the woods. Now the first one that bags three rabbits will fire three shots and that'll be the signal to meet back here by the truck." Holding her gun crooked in her arm, she started up the path that led to the crest of the hill. Bucky and Junie, each thinking that Lizzie's plan was made so that he could sneak back to the ridge and be alone with her, turned and went their appointed ways.

Lizzie climbed, humming softly, feeling hot and sweet and heavy. Small drops of perspiration dewed her forehead. When she wiped them off with her forearm, the feel of herself on her own skin sent a familiar tingle through her body. Oh, God, it was so hot; she was so hot.

She thought about the things that Brother Clay and Mr. Dagostino had done to her and how she was going to teach Bucky and Junie to do them. Her breath started coming heavy, and she stopped and sat down in the shade of a big oak. Leaning against the bumpy bark, she slowly rotated her back on the rough surface and began fondling her breasts. Her nipples rose turgidly in response to her caresses, and she closed her eyes and began breathing through her wet, open mouth. Her fingers opened her blouse buttons, and her full, erect breasts jumped out, the pink nipples eager to be gently rubbed with her palms. She opened her eyes to see Junie standing across the path from her.

Smiling at him, Lizzie continued to stroke herself. He started to move toward her, but she stopped him, saying, "No, stay there, Junie, and watch me." He remained very still, flushed and panting.

Snaking up the trunk of the tree, Lizzie stood erect, and began unbuttoning the fly of her pants. She inched them down, stepped out of them, and then began undulating her back and buttocks against the tree trunk.

She knew that Bucky had found her when she heard him moan, "Sweet Jesus Christ." She kept him back by holding up her hand. "Don't move, Bucky, just watch me."

Bringing her hand back to her body, she placed it against her wet, bushy pubic curls and began to move her hips in a circular motion. As she ecstatically fingered herself, she watched the engorged faces and shiny eyes of the two boys. Bucking up and down, she finally shuddered and moaned. She slowly raised her fingers to her mouth and licked each one.

As if given a silent signal, Bucky and Junie advanced toward her, neither saying a word, looking only at Lizzie's wet, shining nakedness. When they stood on each side of her, she whispered, "Take off all your clothes. Let me see what you two boys have for Lizzie."

They finished in a tangled knot of bodies, slippery with sweat and satiated with kissing and licking and mounting. Saying nothing, they rose, put on their clothes, and walked back to the truck. Lizzie collapsed on the running board, legs sprawled open, yawning contentedly.

Junie looked at her and then looked at Bucky, who was walking to the back of the truck to put his shotgun away. A look of hateful understanding crossed Junie's face. "Lizzie," he half-sobbed, "you ain't nothing but a whore. I thought you was all mine, like you told me. You been doing it with Bucky, too, ain't you? All this time you been doing it with both of us and not giving a damn which one it was. You just want to fuck and you been planning to do what we done today for a long time."

Bucky froze at Junie's words and turned to face him. "You mean today ain't the first time you done it with her? You mean you been screwing her all along, too? Why, you dirty, double-crossing son of a bitch."

Lizzie looked at both of them, not comprehending. She then saw the two shotguns rise, heard the almost simultaneous shots, saw the two bodies fall on the dirt road, blood pouring down Junie's chest, blood cascading down Bucky's leg.

Stunned, she continued sitting. She didn't understand this, she didn't understand this one little bit. Maybe if they'd had a fistfight or something like that over her favors, but to shoot each other? Wonder if they're dead? Lord, this could be a moving picture.

That thought galvanized Lizzie into action. The scenario for the movie rapidly spun through her mind. The heroine would first check the two men, attempt to staunch the flow of blood, and then courageously go for help. She jumped up from the running board and ran to Junie's body.

"How bad is it, Junie, talk to me." She began unbuttoning his shirt and he groaned. Pulling the blood-soaked cloth away, she looked down at his shattered shoulder. "It's your shoulder, ain't your chest or heart, thank the Lord. Be still now." Rummaging through his pants pockets, she found the keys to the pickup. "Stay here and be quiet, I'm going for help."

Wiping her bloodstained hands off on her trousers, Lizzie went to check Bucky. The blood still cascaded from his leg, and covered Lizzie as she bent over to examine him. Taking the belt from her trousers, she whipped it around his thigh and buckled it tightly, then ran to the pickup and thundered back down the buffalo trail to the Philpot Plantation.

As soon as she made the turn off the dirt road onto the asphalt, she started blaring the horn and kept her hand on it until the truck screeched to halt before the Philpot house. Lizzie turned off the keys, jumped out of the truck, and, bloody and screaming, ran dramatically up the steps to the waiting Ora, Nora, and Ludie.

"It's Bucky and Junie . . . they done shot each other . . . up on Rabbit Ridge. Somebody help, please get help."

Ora turned in the house and cranked the phone, "Pearlie, get me Dr. Smoot—and I have no time to explain anything to you." Calling out the door, she ordered, "Ludie, go quickly and get some of those old sheets and the scissors. Nora, grab the brandy and everybody get in that truck. Start it up, Lizzie, and have it ready to go. Yes, hello, Abe. Get right out to Rabbit Ridge. Seems as if there's been a shooting accident. The Taylor and Hayes boys. We're on our way there right now. No, that's all I know; we'll meet you there."

In a real tizzy, Pearlie McAfee for once was at a loss who to ring up to tell the latest news. She surely did feel it was her duty to call the families, but Ora didn't say which Taylor boy and which Hayes boy. Certainly wouldn't do to call the wrong folks, and best not call nobody else, either, since she wasn't sure who it was got shot. Why, she couldn't even tell Bob because he was out of the store. Pearlie had never been so frustrated in her entire life.

Arriving at the ridge, Ora quickly surveyed the two boy's wounds and directed Nora to tend to Junie while she took care of Bucky's leg. She cut away the bloody pant leg and poured brandy over the raw, torn-up flesh and bone fragments. The boy screamed. Ludie carefully draped the soft, white sheet over the ugly sight.

"What happened here?" Ora demanded.

"An accident, Miss Ora, that's all," Bucky murmured, and then closed his eyes so that he wouldn't have to look at his leg.

"It wasn't no accident," Junie screamed in rage and pain as Nora poured the brandy over his shoulder. "I meant to kill him and then I was going to kill that whore of a Lizzie. And he meant to kill me, too." He started sobbing, his body heaving.

"She was there in the woods, playing with herself. Her blouse open and rubbing her hands against her tits. She saw me and told me just to watch her, and then she took them trousers off and stood there all naked and, well, she done other things to herself. And then, Bucky was there, and she told him to watch her, too. By God, we took our clothes off and we both done it to her, we done it to her a lot."

Ludie moaned, "Oh, sweet Jesus protect us." Nora raised an eyebrow.

"Then when we come back down here to the truck, she just sat there on the running board, grinning like a cat that swallowed the canary, and it just hit me sudden like. She's been fucking both me and Bucky for a long time, but neither one of us knowed she was doing it with the other one."

Junie's sobs became louder, his face red and swollen. "And she told me that I was the only one she was doing it with because we was going to get married after I finished up my college football. She was supposed to be mine." He turned his head toward Lizzie. "You whore. You fucking whore."

"No," Ora raised her stooped body until it was erect, "that did not occur, Junior Hayes. Do you hear me, do you understand me? It was an accident, just as Bucky said." The big green eyes flashed.

"Now, I will describe the accident to the three of you. Lizzie, Junie, Bucky, pay close attention. This is what happened. Junie, you were in that stand of trees, saw motion across the trail, and, thinking it was a rabbit, discharged your shotgun. Unfortunately, it was Bucky that you shot in the leg. Bucky, as you went down, your gun discharged, unfortunately hitting Junie in the shoulder. Lizzie, upon hearing the shots, you ran down the trail and discovered the accident, took what measures you could, and drove to us for help. That is what happened and that is all that happened."

Nora stood beside her. "And that is not hypocrisy, children, that is discretion. It's not that you have broken the rules of Taylor Springs' polite society. You are old enough to know that perhaps we have all broken those rules. How-

ever, you will not be flagrant about it." She started laughing
as Ora glared at her and told her to hush.

Abe Smoot arrived, and as he examined the boys, Ora
described the accident to him. He'd given both boys a shot
of morphine to ease their pain and they were both unconscious by now. "Hmmm," he said, "Well, looks like Junie's
shoulder is pretty well tore up. Don't think he'll ever have
much use of that arm. And it wouldn't surprise me if Bucky
isn't going to lose that leg."

He looked up at Lizzie. "How you doing, little lady,
you need something for your nerves?" She shook her head
no. "Well, you certainly have a lot of strength, all you been
through and the way you just took hold and went for help
and all. Yes, we're mighty proud of you.

"Now, ladies, what we're going to have to do is get
these two into the bed of that pickup. Best way to get them
back to town. I figure the five of us can do it, even if they
are such big bruisers. Ora, you drive the truck, real slow
now, 'cause we don't want them bounced around. Nora and
Ludie can ride up front with you. Lizzie, I want you to sit in
the bed of the truck between the two boys. They are out
now, but you better be back there just in case one of them
wakes up. We need you back there to watch over them. I'm
going to zip ahead and phone the families, and then phone
the hospital over at Boonetown, so we can get Bucky and
Junie over there as fast as possible. That leg of Bucky's is
really worrying me."

As Ora drove the truck slowly over the ruts of the buffalo trail, Lizzie sat proudly between the laid-out bodies of
Junie and Bucky, a hand on each of their shoulders. She
could just see the attention they'd get when they went down
the main road, everybody staring at her in her bloodstained
clothes as she gravely tended the fallen warriors.

9

Elvira shifted her weight on the hard, teensy little chair that she had placed right next to the hospital bed. Her back hurt and she eased her swollen feet out of the carpet slippers. She was weary, really weary, but that didn't matter because Miss Ruth had left her here by Bucky to watch over him while Bubba took her and Becky and Preacher Clay over to Mary D's Cafe for a bite of supper.

No, sir, old Elvira not going to doze off or even get off this little bitty chair. Sit right here by my Bucky baby just case he wakes up, case he needs something. Her thoughts rambled on. Ludie, uh-uh, Ludie she knows something about all this that she ain't telling. My poor baby lying there, his leg gone, he a gimp for life now, and poor little Junie going to have a crippled arm. Don't need to tell me about no hunting accidents. Why, them two been hunting since they was tads, they don't go shooting unless they sure what they shooting at. Ludie went up there with Miss Ora and Nora and that no-count girl. That her name, for sure, not LeCompte, but no count. At least Junie back at his own house, they just kept him here for that one night. Don't like hospitals, they death places. Time to get Bucky home where we can nurse him proper. Oh, Lord, when that boy waked up and found out they'd done cut off his leg, oh, the whimpering just like he a baby again. But 'til we gets him out of here and back home, least I don't have to worry none about him dying here.

Elvira reached underneath the head of the hospital bed and made sure that the feather and bone charm that she'd gotten from Sukie was still tied firmly in place. The plat man just has to walk on by this bed now, she thought, can't get to Bucky to carry him off, and she felt satisfied that she was taking care of her own. Bucky's eyes flew open and then clouded with panic. His hand flew down like a wild bird and began beating the flat cover where his leg should have been.

Elvira grabbed both his hands, holding them strong, and began to croon. "It's all right, baby. Elvira here, everything going to be all right. Lie still now, we just going to call that nurse to come and give you one of them morpheem shots. That'll put you back to sleep and ease the pain, ease the pain."

Across the street at Mary D's, Ruth Taylor laid down her fork and pushed back her blue plate special. Continuing to fill his mouth with meat loaf, Bubba said, "Now, Ruthie, you have got to eat and keep up your strength. Why, you haven't touched a bite in four days, and you gonna have to be strong when we bring Bucky home."

"I know," Ruth sighed, "but the sight of my boy lying there without his leg is almost more than a body can bear. Can't help thinking, Brother Clay, that we must of done something wrong, that God is punishing us." Ruth could not comprehend how she could have fallen in disfavor with the Almighty. Since she'd become a Taylor she had been careful to do everything just the right and proper way.

"Ruth, you know better than to talk like that." Randall took a sip of his iced tea. "The Philpot sisters told you themselves what happened, just as the boys told it to them. It was an accident and the Lord doesn't cause accidents; people cause accidents. Just praise God that Bucky and Junie are alive. We can't question the Lord's will and workings, Ruth."

Bubba buttered another crusty corn stick. "Yes, and just thank the Lord that the LeCompte girl had enough gumption to see to the boys and then go for help."

"I ain't thanking the Lord for Lizzie LeCompte," Becky said flatly. "It seems to me that no proper young lady would be running around in the woods with two boys, and everybody in town is talking about what she was doing up there with them."

Ruth stared at her daughter. "That's enough of that kind of talk, missy. Remember 'Judge not that ye be not judged.' People like to talk, but we sure don't have to dignify gossip by repeating it. Besides, I'm sure that your brother and Junie won't be seeing any more of Miss LeCompte. It would just remind them of the accident.

"The thing that bothers me the most," she went on, "is that them two boys are never going to get those football scholarships to college now. Why, those poor boys can't ever play football again. I was so wanting Bucky to go to college. Seems only fitting for a Taylor of Taylor Springs." Tears began rolling down her cheeks, leaving wet trails on her Coty face powder.

"Quit your fretting, Ruth." Bubba leaned over and clumsily patted her face with his rumpled napkin. "If Bucky wants to go, I'll get him there someway. It's hard times, that's true. Course, we're lucky around here. We mostly grow our own food and butcher our own animals, don't need much cash money. Besides, our tobacco is a good cash crop. Even if the country goes to perdition, tobacco is still going to sell for a little something. Shoot, we can always sell some of that old furniture and silver that's sitting around from when

the house was the Grand Hotel. Them antique people from
Louisville is always after us to buy that old stuff."

"Good idea, Bubba," Randall said. "Speaking of football, it was certainly thoughtful of Mr. Dagostino to come
over to the hospital and sit with Bucky. You know that he
even canceled all the football practices until after school begins? Of course, without Bucky and Junie nobody figures
he has much of a team anyway."

Mary D. herself served them the lemon meringue pie,
fragrant citrus wedges covered with curlicues of golden-
tipped clouds. "Now, Mrs. Taylor, I want you to eat every
bite of this pie. I made it myself special. And I got one
boxed out in the kitchen for you to carry over to the hospital so's Bucky can have some. I just can't believe a few days
ago he and Junie and that cute little girl was sitting right
here drinking a chocolate soda. They come in after they'd
been over to the picture show. Lord, you just never know."

Randall slowly chewed his pie. That cute little girl,
that's what Mary D. had called her. That wanton temptress
was anything but a cute little girl. He didn't know what had
happened up on the ridge with those two boys and Lizzie,
but he had a good idea. When Aunt Bertha had told him
that he had come in from the church on Friday running a
fever and babbling in delerium, he thanked God that what
he was saying didn't make any sense to her and Colored
Bertha. He was no longer certain what had happened to him
in the church that day, but one thing he was sure of was
what had happened in the church the day before between
him and Lizzie. That memory was burned into every mus-
cle and nerve ending of his body. But so long as no one else
knew, then he could make everything all right.

"Well," he said, pushing back his chair, "if you good
folks will excuse me, I've got to get on back. Got a meeting

with Brother Jordan and Adam Poe to make sure all the
arrangements are made for Saturday night and the Good
Time Gospel Quartet. Maybe this will be a blessing for the
town, help ease us through this tragic time. I'll be back tomorrow, Ruth, to hold prayer with you and Bucky." He
waved to Mary D. as he went out the door.

He drove the fifteen miles back to Taylor Springs, his
hands clamped so tight on the wheel that his knuckles rose
white. Swirling through the open windows, the hot breeze
created by the motion of the car ruffled his hair and burned
his glazed eyes. Winding down through the hills into the
valley, he thought longingly of rain, a torrent of moisture,
cool shards of silver water sluicing the air and earth clean.
He pictured himself standing naked in the torrent, being pu-
rified and restored from sin by the baptism of the cascading
water. His hands relaxed on the wheel and an empty, innocent look of madness came into his eyes. Water, yes, baptism, yes, that was it. That would be the sign from on high
that he was forgiven. When it rained, when it finally rained,
that would be God's tears falling down on him in forgiveness. And besides, water destroyed witches.

Sitting out in the side yard under the big shade tree
shelling butterbeans, Ludie waved as she watched Brother
Clay's car drive by. She reckoned he didn't see her, though,
as he didn't honk or wave back. She continued popping the
yellow-green pods open between her thumb and finger,
scooping the fat beans into a brown crock that rested on her
aproned lap, throwing the empty shells into a bushel basket
that rested at her feet. From out the open windows came the
sounds of Miss Ora and Nora playing the piano and violin,
accompanying Lucille's full and soaring voice.

Ludie smiled, enjoying Lucille's throaty, climbing
notes. Plum-colored sounds, she decided, yes, they is plum
colored, just like heavy, sweet, deep purple plums. Always

did wonder where that child got that voice. Must have come from the Philpot side, Lord knows the Byrds never had no rhythm, leastways not in singing. She chuckled to herself. Course that Roger Byrd, he sure did have some rhythm in another way. Oh, the ways they was all tied together, Ora and Nora Philpot and Lucille Byrd and Ludie Hayes.

Some things supposed to stay secret, she pondered, or at least not talked about. Some things are family things, ain't to be said out loud.

She thought back to the scene she'd witnessed on Rabbit Ridge last Saturday. Something has done happened to some of the folks that supposed to be quality folks in this town. White Hayes ain't supposed to be behaving like that Junie did, the things he was telling. Course, that LeCompte girl just trashy, must come from her ma. Got to be careful of mixing strangers in with our folk, leads to trashy ways. Say one thing, though, Bucky, he done proper, just said plain that it was an accident. Funny now, his ma just like Lizzie's ma—come here a stranger, too. Hard to understand.

Families is so funny anyways. Look at my boy, Khaki. Sure worried me when he was over in France in that war. I know he over there passing for white. She sighed, thinking of Khaki's boy, Ben, her grandson. Now that one really is worrisome. He always probing, asking, not ever accepting what has to be accepted. We all know where we come from, we tell it from one generation to the other. We has our place here, but that Ben don't accept that place. Keeps talking about his real place. Surely hope it wasn't no mistake sending him off to that school. Hope he don't get more uppity than he already is. Can't stand me no uppity niggers in my family.

Just then Khaki pulled the Packard touring car to a stop in the driveway, coming to fetch Lucille back home. He

walked over to pay his respects to his mother before he announced his arrival by knocking on the front screen door.

"Mama, we done got a letter from Ben, says he doing
fine, but surely is homesick. Says to tell his granny hello
and he misses her."

"You know, son, I was just sitting here thinking about
Ben. I ain't too sure Eula and you done right in sending my
grandbaby off to that Lincoln Institute. His head is too full
of ideas already."

"Now, Mama, Ben going to be fine. You know how
Eula sets store in him getting a diploma. Besides, Mr.
Roger paying his way and pushing for him to get an educa-
tion. Ben'll be just fine. He comes from good stock."

Lucille, having spied the arrival of the car from the
house, came waddling down the steps carrying a cloth-cov-
ered plate carefully before her.

"Miss Lucille," Ludie called, "that the pound cake I
done baked for your daddy?" Lucille's chins wobbled as she
nodded yes. "Well, I'm glad you didn't forget it. That
surely is Mr. Roger's favorite. Now don't you go piecing
on it before you get it home, hear me?" Lucille's chins
shook again in affirmation as Khaki helped her into the car.
As soon as the car turned out of the driveway onto the main
road, Lucille daintily lifted the white napkin, dug out a
chunk of the buttery yellow cake, and popped it ecstatically
into her red, gaping mouth.

Lizzie LeCompte was waiting when Khaki pulled the
Packard to a flourishing stop out in front of the Byrd veranda.
Eula had told her to kindly wait outside since she was sure that
Miss Lucille would be returning soon and it was a lot cooler
outside. "No white trash coming in this house," Eula muttered to herself as she slammed the door, "what that girl want
here, anyway? For sure, she ain't up to no good."

Lucille lumbered out of the car. Lizzie jumped up, running down the steps. "Hey there, Lucille. Thought I'd just come by and visit a spell. I just purely needed to talk with someone."

"Hello, Lizzie." Lucille puffed up the steps and turned to hand Khaki the mutilated pound cake. "Why would you pick me?"

"Lucille, I'm telling you that even though you hardly ever say a word, I can tell that you know a lot that these rubes here in Taylor Springs never even dreamed of. Why, it's not like you lived here all your life. I mean, you just come down here three years ago and before that you lived up North. You have been places and seen things and I just know that we got a lot in common. I mean, I ain't never been anywhere but I have got my dreams and can see far beyond this valley. Can't we talk some?"

Lucille glanced at Lizzie and smiled shyly. "I really don't understand. What do you want to talk about, Lizzie?"

"Well, I reckon you know what I've been through the past few days. I can't begin to tell you how horrible it was up on the ridge when Bucky and Junie had the accident. I know people are talking about me being up there with those two boys, but what they don't understand is that we was just good friends. Why, Bucky himself asked you to go to the dance, so you know that there was nothing going on between him and me."

The rocker creaked under Lucille's bulk. "Eula," she called out, "Eula, would you please come here a minute?"

Eula appeared stiff and disapproving behind the front screen door. "Yes, ma'am, Miss Lucille, you be wanting something?"

"Eula, if you wouldn't mind, please bring some Coca-Colas and a little something to eat out here for me and Miss Lizzie." Eula turned with a snort and stomped back down the hall.

"Why, that's awful thoughtful, Lucille. It is mighty hot and a Coca-Cola would go down mighty good right now. Do you know that I was reading in the latest *Photoplay* magazine that Mary Pickford never drinks nothing but bottled spring water. She has such a delicate stomach that anything else just upsets her something terrible. Ain't that something? Course, I'm sure it don't taste nothing like the water out of our springs!

"Anyways, Lucille, knowing that Bucky had started courting you serious by asking you to the first football dance, and that ain't no little thing, you know, being asked to that dance by the captain of the team, I felt like maybe you'd like to go visit him at the hospital. I'd be happy to go along with you. After that, we could probably drop by and see old Junie, too. What do you think?"

Pushing the screen door open with her foot, Eula carried the tray laden with Coca-Cola and chocolate fudge cake, and placed it on the white wicker table. She stood there, hands resting on her hips, looking from one girl to the other.

"Lizzie, soon as you finish that drink, you can get a ride down to the Bottoms with Khaki. Save you a walk. He got to go down that way anyhow with some garden truck that Mr. Roger sending to Professor Sheely. Miss Ruth has already rung up here asking Miss Lucille to visit Mr. Bucky, fact is she arranged the visit for tomorrow. Course, Mr. Bucky is only asking to see Miss Lucille. I'm sure if he ever wants to see you, he'll have his ma get in touch."

While Lizzie rapidly gulped her Coca-Cola, Lucille smiled vaguely and reached for another piece of cake. She lethargically lifted her fudge-covered fingers in a wave as Lizzie was jounced down the road and out of sight in the Packard touring car.

Lucille wondered how Lizzie could know about what she'd seen and where she'd been. Daddy said she was never supposed to tell anything because it was just their secret. Of course, Mama used to be part of the secret, but Mama died.

Mama always looked like a little girl, she was so slight. She wore her black hair down her back tied with a big bow. And Mama always wore ruffled pink dresses covered with organdy pinafores and white stockings and little black patent leather slippers. Lucille couldn't ever remember Mama leaving the house. The servants did all the errands, and Papa always said, "Oh, Maud is so delicate that she must be protected from the world."

So Mama stayed in her room always. It was so pretty, with the pink canopied bed and the pink lace curtains and the little table and chairs with the pink china doll tea set. And the whole wall built with shelves where all Mama's dolls lived. Why, Mama even called Lucille one of her doll babies and used to sit her up on the shelves with all the other dolls and tell her, "Now, don't move, baby. If you are very, very good, I'll bring you down when it's time for the tea party. And we'll have chocolate cake and sugar cookies and little cups of cocoa with gobs of whipped cream just floating on top."

Papa, who was so tall and big and handsome with his big red mustache, loved Lucille and Mama very much. She remembered Grandpa Nash saying, "Thank God for you, Roger. I don't know what happened to make Maud the way she is. Can't really blame it on Lucille's birth, although she completely deteriorated after that. I'm afraid she will be a child forever. Your patience and understanding is saintlike."

When she was little and tiny, Papa dressed Lucille just like Mama in pretty pink dresses and organdy pinafores. When he would come home and find them both in Mama's room, playing with the dolls and having a tea party, he would gather them both in his arms and call them his ador-

able, pretty baby girls. And then he would untie their
pinafore sashes, and unbutton their pretty pink dresses, and
take off their ruffled petticoats and white stockings and they
would all play the tickle game.

Lucille loved the tickle game because Papa would tickle
all over with his big, red mustache and it felt good. It even
made Mama giggle until the day when he got off the top of
Mama and lay on top of Lucille and the glazed doll-like look
left Mama's eyes and she screamed in one, brief moment of
sanity, "For God's sake, Roger, what are you doing?" Papa
got the pink dotted swiss–covered pillow off the bed and put it
over Mama's face. Lucille laughed because it was a new game.

After the funeral, Papa moved Lucille into Mama's pink
room, but he never came there to visit again. Lucille was so
lonesome that she used to have lots of tea parties by herself
and made Cook keep cakes and cookies and sandwiches always ready on the little table. Chewing and tasting and
swallowing felt almost as good as playing the tickle game.

While Lucille was sitting on the porch thinking of
Mama and Papa and the tickle game, Khaki was stopping
the car in front of the LeCompte house. He didn't bother to
get out and open the door for Lizzie. She sat there waiting,
lips swollen in a pout, knowing that she was being snubbed
by a colored man. Just you wait, she fumed to herself, just
you wait and see what little old Lizzie LeCompte is going to
become. Everybody in this dumb town is going to just beg
to know me some day. They're going to say why of course
I knew Lizzie way back when. Always thought she was
going to amount to something. Oh, yes, they'll sit up and
take notice . . . all the dumb niggers, and fat Lucille, and
the Taylors and the Philpots and especially Brother Randall
Clay. They'll see. She opened the door, slammed it shut,
and flounced down the path to the ramshackle porch where
her ma sat waiting by the rusting washing machine.

Steering the car down through colored town, Khaki stopped where the dirt road dead-ended in a circled clearing. He got out and followed the narrow path that led through the woods to the springs. The sulphur burned his eyes and nostrils and he spewed out a mighty sneeze.

Lord a mercy, he thought, best to be quiet around here. Noise like that could easy get a man looking down the barrel of a shotgun. Halfway around the bubbling water, he lit out into the woods, and after traveling about two hundred yards, he stopped and softly gave the whistle of a mourning dove. When the whistle came back to him on the heavy air, he continued walking until he reached a thick copse of blackberry bushes.

Softly, he called, "It's me, Khaki," and parted the bushes to reveal a small clearing that was completely filled with the massive Sukie and her marvelous makeshift still. The yeasty, sour smell of mash hung heavy in the air and the bubbles of liquid gurgled a happy little song as they traveled through the coils.

Sukie hummed as she busily filled her mason jars with the clear liquid. "Howdy, Khaki, what you be doing here this time of the day?"

"Had to deliver some garden truck down to the Sheelys and then Eula done made me drive that LeCompte girl back to her house. How about a sample of that latest batch, Sukie Bee?" Khaki cackled. "Don't you want an expert's opinion?"

Sukie handed him a half-filled mason jar. "Don't need no opinions, man, I knows what I is doing. I been doing this for I don't know how many years and I done learned how to do it from my daddy. Anyways, what that Lizzie girl doing up at the Byrd house?"

"She trying to get Lucille to go with her for to visit Bucky and Junie, do you believe that? Trying to wiggle her way into decent folks' houses by using Miss Lucille. Eula put a stop to that right quick, I tell you. That old Lizzie girl think after what happened Saturday that she going to get into any quality house in this town, she is plumb crazy."

Sukie looked up. "What you think did happen up there on the ridge, Khaki? Whatever it was, I tell you it was the plat man a-working, and I done put the charms all over the place, got to protect people. I done killed the rooster and drank the blood, too, but I'm a scared that it ain't enough. Plat eye get loose, hard to stop him, specially since he done got loose in the church."

Draining the mason jar, Khaki laughed. "Sukie, you are one pure fool when you start that voodoo business. Now you know ain't no such thing as the plat man. What we has here is just pure people devilment. Don't do to talk about it, ignore it is the best thing."

"Plat man is here, Khaki Hayes. You got so much that white blood in you that you don't know about the real nigger things. You ain't even a colored man. You mostly Philpot and Byrd and that makes you the fool."

"Now, Sukie," Khaki placated, "I didn't come here to fuss about no voodoo. We got business to do. I figure with all the folks gathering up at the Holy Roller church tomorrow night, the menfolks going to get mighty thirsty. All you need to do is let me load every bit of the squeezings you have on hand into the car and I can set us up a nice little business in that stand of trees behind the church. All I have to do is stand outside before the singing begins and just let certain people know what we got back there. What do you say?"

"I say that I gets three-quarters and you gets one-quarter of the money and let's start carrying these mason jars out of these woods."

10

While Khaki and Sukie Bee loaded the homebrew into the car, the Good Time Gospel Quartet was on their way to Taylor Springs. The four Shuck brothers sat silent as the bus bumped and swayed along the hilly, country roads. They passed their own jar of whiskey, their eyes closed and heads thrown back as they drank in long swallows. The fat tires hummed on the hot, melting asphalt as the boys wiped the sweat off their pale foreheads and passed the jar again and again.

The Shuck boys had always cast a different appearance. Even when they were little, running around barefoot in dirt-crusted bib overalls like all the other sharecroppers' sons, something set them apart. Part of it, of course, was their coloring, dead white skin and almost white hair. The only thing that saved them from being albinos was that their pink-rimmed eyes were an almost colorless gray. And, too, their whippet, wiry bodies seemed to be constantly in a rhythmic motion, just like they had music in their very bones, as their mother used to say.

Delmer was the oldest and charged with looking after his little brothers, Levi and Reuben and Noble. Of course, being oldest didn't matter all that much when there was only a year's difference between each of them. Their daddy, Harmon, spent as little time possible sharecropping, and as much time as possible drinking and bedding his wife, Hallie.

Hallie's only relief and recreation lay in her attendance at every service and affair offered by the Good Ship Zion Pentecostal Church. It was the place where she could offer up her burdens to a higher power and she didn't have to do it silently. She could sing and scream and twitch her sagging body to her heart's content and her soul's relief. She could dance and throw her arms up to the heaven and even roll up and down the aisles when the Lord visited his spirit on her. And then she could go back to her silent, drab daily existence and the deadening, daily grinding of her body by Harmon, knowing that she could find release the next time she got to church.

She always took her boys with her, scrubbing their faces, slicking down their white cowlicks with water, and brushing the dirt from their one pair of overalls. They shouted and swayed and prayed with her, but their true glory came with the singing. They sang true and full, and soon began singing in parts. Before long, they were performing for the congregation and had begun to add a little strutting to the singing.

Pretty soon word got out in Prattville, Alabama, and the surrounding towns that those little Shuck boys were surely a caution, why, they could sing like nobody's business, and put on a mighty fine show while doing it. Just as cute as they could be, for a fact. Maybe even cuter than Dale Bob Crabb, the boy evangelist.

Of course, the eight-year-old Dale Bob, dressed up in his white silk suit and with fat yellow curls puffed, around his face, had been blessed far beyond his years in his ability to bring a hellfire and brimstone message straight from the Lord, which certainly drew droves of people wherever he was preaching.

Dale Bob would pound the pulpit, prance up and down the aisles, wave the Good Book, and exhort the people until the sweat rolled off his forehead and down his chubby cheeks. The people responded with the clink of coins tossed in the love offering basket passed around at the end of every service.

Hallie had told Harmon Shuck all about Dale Bob Crabb, for he had preached twice at the Good Ship Zion Pentecostal Church, and she declared the little boy to be a real wonder. Hallie's fondest hope was to get Harmon to church to get him born again. Maybe if he got right with Jesus, he'd start doing good works and let her get some rest at night. When she announced that Dale Bob was going to preach a special service on Friday night and that the preacher had asked their boys to sing a special, Harmon said he reckoned he'd go along with her just this once.

When Harmon saw the love offering basket piled high and heard the people talking about how blessed it was that the Lord was moving through little children, moving through the Shuck boys in song and Dale Bob in preaching the Word, he immediately started negotiations with the Reverend Tyree Crabb, Dale Bob's daddy, and the traveling evangel team of Dale Bob Crabb and the Good Time Gospel Boys was born.

For five years they traveled the South—Alabama, Georgia, Louisiana, Mississippi—and the money rolled in. The rickety old Fords were replaced with a shiny bus, and Hallie finally got some rest, for Harmon could find plenty of women who needed some release after getting all worked up by the services. In their own way, Harmon and the Reverend Tyree Crabb were as much celebrities as their progeny.

Unfortunately, Dale Bob got to be thirteen years old, and when the pimples started covering his face and his voice started cracking, and he didn't appear to be too much of a boy wonder in his white silk suit, Harmon kissed him and the Reverend Tyree good-bye and took the Good Time Gospel Boys out on their own.

Delmer and Levi and Reuben and Noble had the grace to remain thin, clear complexioned, and in good voice. Besides, their hair remained white and they retained that extraordinary appearance that continued to set them apart, making people stare at them wherever they happened to be. So, during the next five years, the Good Time Gospel Boys rolled on from church to church and tent to tent. It was in Crossville, Tennessee, that Harmon found the special girl who joined their group and made them famous.

The Crossville Revival had been going on for a full week before the boys were scheduled to appear on a Sunday night. The big tent was pitched in a pasture just west of town and had been filled every night with people from the town and from all the hills and hollows. They came long before the services were due to start and they congregated around the tent, visiting, gossiping, and sharing the fried chicken, cole slaw, pickled beets, corn cakes, and peach pies packed in their picnic baskets. The little ones ran and played, the women exchanged news of births, marriages, and deaths, and the men wandered over to their dilapidated cars and pickups every now and then just to wet their whistles.

When dusk came and the lanterns filled the tent with a beckoning glow, they packed up all their paraphernalia and went inside to sing and shout praises to the Lord. The visiting evangelist, Brother Giltner Malin, was a powerful preacher, and Lord knows how many souls he had already saved during that week in Crossville. Every night when he gave the invitation, bodies just jumped out of the folding chairs provided by Washburn's Funeral Home and swarmed up the aisles. Falling to their knees, they were prayed over by Brother Malin, who cast out Satan and brought them into the eternal joy of Christian fellowship.

Not that this was any easy task. Brother Malin sometimes had to fall right down on the dirt and wrestle with the Devil, especially when he was dealing with a hardcore sinner. And always working right along with him was his wife, Juanita. Not only could Juanita wrestle with the Devil just as well as Giltner, she also had the gift of healing.

Dressed in a long, gauzy white robe that was gathered with a silver girdle that defined her tiny waist and pushed forward her ample bosom, she stood with her arms upheld in invitation for sinners to come and be saved. Her face, haloed by a mass of platinum blond curls hanging down to her waist, made her look just like an angel, at least that's what most of the men said. And the women did say she surely had the sweetest smile on her face.

Juanita would just put her slim white hands on the sinners' shoulders, close her big blue eyes so that the long, curly black eyelashes rested on her pink cheeks, and command in a clear, ringing voice that the Devil be gone from this poor, miserable worm of a sinner. Of course, her healing was a very different matter.

When Juanita healed, she first ran those slim white hands over every part of the afflicted's body, not missing a single place or a single inch of skin. This was because she had to find the source of the hurt, she explained. Then, she took the afflicted's body in her arms and hugged it tight to

her own body, and with her big blue eyes boring into the
eyes of the sick one, she crooned softly, "Come . . . come
. . . Satan come out of this body into mine . . . because my
body is the temple of the Lord . . . and it can know no
disease." And then her bosom would shudder, and she
would fall on the ground, yelling, "Praise God, the Devil
has released your hurt into my body, you are healed." Several of the older boys had to go back two or three times that
week to get healed, they just weren't sure it took the first
time. Juanita always welcomed them in the spirit of holi-
ness.

"So far as I can tell, this had been the best revival the
Lord has done ever sent to Crossville," Aunt Becky Drane
was heard to remark when the crowd was milling around
waiting for the final revival service. Which said quite a bit,
since Aunt Becky was eighty-five years old and had never
missed an event that came to town. "Now, I hear tell that
those young fellers, that Good Times Gospel Quartet that
are a-coming in this evening, are supposed to be fine, but
I'm telling you they're going to have to go some to beat out
what's been happening here."

Suellen Swofford offered Aunt Becky one of her dried
apple fried pies. "Go on and have one, you know that it's
not going to give you a bit of trouble to chew it. Lord
knows you've had enough of my pies to know how tender
they are, not that I'm given to bragging, but facts are facts."

"I surely agree that the spirit has been moving during
this revival, Becky, but I must say that I'm really curious to
see these Good Time Gospel Boys. They was over to Cove
Lake last year and Flora Jenkin's sister-in-law seen them and
said it was better than a picture show. Said those four boys
is good-lookers but in a real different way, like they're all
white and shining. She said they all got white hair, and real
white, almost alabaster skin, and their eyes almost got no

color. Said all the young girls just went crazy over them. Course, they're real young, like the oldest one ain't no more than seventeen or eighteen. Anyway, Flora's sister-in-law said they sing to beat the band, and while they are a-singing, they strut and kind of dance, even go out into the congregation and pull people up on their feet to sing along with them. Mostly it's women they do that to."

Aunt Becky gummed her pie and nodded her head. Swallowing quickly, she gulped. "Look a there, Suellen. Well, I never in all my born days, ain't that that Amish girl from over Loudenbeck's Holler? I can't believe my eyes."

"That's her all right, look, she's even got on that little white net bonnet. Yep, that's the youngest one. What's her name, now? Something real foreign."

Brunhilda Loudenbeck walked decorously through the crowd, eyes demurely looking at the ground, carrying a small covered basket. Her petite body was covered with a dark-gray shapeless dress and her golden hair was bound in the white net cap. She entered the still empty tent and sat on the aisle chair of the right back row, placing her basket at her feet.

She sat very still, but inside her blood was boiling. At last, she had left the holler and come out into the world on her own. The Good Time Gospel Boys were going to be in this very tent and she was going to see them and hear them. And they were going to see her, too. For three years now, she had been waiting for this moment. She had known the Lord would let her know when it was time for her to be recognized. After all, it was the Lord who had told her what to do to prepare herself to escape from Loudenbeck Hollow.

She had never understood why, ten years ago, her family, along with the Durst family, had packed up all their belongings and made their way from the large Amish settlement in Plain City, Ohio, to settle by themselves in an iso-

lated hollow located in the Cumberland Plateau of
Tennessee. She could not even remember the trek itself; she
had been only five years old.

Her first memories were of Loudenbeck Hollow itself,
a large clearing ringed by hills, and of the two large farm-
houses that sat side by side. The huge barn and the other
outbuildings and the patterned fields that filled the rest of
the clearing were held in common by the two families.
They worked the fields together, tended the stock together,
gathered the harvest and preserved the food together. The
women shared the bread baking and the canning, the men
shared the butchering and meat preserving chores, and they
all kept to the Amish ways of their ancestors.

The Loudenbeck household contained her grandfather,
her father and mother, her sister, who was older by two
years, Brunhilda, and the three younger brothers who had
been born after they came to the hollow. The Durst house
was filled with six lively boys and their family. None of the
children went out of the hollow to the schoolhouse six miles
up the road. School was against their ways, said the grandfather, and they were to follow the ways the Lord had set
down for them, which was to work and live off the land,
and to keep pure unto themselves.

When the grandfather would take down the heavy family Bible and read the Word to them and then tell them of
the faith and stories about their own family history,
Brunhilda would always question why they had left and
come so far away to live here by themselves. The only answer she ever got was that it had to do with an interpreta-
tion of the Word, and that all those people left back in Plain
City were living in error.

Adolph, the oldest Durst boy, once told her that the
two families had been made to leave Plain City because they
questioned the rest of the community's use of mechanical

tractors and threshers, which was clearly against the faith. Brunhilda didn't understand what that meant, so she never did come to understand why they all were where they were.

She had been allowed to go into Crossville twice with her father and older sister to fetch some plain cloth and white muslin so they could refurbish their wardrobes. Both she and Marlena were admonished that they were to keep their eyes down, not gaze around, and were to speak only necessary words. However, any time her father was not watching her, Brunhilda stared as much as she could at everything and committed all the new exciting sights, smells, and touches to memory.

Back in the hollow, she spent as much time as she could back in the woods in the hills. Her family was forever calling her and she was forever hiding from them. She roved the mountains until she was at home with every tree, every spring, every critter. Such things were infinitely more exciting and satisfying than the white dough sameness of the days and people back in the hollow.

Three years ago, the grandfather had pronounced Marlena and Adolph Durst husband and wife, and Marlena had moved over to the Durst house with her new husband. Marlena had said, "Don't you fret, little one, soon you'll be wedding one of the Durst boys. Why, you're already twelve years old, it won't be long."

The whole idea of marrying one of the Durst boys and being stuck in the hollow forever so disgusted Brunhilda that she ran off into her mountains down to her favorite spring. She stroked and tickled the snakes that always nested there, and picked them up and wound them like shiny necklaces and bracelets around her. It was then the Lord revealed to her how she was going to get out of Loudenbeck Hollow.

That night, when the Good Time Boys entered from

the back of the tent and strutted up onto the wooden platform singing and swinging to the chorus of "Beulah Land,"
a collective *aah* came from the folk sitting in the tent. There
the boys stood, white on white, gleaming with glory and
glamour, and as they sang and stomped and sweated, the
crowd rose to its feet and clapped their hands and swayed to
the beat, shouting "Glory, glory." The heady fumes of
body heat and the smell of ecstasy filled the tent.

When the Good Time Boys suddenly went quiet and
then shifted tempo by beginning to quietly croon "Just as I
Am," the crowd sighed and began to sit down, all except
the small figure wearing a white net cap standing at the back
of the tent. "Just as I am," the boys sobbed and the girl
picked up her basket and began to slowly sway up the aisle
toward the platform. "Without one plea," she reached the
platform, turned to face the crowd, and put down her basket. The boys, fascinated, didn't miss a beat and added
more bathos to their music. "But that thy blood was shed
for me." She took the white net bonnet off and the golden
hair swung loose and long. Kneeling before the basket, she
raised the lid and took the silvery-black snakes out, wrapping one around each thigh and the other two placed on her
chest. She arched her body back into a taut bow and the
plain gray dress rose high, revealing her thighs. The boys
sang on with an increased fervor. The girl swayed and
writhed as the snakes twisted around and up her body and
the Good Time Boys boomed out, "Oh, Lamb of God, I
come, I come."

Practically everybody in the tent got sanctified that
night, and they still tell about it in Crossville to this day,
although the Good Time Gospel Quartet has never been
back. Seems as if Harmon Shuck, knowing a sure winner
when he saw one, rounded up the boys, Hallie, and
Brunhilda and her snakes, and was out of Crossville and

already in Nashville before the Loudenbeck family had even realized that Brunhilda wasn't at home that night where she was supposed to be.

After that, there wasn't a camp meeting or a revival or a church throughout the whole South that didn't try to book the Good Time Gospel Quartet. The act never changed; it was always the boys singing "Just as I Am," Brunhilda rising from the back of the crowd in plain dress and white cap, kneeling in front of the crowd, the snakes slithering over her arched body. Harmon did change the color of the dress from gray to white, to match the boys, as he said. And he did have Hallie change the high neckline to a real low scooped-out one, to give more of a dramatic effect, he explained.

Soon, they were traveling as far as Texas and Oklahoma, even into Florida and South and North Carolina. Oh, they were famous all right, and they were rich. In fact, they got so rich that Harmon took Hallie back to Prattville and built them a fine mansion, one of those plantation kinds with big white columns in the front up on Camellia Road, and became one of the pillars of the community and the Good Ship Zion Pentecostal Church. Hallie's prayers had been answered.

"You boys," Harmon explained, "are old enough and been watching me long enough to know how to conduct this business. Your ma and I been traveling around long enough. It's time we took our ease. Just always remember that the folks are going to dig in their pockets when they get a good show, and they are going to feel real righteous about paying for a good show when it's given in the name of the Lord and they think it's saving their souls to boot. You got to look at it this way, boys. All them people in all them godforsaken little places ain't got nothing in their lives but dirt-scrabbling hard work, doing the same dreary thing day after day. You got a chance to bring them some excitement, some glory, something to dream on."

"But what about Brunhilda, Pa?" Reuben asked. "Don't you think one of us ought to marry up with her so's it would look respectable, her traveling with us and all. With Ma along, that made it seem all right, but without Ma?"

Harmon looked hard at all four of them. "Boys, nobody is to marry up with Brunhilda. Why, it would ruin the act. Brunhilda has got to remain the virgin so far as the public is concerned." He hawked and turned to spit on the ground. "No need to try to give your old daddy any shit. I know that each one of you been diddling Brunhilda and I know that she loves it and you love it.

"Now here is what you do," Harmon continued. "Everywhere you go, you boys continue to sleep on the bus like we always done, but you find some good Christian family who will take Brunhilda in for the night. They'll fight for the privilege, and Brunhilda and you boys will remain pure and godly in the eyes of the public. You boys and Brunhilda can do your screwing around where nobody ain't aware of it."

And that's just the way they did it, just like Harmon told them to. The bus rolled, the Good Times Boys sang, Brunhilda carried her basket of snakes, and they all got richer and richer. The paper money went back to Prattville, where Harmon immediately converted it into silver and gold coins, which he buried in the cellar of the new house.

It was in Kentucky that the Good Time Boys lost Brunhilda. They were playing an engagement at Camp Crestview, a Southern Methodist Episcopal church camp located just outside PeeWee Valley. Why, those Methodists had built a fine campgrounds with cabins and a big dining hall and a huge meeting house, and every summer they filled it with folks coming from all over the state to stay a week or two to listen to lectures and sermons and enjoy music. It was a real cultural experience to be able to go to Camp Crestview.

What the boys and Brunhilda didn't know was that the night that they performed there—and they did give it their all since they knew they weren't dealing with just the usual one-town, easily pleased crowd—David Wark Griffith was sitting in the audience.

In fact, nobody in the crowd recognized D. W. Griffith, although most of them could have told you that they knew he was the famous Hollywood movie director because they all had seen *Birth of a Nation* and knew all about Lillian Gish and Dorothy Gish and Mary Pickford. It was no sin to see the kind of moving pictures that D. W. Griffith made because they were moral. Good always won out in the end.

What most folks didn't know was that D. W. Griffith had been born right there in PeeWee Valley, one of their own, being as he was always associated with that mythical place called Hollywood. But he was there at Camp Crestview that night, sitting right there in the midst of his family, which he was visiting. When Brunhilda rose from her seat in the back of the meeting hall, let down that golden hair, and arched that body, D. W. knew he'd found himself another movie star.

Brunhilda left with D. W. Griffith that night with no more hesitation or good-byes than the night she left Loudenbeck Hollow forever. She did, however, leave the boys her basket of snakes.

Well, the boys kept singing and had no trouble getting engagements, but the clincher had gone from their act. They would have been just another traveling quartet, except that their appearance still set them apart and made them remembered. They kept looking for another Brunhilda, but

no one had the air of decorum and purity that suddenly became charged with holy orgasm as the snakes slithered over
her body. Besides, they could never find any girl who
would even touch those snakes.

Every now and then, the boys would stop at a moving
picture house when they'd see Brunhilda's picture out front
advertising her latest movie. They loved to watch her being
rescued from ice floes or from in front of locomotives or
from going over raging falls by the handsome hero. After
the picture, as they walked back to the bus, one of them,
either Delmer or Reuben or Levi or Noble, would always
sigh, "Jesus, do you remember how that girl loved to fuck?
And always wanted them snakes crawling around on her
while we was doing it?"

When the big crash of '29 came, it didn't bother the
Boys or Harmon a bit. After all, Harmon had all the silver
and gold coins buried in the cellar and the boys just kept on
traveling the circuit. Of course, the pickings were leaner or
at least seemed that way, but you had to remember that a
quarter bought a lot more than it did before. The thing was
that the boys were really men now; but they stayed slim and
white and nobody ever thought on them being men, not
even the boys themselves.

That Sunday afternoon, when the bus pulled up beside the
Taylor Springs Pentecostal Church, Brothers Jim Jordan,
Adam Poe, and Reverend Randall Clay were waiting in the
parking lot as a proper welcoming committee. The boys
stepped down, dressed in white shirts and trousers, and
Brother Jordan exclaimed to the others, "Well, I never in all
my born days, will you look at that! White clothes and
white hair and white eyebrows. Looks just like four of the

Angel Gabriel. Oh, there'll be a blessing here tonight, I just feel it."

Randall, befitting his role, stepped forward to shake the hands of each of the boys and introduced himself and his colleagues. Jim Jordan directed them to park the bus right in back of the church, they'd be just fine and dandy there, and told them they'd be back to fetch them in about an hour.

"That'll give you a little time to rest a spell," he continued. "We'll be back to take you over to the McAfee house, where Pearlie is going to give you a good meal and you'll get a chance to meet some of the finer Christian folks of the community. Can't tell you how we are looking forward to this special service of music tonight. We have had such tragic moments during this past week that I just know the Lord directed you to be here tonight."

Delmer, Levi, Reuben, and Noble climbed back on the bus, and Delmer gunned the engine to run the vehicle to the back of the church. "If I have to hear one more time," Levi complained, "about tragic moments preceding our performance, I swear to God I am going to puke."

"Shut up, Levi," Noble commanded, wiping the sweat off his face with his white shirt-sleeve, "it's so damn hot here that nobody gives a damn anyhow. The only thing I want to know is if there's any pussy in this godforsaken place. I am hornier than hell. Besides, tragic moments mean more money in the love offering."

Pearlie McAfee had really outdone herself. From the moment she had heard that the Good Time Gospel Quartet was coming to Taylor Springs, she had been busy planning her guest list and the supper.

She had invited the Philpot sisters, but, of course, they declined just as she knew they would. She'd had to invite them, even though she knew they thought they were too far above the rest of Taylor Springs to even consider attending a supper in honor of a Holy Roller singing group. Bubba and Ruth Taylor had accepted, even though poor little Bucky was still in the hospital. Ruth had phoned up and said, "We'll certainly be there, Pearlie, because Elvira is going to be with Bucky and I just have the feeling that the Lord means for Bubba and Becky and me to be there." Pearlie certainly admired such a spirit and told Ruth Taylor so.

She had, of course, invited the Byrds, Myna Smoot, Tony Dagostino, the Jordans, the Poes, and Randall Clay and his Aunt Bertha. Pearlie chuckled when she considered how Bertha Hayes was just fuming because she thought it was her proper place to be holding this supper for probably the most distinguished group that had visited Taylor Springs in many a year. Folks around here shouldn't forget that the McAfees was one of the founders of this town. The Clays and the Hayes come later.

Pearlie McAfee showed them all how it was supposed to be done. She stood at her front door and received them like the queen of Taylor Springs; she even wore the white lace mitts that had been handed down from Robert's great-great-grandmother. When the Good Time Gospel Boys came to her front door, they bowed and kissed the hand that wore those mitts.

And it was a sumptuous repast that she served them. There were thin, pungent slices of baked country ham, redolent of cloves and brown sugar, piles of crunchy, buttermilk-battered fried chicken, pork tenderloin simmered with cinnamon and apples, string beans fragrant with bacon, fluffy mounds of buttery mashed potatoes, brussel sprouts mixed with mealy chestnuts, small ruby beets flecked with orange peel, and Pearlie's famous stack pie, seven layers of fabulous pastry slathered with dried apple filling.

After supper, Pearlie asked Lucille Byrd to sing while

the rest of them enjoyed their coffee. Blushing, Lucille sat down at the old pump organ, and accompanied herself while her honeyed voice dripped the words of "Amazing Grace" throughout the room.

"Miss Lucille," Delmer broke the silence after the last note faded away, "we'd be mighty honored if you'd sing that song with us tonight during the performance. And we'd also like you to join us on our bus after the service so's we could talk to you about the tour."

After the service, the boys waited back by their bus for Lucille. "I sure hope she comes," Reuben said. "I never saw anything like her in my life. She is big, she is majestic. She is just like a power come down from Heaven, and oh my God, that voice. Lord grant that she wants to go along with us. She's the only one we found who could ever replace Brunhilda."

Lucille came lumbering through the darkness, up to the bus. "Good evening," she murmured. "My daddy couldn't stay, but Khaki's waiting out by the car to drive me home. I did enjoy singing with you tonight and I hope you come back next year so I can sing with you again."

Delmer took her huge marble arm. "Miss Lucille, what we wanted to talk to you about was joining up with us, traveling with us."

Lucille smiled shyly. "Oh, I couldn't do that even though you boys are so pretty, so white. I never saw anything like you, why, I just get the funniest feeling when I look at you and hear you sing. You see, I have to stay here with my daddy."

She looked around at the four boys and grinned. "Tell me, do you boys know how to play the tickle game?"

The bus rocked and creaked as the Good Time Gospel Boys tickled and mounted Lucille. Lightning flashed and danced across the night and the echo of thunder rumbled from the ridge down into the valley. The fresh electric smell of ozone lifted the odor of sulphur from the air and slow fat drops of rain began to bounce on the arid earth of Taylor Springs.

Soon the drops became a shower and then a solid curtain of cool water. A vivid flash of lightning illuminated the figure of Mary William Sheely spinning in windmill circles in the clearing by the springs and also the naked figure of Randall Clay, standing rigid in front of his church, his arms upraised to heaven, a beatified expression on his uplifted face.

PART THREE

1940

11

She woke when it was still very early. A slight breeze blew the starched lace curtains out from the open windows and she could see the slight edgings of pink on the horizon where the sun was just beginning to rise. As she raised her arms over her head, throwing her firm breasts into points, she heard the faint crow of a rooster and the soft closing of the kitchen door as Colored Bertha came into the parsonage.

She stretched luxuriously and then rolled herself over against her still sleeping husband. She began to rub her hand in slow circles over his belly, and when he groaned, she inserted her fingers under the elastic of his pajama bottoms and began to caress him. When he grew turgid, she pulled down the pajamas, stripped off her nightgown, and lowered herself slowly onto him.

He opened his eyes, and looked at her as she triumphantly rode him to climax. He shuddered and moaned loudly. "Ssh, Randall," she laughed softly, "remember a Presiding Elder of the Southern Methodist Episcopal church is sleeping right in the next room, wouldn't be seemly for him to think that one of his ministers is right next door enjoying the lusts of the flesh."

He pulled her down to him, and started suckling her still pink-tipped breasts and kneading her luscious ass. Flipping her over on her back, he began biting her pouting lips and then kissing her ears and nuzzling her throat. As she raised her legs over his shoulders and guided him inside her sweet wetness, he repeated silently to himself with every thrust, "You're a witch, Lizzie, you're still a witch."

Almost ten years ago, the night the Good Time Gospel Boys had first come to Taylor Springs, when the long drought had ended and Randall Clay had stood naked in the downpour before the door of his church, he was certain that he had been cleansed of his sin, his copulation in the house of God with that witch Lizzie LeCompte. He had asked God for a sign, for a baptism of rain, and God had answered him with lightning and thunder and sheets of water.

The next morning he had risen to a world of fresh-washed air and a soul cleansed of its sin. With a light heart and a clear purpose, he resumed the business of leading his flock. One of his first tasks was to visit Brother Jim Jordan to discuss Lizzie LeCompte.

"Brother Jordan, what with the accident that happened to Bucky Taylor and Junie Hayes and all the gossip about Lizzie's part in it, I was wondering if, perhaps, it wouldn't be the best thing for the girl to transfer her membership here to your church, the rest of her family being members here now. Seems as if with the Taylors and the Hayes attending my church that it just might be a more Christian atmosphere for her with your congregation."

Brother Jordan leaned back on his chair and rubbed his stubbly chin. "Probably the best thing for all concerned, though, mind you, I don't set no store in all them stories about the girl. I just have the feeling that that girl is capable of great, spiritual things. Yes, just looking at her, I wouldn't doubt that she could be one that the Lord could visit with the gift of tongues." He licked his lips. "Surely wouldn't mind seeing her sitting out there in my congregation every Sunday."

"Would you talk to her then? It would be like you were seeking her out special like. And you could tell her that you had already discussed the matter with me and that I certainly could not stand in her way in finding her true religious home."

"Be happy to, Reverend Clay. Thought probably you come up here this morning to talk about the Quartet singing. Wasn't that a sight, though? Everybody in town here and the glory of the Lord holding full sway. And I tell you Lucille Byrd's singing was a visit of the spirit. You know them boys wanted her to go on the tour with them? Course they don't know nothing about her being part of one of the best families in town and that her daddy and her wouldn't never consider such a thing, that sort of thing being beneath the Byrds. However, she is a real lady. She went out to the bus and talked it over with them real polite like. Said she'd be happy to sing with them whenever they come back to town."

"Yes, Lucille has a remarkable voice. Did you book the boys to come back here next year?

"Certainly did . . . and every year after that. Even set up the date, the last Sunday in August, we are guaranteed that. And I want you to know that it didn't cost us one red cent. The love offering covered it all." Jordan didn't bother to add that he had twenty-five dollars as the host church's part of the take in his pocket.

And so as autumn colored the trees on the hills in shades of gold and orange and red, and frost rimmed the buffalo paths that led down into the valley, the town seemed to return to its normal, uneventful tempo, and Randall Clay's spirit, if not his flesh, was less troubled, until the day he looked up from his desk and saw Lizzie LeCompte standing in the doorway of his church office.

"What are you doing here, Lizzie?" His eyes were hard and his voice stern.

She raised her pert chin, tossed the brown curls, strode rapidly to the desk, leaned over, and placed both hands on it, pushing her face directly before his.

"I am going to have a baby, Randall Clay, and I want to know what you're going to do about it. You can either marry me or you can find me some money so I can get rid of it."

Of course, he married her. He was already carrying the burden of the dead Boopsie on his soul, so what else could he do? Never mind that the baby probably wasn't his. Lord knows who the daddy was. But he could not have the guilt of another bungled abortion laid on his soul.

The next morning, a Saturday, he drove her to Jeffersonville, Indiana, where there wasn't any waiting period for a license, and they were made man and wife and returned together to the parsonage that night. As he preached his sermon the next morning, Lizzie sat demurely, flanked by Aunt Bertha on the right and the Philpots on the left. After the services, as Randall stood by the door shaking the hands of his congregation, she stood beside him as he announced their marriage. The twins were born seven months later, but then, as Doc Smoot said, "Twins always come early, always premature."

Lizzie, overnight, had become Mrs. Randall Clay, the preacher's wife, and was immediately surrounded by Aunt Bertha, Colored Bertha, and the Philpot sisters, a protective covey that rapidly taught her the proper way a Clay behaved. Myna Smoot had the wedding shower, which was

followed five months later by the baby shower held at the
Philpot Plantation. Lizzie always was a quick study, and by
the time the twins were six months old, their mother was
firmly fixed in the social order as a respectable young ma-
tron of Taylor Springs.

The only unusual thing in the whole affair was that
Randall continued as pastor of the Taylor Springs Southern
Methodist Episcopal Church. The Methodists usually reas-
signed their pastors every four years to a different church,
which was just their way of keeping things lively. No use
letting either a preacher or a congregation get stagnant, and
besides it was a method of promotion or demotion.

Randall was never moved, and he never asked why. He
had the feeling that the Conference felt that perhaps he'd
better be kept where his sudden marriage was accepted and
not sent where questions might be asked. Actually, for the
first time in his life, Randall was happy. He was fixed
firmly in his place with his people and his church and his
wife, who had become a model of public propriety and the
perfect preacher's wife. But in bed, she was still Lizzie
LeCompte, the most luscious piece of ass in town. Randall's
problem was finally solved. He could be good, just like his
mama always wanted him to be, and he wasn't horny anymore.

He rolled off Lizzie with a contented sigh, and lay back
with his head pillowed on his arms, watching her as she
poured water into the china wash bowl and scrubbed her
body until it glowed.

"Wonder if Colored Bertha went out and picked those
green tomatoes this morning like I told her? I declare, I
never saw anybody that liked fried green tomatoes as much
as Reverend Merritt does. And he is the only living soul that
I know who puts milk gravy right on top of them. Thought

Colored Bertha would die when she saw that. But we do aim to keep him happy, don't we, Randall?"

She slipped the prim blue cotton house dress over her head and buttoned it up to the high neck. Standing on one foot at a time, she guided the brown cotton lisle stockings up her legs and rolled them down midthigh with the elastic garters. Slipping her feet in the brown midheeled oxfords, she quickly tied them, and then took a brush to her curls.

"I can't dally. Have to check the dining room table. I tell you Colored Bertha is getting old, Randall. Why, yesterday morning, she'd left the dinner tablecloth on and was going to use it for breakfast. We got to think about getting some younger help in. Not that we'd ever get rid of Colored Bertha, but maybe get somebody in to help her."

"Lizzie, you know that Colored Bertha would have a fit if she thought somebody was coming in here because we thought she couldn't keep up with the work anymore. Maybe if we approached it like we wanted her to spend more time with the twins, make sure they're behaving proper and learning their manners? You know how she is about the twins, far as she's concerned they're her babies."

Lizzie looked at herself in Aunt Bertha's pier glass and nodded approval. "Wonder if those rapscallion twins are up yet? Yes, I think that's a good idea, Randall, we'll just approach it that way. Being as I have all my duties with the church what with leading the Missionary Society and all that, why I'm sure Colored Bertha will see the need."

He looked at her and grinned as she started toward the door. "You look as young as they do, and I want you to know that your buttoned-up dress and your cotton stockings and your brown oxfords are a good try, Lizzie, but they still can't hide what's underneath."

Turning, she stuck out her tongue. "Never you mind, just get yourself out of bed and ready to have breakfast with the Presiding Elder. I have a busy day what with meeting with the Altar Committee to get the flowers arranged for Reverend Merritt's special prayer meeting tonight, and I have to get the twins up to the Taylors for Thelma's birthday party and then go by Byrd Farm. Lord, Randall, look out the window. It's a beautiful, perfect June day, just like in a movie."

When Lizzie flounced into the kitchen, Colored Bertha turned, grumping, "They gone again, Miss Lizzie. I tell you, them two is a case. I go up to make sure they is dressed proper for to have breakfast with that Sliding Elder and they ain't there. Gone slick as a whistle and Lord knows where."

"Don't fret, now, Colored Bertha, they'll show up. Not much place to go in Taylor Springs. They're probably either down in the barn or maybe over at Mama's. But you're right. Those two girls are nine years old now and they have got to quit all this roaming around. It doesn't look proper. I was talking to Reverend Clay just a few minutes ago about this, and we decided what we need to do."

The twins weren't down in the barn or at Mawmaw LeCompte's. For over an hour they'd been down at the springs, back in the clearing, watching Sukie Bee operate the still.

They sat perfectly still, cross-legged on the ground, big brown eyes concentrating on memorizing her every movement, the proportions of grain to water to sugar, the stirring of the mash, the intensity of the fire.

"Jesus loves the little children, all the children of the world," Sukie sang softly as she worked, looking up every now and then at the twins. They were surely a caution; the whole town agreed on that. They sat there wearing overalls, no shirts, no shoes, and the only way to tell them apart was to remember that Vashti had a little mole on her right cheek along with all the freckles while Vangie just had the freckles.

"Red and yellow, black and white, they are precious in his sight," Sukie continued her singing and stirring, "Jesus loves the little children of the world."

"You know what I think, Sukie?" Vashti piped in. "I think you've done put too much sugar in. It doesn't smell right."

"Child, who are you to be telling me what I'm doing? I've been doing this before you was born and before your daddy and mama was born and even before that. You talk to me like that, I'm liable to turn old plat eye loose on you." Sukie raised her paddle and made a menacing gesture.

Vashti and Vangie both squealed with delight. Vangie crowed, "No such thing as the plat man, Sukie Bee. You can't scare us. Khaki and Ben both told us that was just a bunch of old nigger nonsense you used to try to scare them with."

"You better believe there's a plat man. Why, neither one of you would be here today, if'n I hadn't laid the charms and chased him right out of Taylor Springs. You'd have never got born. The only thing I wasn't able to save you from was that bright red hair you got all messed up on your heads. That was the sign he done left. Better not be laughing at no plat man, missies."

"Shoot, Sukie," Vashti said, "Red hair ain't got nothing to do with it. Thelma Taylor has hair just as red as ours. So there."

"That's just what I'm talking about, 'cept you too young to understand." Sukie touched her finger to the upraised stirring paddle and then popped a drop of the mash into her mouth.

"Hmmm," she pondered, "I think there's just a touch too much sugar. Vashti, you may have the gift after all.

Maybe, just maybe, I'm going let you mix up the next batch."

Vangie jumped up from the ground, putting her grubby fists on her skinny hips. "Well, what about me, then? Why should Vashti get to do it all by herself? It's not fair, Sukie Bee."

"Hush, child. Listen, certain people got certain gifts, and it 'pears like Vashti might have the feeling for making the mash. Now, you probably got other gifts, don't know yet, but when we out gathering in the woods for charm makings, seems like you know just what to look for and where to find it. We just have to wait and see."

Vashti looked up at the brightening horizon. "We got to get going anyway, Vangie. Bet Mama's already up and Colored Bertha's probably raising cain 'cause she's done checked our room and we aren't there. Won't even have time to stop and see Khaki or check the barn for Mary William." She took Vangie's hand and they silently crept through the blackberry bushes, down the path to the clearing by the spring, and then scampered up the dirt road, laughing and singing, "red and yellow, black and white, they are precious in his sight, Jesus loves the little children of the world."

Khaki, sitting on his front stoop, hollered and waved to them as they ran by.

"Can't stop now, Khaki," Vangie hollered back. "We think we're already in a heap of trouble. We'll try to come back this evening before supper."

They puffed by Mawmaw LeCompte's house. Mawmaw was out front pinching back her peonies, her back to the road, and didn't see them. She was totally occupied in surveying her neat flower beds and lush lawn. Ever since Lizzie had done so well by herself by marrying into the Clay family, things had certainly gone better for Bethany LeCompte.

First thing, her new son-in-law come right down to the house and before they knew it, had taken her shiftless husband Peter right out to the Philpot Plantation and Miss Ora and Miss Nora had hired him right on to be their regular handyman. Course, they called him their general manager, but that was just fol-de-rol talk. He took care of the grounds, and them big dogs, and did all the painting and repairing and things such as that.

Miss Ora explained, "Ever since Khaki started working regularly for Dr. Byrd, things have just been slipping here at the plantation. Now, Peter, we need you as a full-time employee, every day, except Sunday, of course. We are certainly willing to pay well, but we expect full measure for our money, and naturally know that we'll get it since you are a LeCompte."

Pretty soon, Randall had arranged to have Bethany's house fixed up, painted a pristine white, even had running water put in, nicest pump you ever saw right in her kitchen. Put up a new privy, too, right out in back of the garden. And brought in some real nice furniture. "This stuff is just sitting up in the parsonage attic," Randall said. "Might as well be used." Yes indeed, being Bethany LeCompte of LeCompte Bottoms was something else now.

But that Vashti and Vangie was some children. Tomboys, that what they was and about as wild as any wood critters. Her granddaughters came to see their mawmaw practically every day, begging her for baloney and cheese on store-bought bread and for stories about their mama when she was a little girl.

And Bethany told them about how their mama was the prettiest and smartest girl that ever lived in Taylor Springs. And good, she was such a good girl. Why, she even taught the

Little Angels Sunday school class, the very one that Vashti and Vangie went to until, of course, they got to be older and graduated to the Cherubims. And how being that their mother was so sweet and pretty and good, their papa just one day swept her off her feet and carried her off to marry him just like a prince in a fairy story. And how they should keep their hair brushed and mind their tongues and try to grow up to be as good as their mama.

But today, Vashti and Vangie didn't even holler howdy to Mawmaw. They ran on up the road and ten minutes later appeared at the door of the dining room, just as Randall was inviting Reverend Merritt to say the blessing. Heart-shaped, freckle-covered faces scrubbed clean, long red curls brushed shining and held back with white ribbons, blue-checked dresses covered with ruffled white pinafores, they chorused, "Morning, Mama, Papa, Reverend Merritt." Their bottoms still stung from where Colored Bertha had administered a whomping whack to each one.

Charley Merritt forked a mound of fried pork tenderloin and four eggs onto his plate. "Randall, I tell you there is going to be war. Armageddon is upon us, every sign is there in what is happening in Europe." He helped himself to a liberal portion of fried green tomatoes from the serving plate extended to him by Colored Bertha. "There is no way the United States can remain in this isolationist position."

Bertha returned with a bowl of milk gravy. "Colored Bertha," he exclaimed, "there's nobody in my whole Conference who treats me the way you do. You surely do spoil me. Never come here without you fixing me my fried green tomatoes and milk gravy."

Gesturing with his fork, Charley continued. "Satan is loose, and his name is Hitler. Now, you mark my words, there is no way we can stay out of this. God will not be mocked by all this wickedness let loose in the world, and we will have to go forth to battle Satan in God's name."

"Reckon this has anything to do with Sukie's plat man?" Vashti whispered to Vangie.

Lizzie turned her gaze to them. "Girls," she gently reprimanded, "you know that it's not polite to whisper in front of others."

The red heads bowed, "Yes, ma'am." Inside they were giggling, and they both knew it. Ever since they had been born, they'd really never needed words. Just like they knew right now that each of them was thinking how vomity it was that the Sliding Elder could be sitting there stuffing his mouth with fried green tomatoes with milk gravy poured over them.

Lizzie put down her napkin. "Reverend Merritt, Randall, if you'll excuse us, please. I can tell that you have serious matters to discuss what with the world situation and the church's role, and the girls and I do have some visits to make." Lizzie felt like Myrna Loy couldn't have played the scene in a more ladylike manner. Taking each of her daughters by the hand, she knew they made a pretty picture as they exited from the dining room.

"Randall"—buttering two more biscuits, Charley Merritt popped one in his mouth. Swallowing. "Randall, I must say that you have a fine family there, and to tell the truth, an extremely pretty wife and two pretty little girls. You must be quite satisfied with the way things turned out."

"Can't question the ways of the Lord, Charley. Seems as if what is meant to be will be. I must say that no preacher's wife ever took her congregational duties more seriously than Lizzie. And since she is still a relatively young woman, what with her just being seventeen when we married, that makes it all the more exceptional."

"The church seems to be in fine shape, Randall. No

financial problems, thanks to the Philpot sisters, and you have an active congregation. The Conference feels that you should be appointed here for another four-year term, well, since things are going so smoothly. Now, I know you've been here for a long time and that's not generally the way things are done. Do you have any feelings about never having been appointed to a larger church in a larger city?"

Randall leaned back and took a swig of his coffee. "No, sir, I feel like I'm where the Lord means for me to be. By the way, Aunt Bertha said to be sure and give you her regards and that she expects us all for supper tomorrow night. Hope that's agreeable with you?"

"It certainly is, a fine woman, Bertha Hayes. Though I reckon I shouldn't call her Hayes anymore. But, old habits die hard, don't they? Who'd ever think that Bertha would have gotten married after all those years? The Lord does work in mysterious ways."

12

Lucille Byrd lived down at the post office now. Well, not really the post office, but the room at McAfee's General Store that housed the telephone switchboard and the post office. And Lucille was very content there, what with curtaining off the back of the room and putting in her bed and bureau and washstand, it made just the right size living quarters for one person. Besides, at night, when the store shut down for customers and she had the whole place to herself, she could help herself to all the baloney and cheese and pickles and anything else in the stock that her heart desired because Mr. Bob said she was just to consider the place her home.

Two things had moved Lucille out of Byrd Farm into her own place at the post office. First of all, Randall Clay went off to Indiana and married Lizzie LeCompte and brought her into the parsonage with Aunt Bertha, and secondly, Miss Pearlie McAfee just up and died all of a sudden like, two days before Christmas, sitting right at the switchboard getting ready to plug Myna Smoot into Ruth Taylor. Thing of it was, it certainly destroyed the spirit of the season having to plan the viewing and the funeral just when everybody was getting ready for Santa Claus and the birth of the Baby Jesus.

When Randall brought Lizzie LeCompte back to the Southern Methodist Episcopal parsonage as his bride, the whole town declared that it was a wonder the way Bertha Hayes just took that girl in and started to make a lady of her. You certainly had to give Bertha credit for that.

"I'm telling you right now," Ruth Taylor was overheard saying to Myna Smoot down at the store, "that Bertha is a real saint. It's not easy to have been the mistress of a house and all of a sudden have your place taken by a mere girl. And I must say that Bertha has made that girl into a right proper preacher's wife, well, considering how she was and all."

"You know, of course," she continued, "that Bucky did court that girl a little bit, but, of course, now with him off to college, he has the opportunity of meeting a lot of girls in good social standing. What with that artificial leg them doctors down in Louisville fitted on him, you can't hardly tell he's missing a leg. He's just doing real fine and writes home all about this sweet little girl he's been going out with a lot."

Myna tittered. "Sounds like you got two doing some serious courting, Ruth. My Mr. Dagostino surely does spend a lot of time up on the hill at your house. Says he's helping your Becky with her algebra homework. I must say if a good-looking man like that was around me, my mind certainly wouldn't be on no algebra."

"Really, Myna, you are a sight. You know that Becky ain't but sixteen, even if she is a little ahead of herself in school, being a senior and all this year. Course, she was only five when she started in school, such a smart little tad. But much too young to even be thinking about courting serious. Tony Dagostino is just such a dedicated young teacher and I think he just likes to visit up at the house. He is fascinated with all the furniture and silver and all that stuff that is there from the days when it was the Grand Hotel. He does have such an interest in history."

Bertha continued her mentoring of Lizzie through the birth of the twins. Along with Ora and Nora, she taught the girl how to properly run a quality household, how to preside at various church functions, how to speak like a preacher's wife, and the way a lady groomed herself. When Vashti and Vangie were six months old, and Lizzie received her final acceptance into the social elite of Taylor Springs with an invitation to join the Literary Guild, Bertha Hayes accepted Dr. Roger Byrd's proposal of marriage and left the parsonage to become the new mistress of Byrd Farm.

It was in the spring of 1931, right after the twins were born, that he had first come calling on her. Thinking back on it, she had to admit that her calm, ordered life had become upset since Lizzie had moved into the parsonage, although as far as Taylor Springs would ever know, Bertha Hayes thought Randall's marriage to that girl was the best thing that could have happened.

But she couldn't help remembering that August night when Randall had come delerious into the parsonage, screaming of his punishment for fornicating with Lizzie in the House of God and throwing plat man charms out of his pockets. And she couldn't help but remember what had happened up on the Ridge with the Taylor and Hayes boys and Lizzie. Every time she looked at Lizzie, she thought of those events. Then, when the twins were born, the dearest little things in the world and she did love them, but she knew they weren't Randall's. All that red hair—they were Taylors through and through.

So, when Roger Byrd started calling on her and they started visiting together, she had to admit it was a thrill to get out of the parsonage, out of Lizzie and Randall's way, far from the squalling and care of two babies. She and Roger even went all the way to Louisville to the Philharmonic Concert and to Keeneland to the horse races.

She'd look at him, white hair and mustache with a few faded red threads running through them, and still see in her mind's eye the sixteen-year-old Roger who had handed her down from the buggy when they came clipping up to visit Philpot Plantation so many years ago. She'd been curious about him then and she was curious about him still.

When he proposed marriage to her, Bertha listened to him attentively, listened beyond his words.

"Bertha," he began, "I have been a widower for many years, my only child is an adult now, and I feel the need for companionship with a lady of taste and refinement during my declining years. I am beyond the age where I look for conjugal delights, but instead am searching for the delights of feminine conversation and grace in my household."

"Roger, we must speak plainly to each other. When you talk about conjugal delights, I assume you are speaking of bed. You know I am a spinster. I have never had a man, nor do I ever want a man in that manner. Now, you notice I did not say that I was totally innocent of sexual knowledge. Besides, I am well aware that although Lucille is your only legitimate child, you do have other offspring right here in town."

He looked at her. "Oh, Bertha," he laughed, "would that the whole world was as innocent as you are. Would that I were. No, Bertha, sexual union is not what I propose. Even if we were still young, I doubt that we would satisfy each other that way. I suspect that we both know some things about each other, things that are never said aloud in a place like this. By saying them aloud, it would give them credence. No, my dear, I only propose that we enjoy each other's company and establish a harmonious household for our declining years."

"Good." Bertha planted an affectionate kiss on his cheek. "I think June would be a lovely time for a wedding. We'll have it in the garden at the farm. The roses will be in bloom and I'll wear a chiffon dress and a large, sheer straw hat . . . mauve, I think, or do you think blue would be more becoming? A small ceremony, in good taste. I'm sure Ludie will want to do the wedding cake and Eula can handle the other refreshments for the reception. And Lucille will sing, naturally."

It was a lovely wedding, everyone in town agreed to that. The roses were in bloom, the sky was a soft azure dotted with cotton puff clouds, and there was just enough of a fresh-smelling breeze to gently tease the chiffon ruffles on the bride's gown. Lucille sang "Oh, Promise Me," and the Reverend Randall Clay performed the ceremony uniting his Aunt Bertha and Roger Byrd in holy matrimony.

In the front row of folding chairs, borrowed from McAfee's Funeral Home over in Nelsonville, sat Miss Ora, Miss Nora, Mrs. Randall Clay, Ruth and Bubba Taylor, Myna Smoot, and Bob and Pearlie McAfee. The rest of the rows were filled with the rest of the town, with all the coloreds standing in the back. Colored Bertha was holding one of the Clay twins, while Ludie held the other.

The infants were dressed in elaborate white batiste gowns, ruffled bonnets tied over the red curls. "They sure are the prettiest little babies I ever saw," Eula whispered as she chucked one under the chin. "Can't tell which one is which, they so alike."

Elvira grumped, "Makes no nevermind which one is which. Tell you right now they the spitting image of Bucky when he was a baby and nobody could know that better than me. Surely hope they going to get raised up right what with their mama being what she is, and then everybody know that Colored Bertha never did raise no children."

"Sssh," Sukie cautioned. "No call to be saying out loud them kind of things."

"I now pronounce you man and wife," Randall intoned. "You may kiss the bride."

Ludie placed her twin in Elvira's arms. "Take this young'un for now. I got to get into the house to help Eula with the refreshments. Course, it was me who had to make up the wedding cake. Mr. Roger wouldn't have it no other way." She turned and motioned to Khaki. "Come along, son. You got to fix up that punch for me. After all, this here is a family celebration."

Bertha Hayes Byrd danced right into her role as the doyenne of Byrd Farm without skipping a beat. She refurbished what was necessary, maintained what was valuable, and marshaled her forces with driving energy and skill. Her only goal in life was to provide a proper home for Dr. Roger Byrd, one that befitted his breeding and social station.

Khaki and Eula became her fervent allies, particularly in her attempt to do something about Lucille. Roger was greatly disappointed when Lucille refused to leave Byrd Farm to go on to school to further train her voice. Even enlisting the formidable aid of the Philpot sisters was to no avail. Lucille just shook her moon face in a silent no and said, "I could never leave Taylor Springs now." Not now, she thought, not with the Gospel Boys coming back every year.

"Eula," Bertha sat at the big, wooden kitchen table peeling apples, "we must do something about Lucille. I know in my heart that the girl is shy because of her heaviness. That is why she will not go for voice training. Now, I know a young person needs to eat to keep up their strength and needs a little flesh on their bones, but . . ."

"You right, Miss Bertha, you don't know the times I tried to get that girl fixed up. That time Mr. Bucky invited her to that dance, that the only time I ever thought they was a chance. Just not natural for her to do nothing but to eat and sing. Course, now with Bucky going off to that college, no hope there. Don't know what happened to her, but something done happened way back, maybe when her mama died."

Bertha popped a slice of apple into her mouth. "These apples won't take too much sugar, Eula, they're very sweet. What we must do is cut down on what Lucille eats. Now, what we'll do is not serve the food at the table; you'll serve the plates right here in the kitchen and we just won't have any second helpings. And you and Khaki and I will watch her so we can control what she eats between times."

Lucille never said a word about the new regime. She ate what was placed before her and then, after Papa and Bertha were sound asleep, crept down to the kitchen and ate and smiled as she thought about the Good Time Gospel Boys. No, she would never leave Taylor Springs now, but it would certainly be nice if she could eat whenever she wanted to, like it used to be before Miss Bertha came to the house.

Then, right before Christmas, Pearlie McAfee just keeled over at the switchboard and died right in the store. Lucille was standing at the counter, having been driven over by Khaki to pick up some flour and sugar for Eula's baking. She had just told Mr. Bob to include six Moon Pies in the order and had already opened one, ripping the crinkly cellophane, popping the marshmallowy, chocolately sweetness into her mouth.

Miss Pearlie hit the floor with a thud, Mr. Bob rushed

over to her, Lucille rapidly waddled over to the switch-board, took the headset from Pearlie's prone head, and rang Doc Smoot. She remained at the board and told Khaki to go on home and tell her papa that she was obligated to stay there and help Mr. Bob.

"I never," Bob McAfee exclaimed later, "seen anything like the way you took over that switchboard, Lucille. And took over the mail the next day. Never even knew you knew how to do anything like that. You surely was a savior to me that day. And right now."

"I always watched how Miss Pearlie did it, Mr. Bob. Nothing to it, besides, I like having this job."

Khaki drove her to the store every morning and picked her up every night. Roger Byrd was distressed to think that his daughter was working in a store, but Lucille would only smile when he insisted that it was not her proper station in life and that it must stop.

"Papa, I am being of service to the town. Besides, I am going to move into the post office. There is plenty of space for me to set up a nice room, and that way, if there is any emergencies at night, I'll be there to answer the switch-board."

"Are you out of your mind, Lucille? My daughter living in a room in a general store? Remember who you are, girl, and your breeding."

"That's just what I am remembering, Papa. When I'm busy with my switchboard and post office, I don't have too much time to remember my childhood."

Dr. Byrd paled and stared at his elephantine child, the black curls wild around the fat-swollen face. He then directed Khaki to move whatever furniture Miss Lucille wanted into the post office. "However," he harrumphed, "Bertha and I will expect you to visit us regularly, and, of course, you will take Sunday dinner, as we always have, with Miss Ora and Miss Nora at Philpot Plantation."

So for eight years now, Lucille had lived at the post office, taking Wednesday night supper with her papa and Miss Bertha at Byrd Farm, taking Sunday dinner at Philpot Plantation, and happily joining the Good Time Gospel Quartet the last weekend of every August.

A visit with Lucille was part of the daily routine of Vangie and Vashti Clay. Every day, whether it was summer or winter, for the twins knew no other seasons as they believed in and felt only hot or cold, they followed a fixed pattern of visits through Taylor Springs. Their voyaging ritual always included a few minutes with Mary William Sheely, a stop in Colored Town to see either Sukie or Khaki, and a visit to McAfee's General Store to sit comfortably in silence with Lucille, sharing a Moon Pie or a Baby Ruth candy bar.

Lucille would then permit them to pull back the flowered chintz curtain and go into her living quarters, where Vashti and Vangie would plop down on the goose-down comforter that covered the bed and look at the silver-framed picture of the Good Time Gospel Boys sitting on the bedside table. It was a source of never-ceasing wonder to look at that picture of those singers—well, they were just like movie stars—and see written right on it, "To Lucille, with gratitude for everything. Love, Delmer, Levi, Reuben, Noble."

When they would ask Lucille about the picture, and how it felt to know somebody so important as the Good Time Boys, and what it was like on their traveling bus, she'd just smile, hug the two wiry little bodies, and give them another Moon Pie.

Lying back on Lucille's bed, Vangie pondered, "Still and all, Vashti, Miss Lucille is the only person we know who knows somebody really important. Now, Mary William's brother don't count. Even though he is a movie star, and Professor Sheely says that even better than that he was a big stage star in New York City and he is married to another movie star, we never seen him and Mary William don't really know him. The only thing Mary William knows is what we guess is going on in her head, and that is only things like hungry and happy and sad and glad."

"Sure, but Mary William thinks some good things," Vashti interjected. "She has feelings about the springs and Sukie Bee and, well, just everything. But you're right, she don't even know she has a brother, much less that he is famous."

Vangie popped another piece of Moon Pie in her mouth. "I tell you one thing, Vashti, the next time the Good Time Gospel Boys come to town, I aim for us to get on that bus. I can just picture it in my mind. It must be purely marvelous."

The two girls heard the bell tinkle as the front screen door of the store opened, and then the sound of their mother's voice. "Lucille, I just know those two rapscallions are here. There's not a day that goes by that they don't come visit you. I surely think that you must spoil them to death."

"They're in the back, Lizzie. I think they just like to come to go back into my little room. Must be like a nice little hidey-hole for them."

"Like I've told you a thousand times, Lucille, if they become a bother, you just send them right on home. Vashti, Vangie, come on out of there. You know Lucille is busy and has plenty of work to do without putting up with you two. Come on now, we have to get back to the parsonage and you have to get ready to go to the Taylors' for Thelma's birthday party."

The girls popped around the curtain, smiling winningly at their pretty mama, and then ran to the switchboard to give a hug to Lucille.

"I just love to hug you, Lucille." Vangie sighed. "It's just like sinking into a big bowl of Jell-O."

The bell jangled again and Bucky Taylor stepped inside the front door. He stood, the artificial leg holding him stiffly erect, looking at the red-haired little girls. He turned his gaze to their mother, the buttoned-up-tight Lizzie LeCompte Clay, and then to the awesome massiveness of Lucille Byrd.

"Morning, ladies." He cleared his throat.

Vashti and Vangie ran to him. "Howdy, Mr. Bucky. We'll be up soon to Thelma's party. Is she all excited? Did she get some presents yet? Did you and her mama get her that Shirley Temple doll that she really truly wanted?"

Bucky put his hands on the two red heads. "Whoa, now. No, Thelma ain't getting any of her presents until the party, and yes, she is all excited, and I wouldn't tell you two what her mama and I got her 'cause you'd just go and spill the beans."

They giggled as Lizzie came and took them both by the hand. "If you two don't get home and get yourselves ready you're going to miss the party. Bucky, tell Alice we'll be there right on time and that Khaki will be bringing up that freezer of strawberry ice cream that Colored Bertha is fixing. Randall isn't going to be able to bring it up himself what with the Presiding Elder being here."

"Why, I could have come down and picked it up, Lizzie, or Tony could have come. No need to bother Khaki."

"I know, Bucky, but he'll probably stay around and dish out the ice cream and have himself a good time."

"Reckon you're right at that, Lizzie. Tell you what, Lucille, since I know you won't leave this switchboard come hell-o or high water, I'll just have Khaki fetch you some refreshments by here on his way back."

Lucille smiled. "That would be nice, Bucky." She called good-bye to Lizzie and the twins as they swept out the door.

Bucky studied her crinkly brown eyes for a minute, wondering what would have happened if he and Lucille had been able to go to that football dance together.

Lucille smiled at him and then watched Bucky walk to the back of the store. Maybe, she thought, just maybe, if we'd been able to go to that football dance together, Junie Hayes wouldn't be moldering in the cemetery and Bucky wouldn't be a one-legged man and Lizzie wouldn't be a preacher's wife and Bertha Hayes wouldn't be married to Papa and Vashti and Vangie wouldn't exist and I wouldn't be living in the post office just waiting until August for the Good Time Boys.

13

Elvira stood on her swollen, aching feet, hands planted on her hips, head cocked to one side as she looked over the array of food stretched across the big kitchen table.

Let me see now, we got them fancy little sandwiches all cut and done, we got the cream cheese and nut, and we got the benedictine, and we got the cucumber and watercress. All the crusts are off and cut in them fancy little shapes and covered up with them damp tea towels for to keep them fresh. And we got the baked country ham and the beaten biscuits. Lord, nearly blistered my hands off beating that dough yesterday, good thing Mr. Tony come by and helped me or I'd still be beating. And we got the Lord Baltimore cake and the devil's food cake and course Thelma's birthday cake, white cake with sugar icing and pink roses. Lemonade and iced tea is fixed, just got to chip some ice to put in it come the last minute.

"Miss Alice, Miss Ruth, I think everything ready," she hollered out. "You all want to come check it now?"

Ruth Taylor called back from the dining room, "Just as soon as I finish straightening this lace cloth, Elvira, be right there. I sent Alice upstairs to lie down for a little bit. I swear that girl is so delicate, don't seem to have much endurance."

The first time Bucky Taylor brought Alice home to visit, Ruth knew that she wasn't about to lose her son. She'd never forget the sight of the two of them, standing there in the parlor. Him on that artifical leg, saying that one year of college was enough and he'd fetched Alice home with him, as they were going to get married. And Alice, what a puny little thing she was, tiny and birdboned, with that pale skin and mousy hair. Course, with her being a Todd from Lexington, she was bound to be delicate because of her fine breeding. Ruth knew right then that Bucky and Alice were going to live in the big house with her and Bubba, being as they both needed taking care of.

Lord knew the Taylor house was big enough to hold an army, plenty of room. Good thing, too. First there was Bucky and Alice and little Thelma, and then when Becky married Tony Dagostino, of course they moved in. Becky Taylor wouldn't consider living anywhere else but on Taylor Hill. Two years ago, Becky presented Ruth and Bubba with their first grandson and now Alice was expecting again. Ruth Taylor was in her glory as she supervised the flowering of the first family of Taylor Springs.

Ruth swept into the kitchen and inspected the refreshments. Bending over the kerosene stove, Elvira was inspecting the wicks underneath the burners, mumbling that they was burned down to nubbins and that Dagostino foreign man done promised he'd pick her up some in Nelsonville and he never done it.

Ruth looked at her and scolded, "Really, Elvira, the older you get, the more impossible you are. Now how many times have I told you to quit calling Becky's lawful wedded husband 'that Dagostino foreign man'? Tony has done very well and is a leading citizen of this community.

Taking over as principal of the school when Dr. Byrd retired and still being the football coach."

"Well, he still foreign acting," Elvira grumbled. "But I
guess it's for the best that him and Becky living here with
us where they belong. But I'm telling you, Miss Ruth, if
Becky don't start doing something with that boy of theirs,
they going to be the devil to pay. That little booger only
two years old and wild as he can be."

"You know you're crazy about little Alex," Ruth
laughed. "You're the one who spoils him rotten, Elvira.
Why, you just trot around after him and wait on him hand
and foot."

"Somebody got to look after him what with Miss
Becky down there teaching at the school. Don't understand
what any respectable married woman with a baby is doing
working outside of her home. Ain't fitten."

"Well, the world has changed, Elvira. Becky said she
spent four years at college to be a teacher, and she intends to
be a teacher. Besides, I think she likes to be down there
working alongside Tony. Anyway, all the food looks just
fine. You can start carrying it into the dining room while I
go upstairs to get myself ready. I better see what Thelma is
up to, too. Make sure she's ready. After all, it is her birthday party."

Thelma Taylor was up in her bedroom looking in the
mirror and wishing that her fine, light red hair that was cut
in a Dutch bob was blond and curly like Shirley Temple's.
Maybe, she thought, I'll look like her when I grow up. She
turned toward the little rocking chair where she had tied up
her cousin, Alex. His fat body, clothed in short white pants
and a fancy white shirt, was squirming as he tried to get
loose. Since she had tied a white handkerchief over his
mouth, his enraged cries were muffled.

"Alex, you might as well be still. I'll let you out in a

minute. Can't imagine why anybody would tell me I had to watch out after you when I'm supposed to be getting ready for my very own party on my very own birthday."

She unloosed the fat little body, and as she undid the handkerchief gag she popped a Hershey kiss in the red mouth. Alex immediately began chewing. Taking him by the hand, she led him down the hall to her mother's bedroom.

"Mama," she called softly at the open bedroom door, "Mama, are you awake? I'm all dressed for my party and I got Alex all ready, too."

"Come on in, darling." Alice Taylor raised her swollen body to a sitting position on the bed. "Why, don't you look just beautiful. I can hardly believe that my baby is a big girl, eight years old today. Turn around, now. Oh, you look just fine, a perfect little lady."

She grimaced as a dull pain shot through her extended belly, and placed her hand over it. "And Alex looks just perfect, too. Honey, real quick, get one of Mama's handkerchiefs and wipe his mouth before that chocolate dribbles down on his little white shirt."

Wiping Alex's mouth, Thelma asked, "Are you hurting, Mama? Will you be able to come to the party?" Alex started jumping up and down, his fat legs pogo-sticking, yelling, "Candy, candy."

Alice laughed, "Of course, I'll be down to the party. I wouldn't miss it for the world. Now you take Alex down to Elvira, Lord knows she's the only one who can do anything with him, and you get into the parlor and get ready to receive your guests. Grandma Ruth should already be down there, and your daddy and Gramp Bubba and Aunt Becky and Uncle Tony should be there any minute now."

Thelma pirouetted one more time, grabbed the jumping, yelling Alex, and went down the stairs still thinking about Shirley Temple.

Tony Dagostino stood on the wide veranda, the same one where Georgette LeCompte Taylor once sat, rocking and chewing tobacco, and looked down on Taylor Springs, just as she once had. He heard his yowling son being dragged down the stairs by his niece and then Elvira's soothing tones as she packed the rambunctious Alex off into the back part of the house. He heard the cooings of Thelma and his mother-in-law as they surveyed the refreshments laid out in the dining room, and the firm, staccato steps of his wife as she descended the stairs to join them.

He lit a cigarette and glanced out to see his father-in-law rushing in from the spring house. Tony grinned. The old coot was probably out there sneaking some of Sukie's brew into the house to liven up the punch for the menfolks. The stiff-legged thump of Bucky and the shuffling drag of Alice's footsteps were next down the stairs. Their voices mingled in a chorus with the others in the dining room.

God, he thought, who in hell would ever believe that Tony Dagostino would be at a party like this? A birthday party for a little eight-year-old girl that was the social event of the summer in this misbegotten place, with a misbegotten cast of characters.

Miss Ora and Miss Nora Philpot would be attending, of course. It would not be a social event without them. And naturally Ludie would be accompanying them. She would remain in the kitchen, ostensibly to help Elvira, but, of course, when it came time for Thelma to cut the cake and open the presents, all the coloreds would be clustered in the doorway: Ludie and Khaki and Eula and Colored Bertha and Sukie and Ben and Cora. After all, they belonged, they were family.

Myna Smoot had volunteered to help Professor Sheely

get Mary William ready. The Professor was "just getting old," as Myna put it, and practically senile, and heaven knows how he'd let Mary William show up if she didn't go down there and try to do something with the girl. Dr. and Mrs. Byrd would arrive in that same Packard touring car that took Tony on his first visit to Byrd farm, but Lucille would be missing. Lucille rarely left her room at the post office. And, of course, the luscious Mrs. Reverend Randall Clay would be present with her twin daughters. Thank God, those girls had red hair and not black curls and Roman noses! Add to the list of guests Lizzie's mother and brothers and sisters, who had become acceptable by marriage, Mr. Bob McAfee, Preacher Poe and his family, who were in some way kin to Bertha Hayes Byrd, the Pentecostal Jordans, because Ruth Taylor's daddy had been that Holy Roller church's first preacher, all the acceptable children of Taylor Springs, and old Doc Smoot, who had birthed all those children.

Tony flipped his cigarette over into the peonies, hoping that Ruth didn't see him. The only one missing would be Junie Hayes—big, bumbling, happy, honest, gullible Junie. Tony could still remember him from that August of ten years ago, his shattered arm and his dream-shattered eyes. Bucky went off to college on his wooden leg, Lizzie moved into the parsonage as a respectable married woman, Tony Dagostino married himself into the big house on the hill, and Junie Hayes drove his daddy's pickup truck into the waters of the Taylor Springs.

The town talked of the terrible accident, poor Junie sitting there in the truck's cab, drowned. Being as it was January, and ice on the roads, probably slid right into the springs and hit his head on the steering wheel or something. Must have been unconscious, for there were no signs of him trying to get out or anything. Tony never believed that. He always felt deep in his gut that Junie knocked back about a quart of Sukie's homebrew and deliberately drove himself into the cold waters. Without football and Bucky and Lizzie, there was nothing left for Junie.

Yes, he thought, here I am, Tony Dagostino, king of the hill, king of Taylor Hill anyway. He had carefully courted Becky, very properly, through her last year of high school and her four years of college, knowing that they would marry and move into the Taylor house. And he also knew that one day the house would be his.

Bucky had lost all his guts and hopes when he lost his leg. He made a pretense of helping his father manage the land, but in reality he wandered through his days lost in a fog of morphine and memories of what he once had been, the golden boy of Taylor Springs. Even the girl he married was a pale, petite ghost, sickly and always taking to her bed as a delicate Southern lady should. Tony was amazed that the two of them had managed to produce tough little Thelma. Probably, he mused, this baby that Alice is carrying now will never make it to full term.

He walked down the steps as the Byrd's Packard, crammed with the Philpot sisters, Ludie, Eula, Dr. Roger and Bertha, chauffeured by Khaki's boy, Ben, swept up the driveway. Yes indeed, as soon as old Bubba Taylor passed on, this whole place would be in the hands of the dago from Chicago. He smiled in welcome as he helped the ladies from the car. "Beautiful day, isn't it? Just a perfect day for Thelma's birthday party."

Khaki, dressed in the same black Sunday suit he had worn for twenty years, the one Dr. Clay passed down to him, sat on the front steps of his cabin and waited on Sukie Bee. He peered up and down the dusty road. Fretting, he called, "Sarah, where in the tarnation is that woman? She know that we got to stop by the parsonage and pick up the ice cream and Colored Bertha."

"Quit fuming now, Pa Khaki. We got plenty of time, you know Sukie'll be here. She wouldn't miss this for the world. According to her, none of us would be here or even having this party if it wasn't for her and her voodoo charms."

Khaki chuckled as his daughter-in-law came out on the porch. That Ben surely did marry himself one fine woman. She was as light and pretty and curved sweet as could be, and besides she was smart. She finished up at Lincoln Institute just like Ben done. Just to think that there was two high school graduates living right in his house.

Course, he and Eula were both surprised when Ben and Sarah came back here. True, the gas in his lungs had finally got to him and he knew he couldn't do much more work for Mr. Roger, but he never figured Ben would come back to take his place. But Ben just said, "Pa, this is my place here. I've just come to claim my part of it."

Khaki just told the boy right then some things was better left unsaid. Ben replied flatly, standing tall and proud, that he'd come to take Khaki's place, do Khaki's job. There was a depression out there and no work for most white men, much less a colored boy. Mr. Roger would pay him good and take care of him and Khaki and Eula and Sarah. After all, Dr. Roger Byrd owed them.

Sarah plopped herself down on the steps and put her arm around Khaki's stooped shoulders. He was surely going to miss her when she went to work up at the parsonage. It was nice having company here at home and he knew Eula surely appreciated Sarah redding up the house since Eula was still working out at Byrd farm. But Miss Lizzie thought Colored Bertha needed somebody else in to help with the housework, too much doing all the housework and having to watch after the twins, too.

Khaki chuckled, thinking that if Miss Lizzie wanting
Bertha to rest, she sure didn't want her spending more time
with them twins. Those girls would fret a person to death.
Visited him most every day and both of them was full of
the Old Nick.

Sukie Bee finally waddled into sight, puffing and carrying a covered wicker basket. "Hey, Khaki, hey, Sarah."
Her girth was covered in purple georgette, a dress handed
down from Lucille Byrd, and she wore a planter's straw hat
rammed straight on her head. She turned slowly for their
perusal, "Now, don't you tell me that Sukie ain't turned out
for this party."

Sarah and Khaki walked down the path toward the old
truck. "What you toting in the basket, Sukie?" Khaki asked
as he stowed it in the truck bed.

"Just a little something for Mr. Bubba to put in the
party punch," Sukie chuckled. "Sarah, get around here and
give me a push so I get my big behind up in this truck and
on this seat."

When Khaki delivered Sarah and Sukie and Colored
Bertha and the freezer of strawberry ice cream to the
kitchen door of the Taylor house, the men were in the parlor discussing how FDR was leading the country to so-
cialism and directly into a foreigner's war. The talk was
wetted down with copious cups from Bubba's punch bowl,
which tended to make the conversation very spirited. Miss
Ora and Miss Nora sat on the sofa, spines erect, feet placed
on the floor, watching Ruth and Becky direct the children in
a game of pin the tail on the donkey.

"Sister," Nora whispered, "I certainly do wish that
Bubba would bring me a cup of that punch. I do believe I
would enjoy it much more than this glass of lemonade that
Elvira served the ladies."

"Nora, please do behave yourself. You are eighty years

old and you still carry on like an incorrigible child. And quit sitting there chuckling to yourself."

"I am just enjoying myself watching the children, Ora. When I look at Vashti and Vangie Clay, I'd swear I was looking at our mother. Isn't it amazing how they resemble the Taylors?"

Ruth clapped her hands. "It's time for the birthday girl to open her presents and have her cake. Come and gather round, everybody. Here, Thelma honey, you sit right here in the big chair and Vashti and Vangie, you can fetch the presents. Alice, you sit down there by Thelma. You look worn out, can't be too careful now in your condition."

The twins solemnly transported the presents, one by one, and Thelma carefully unwrapped and admired each gift, properly thanking the donor. The last big box the twins carried together, the present from Thelma's mama and daddy.

When the pink tissue paper and ribbon were torn off and the box lid lifted, Vashti squealed, "It is. You did get the Shirley Temple doll." Thelma held it aloft, and then hugged it in her arms. All the adults smiled and Alex, wiggling out of Elvira's arms, came running over and tried to tear off the doll's leg.

Tony swooped the round little boy up in his arms and held him upside down by his ankles, which made Alex squeal with joy. Thelma clutched the saved doll to her chest, the twins broke into a chorus of "On the Good Ship *Lollipop*," Mary William started flapping her arms and cawing along, and Myna Smoot laughed until pearly little tears rolled down her plump cheeks.

As Thelma made a wish and blew out the eight pink candles on her birthday cake, the Reverend Randall Clay and the Presiding Elder arrived just in time to ask the blessing before the partaking of refreshments.

14

The Clay twins and Thelma Taylor were hiding down in the parsonage privy. It was their favorite meeting place, and since it was a three-holer and the door locked from the inside, there was plenty of room and privacy to sit and scheme away from inquisitive adult eyes.

"Vashti, Vangie, where you all at?" Colored Bertha's voice called from the parsonage back porch. "You two better answer me. Your mama been looking for you."

"Hell's bells," Vashti cussed. "Ever since Mama hired Sarah to do most all the work, Colored Bertha follows us around like an old bloodhound. Can't get away anymore. Can't hardly get down to the springs with Sukie or out in the woods."

"You just better quit that cussing, Vashti, or my mama won't let me play with you anymore." Thelma giggled. "My mama says I am to be a lady just like she is. And ladies don't go around cussing."

"How's your mama going to know about Vashti cussing unless you tell her?" Vangie asked. "Besides, your mama is lying around in bed all the time getting ready to have that baby. Why, her stomach is all swollen up like she swallowed a watermelon. If that baby don't come soon, she's just going to bust open, least that's what Elvira told Colored Bertha."

Thelma stuck out her tongue at Vangie. "Just you shut up, Vangie Clay, about my mama. She told me that soon Doc Smoot would come and bring me a baby brother or sister in his doctor bag."

Vashti snorted. "Thelma, you surely don't believe that Doc Smoot brings any babies in his black bag? Don't you know that baby is in your mama's big stomach? Don't you know nothing?"

"Bet you don't even know how babies get in the mama's stomach." Vangie went on to explain. "The daddy puts his thing, you know like little Alex's pee-pee, in the mama's hole and that puts the baby in the Mama's stomach. And then when the baby is ready to come out of the stomach, it comes out of the mama's hole."

Thelma squirmed uneasily on the smooth wooden plank. "Why, that's the dumbest thing I ever heard in my life. Why would anybody want to do something like that?"

"Sukie Bee says that grown-ups do it because it feels good and that's how you get babies," Vangie gravely proclaimed. "And it is the truth, because Vashti and I peeked in the bedroom door and we saw Mama and Daddy doing it."

"Well, I don't believe it." Thelma stomped her feet on the privy floor.

Colored Bertha's voice called again. "Girls, you down in the barn again? You better come out wherever you are, time for you to get ready to go for your piano lesson."

Vashti grabbed Thelma's fine, red hair. "You just keep quiet about what Vangie told you. And don't stomp your feet and try to hold your breath until you turn blue in the face. You know that don't scare Vangie and me like it does the grown-ups."

Thelma's eyes watered from the hair pulling. "Well, I won't tell, but I still don't believe you. Besides, Colored Bertha is looking for you and we still haven't even decided yet about how we're going to sell the plat man charms. That's what we're supposed to be doing."

Vangie cautiously cracked open the privy door. "She ain't nowhere around. Quick, everybody out, and run behind the privy and back into the garden. We'll act like we've been playing out there and didn't hear her."

Bent over double, the girls sneaked out the half-open door and ran laughing back into the corn rows in the garden. Panting, Vashti said, "We'll come up to your house tomorrow morning, Thelma, and decide about the plat man charms. Come on now, let's go on back to the house, Mama's even started calling us."

The three girls, holding hands, ran out of the garden into the back yard. "Here we are, Mama," Vashti called up to Lizzie, who was waiting on the back porch. "We was just back in the garden playing hide and seek."

While Colored Bertha was herding the twins up the parsonage stairs to get them dressed proper for their piano lesson, Thelma crossed the road and ambled by the church, glad to be going to pay another visit. It was surely boring up at her house these days what with Mama always lying in bed sick and Grandma Ruth shushing everybody so's poor little Alice could rest, and Aunt Becky spending all her time chasing after that dumb Alex, and Elvira thumping around the kitchen complaining about the heat and how, even up here on the hill, the air so stinky from the sulphur in the springs.

Shoot-tee, she thought as she climbed the steps to Miss Myna's front door, what does dumb old Elvira expect. Every July it gets hot and every July the dumb old springs smell.

"Yoo-hoo, Miss Myna. Cora," she called through the screen door. "It's me, Thelma."

"Come on in, honey," Myna Smoot called back. "I'm on the telephone right now. Just run on back to the kitchen. Cora's been waiting on you."

Thelma walked down the cool, dark hallway to the kitchen and Myna resumed her conversation. "Yes, Bertha, it was Thelma. I told Ruth just to send her on over here this morning. No, nothing's happening with the baby yet, but Ruth does say that Alice is feeling so poorly. What? Well, I certainly hope they don't have to take her to the hospital. That's no natural place to be giving birth. Well, Cora and I are just going to teach her how to make a pound cake. That'll keep her busy and besides, right now, Elvira and Ruth just don't have the time to be teaching her things like that. All right, yes, I'll see you tomorrow at the Literary Guild. Bye, now."

Myna put the sweaty receiver back on the hook and wiped her hands on her pink polka-dotted apron. Surely was hot, but then every summer was hot in Taylor Springs. Well, what would you expect, she told herself, being down in a valley surrounded by hills. Just like being in an upside-down teacup. Then, with the springs getting so low in the summer, naturally the sulphur smell was going to be bad, what with no breeze or anything. Makes a body wonder why those first people who came here decided to stay. Lord, Bertha said that Ora was going to give a paper tomorrow at the Guild on the first settlers and I said, what, again. Now that wasn't very Christian of me, but if we have to hear about those buffalo roads again we're all just going to die of boredom.

Thelma stood on a wooden stool pulled up to the kitchen table, one of Cora's white aprons wrapped three times around her and tied tight in the middle, industriously attacking a mound of yellow, dewy butter with a big wooden spoon.

"Hey, Miss Myna," she said as Myna puffed through the door, "Cora says that I have to work at creaming up this butter until it is as light and fluffy as a down comforter. Then, we get to put in the sugar, just a teensy little bit at a time, and then beat the butter and sugar just like we were beating the devil out of our hearts."

"That's exactly right, child." Myna walked over and looked into the big crockery bowl. "You're doing fine, but you still got a ways to go. It takes a lot of effort to make a fine pound cake, and Cora does know how to do that. Probably the only one that can pass her is Ludie. Now Ludie is known to be the best at pound cake, nobody in town disputes that."

"Humph," Cora grumbled, "that surely be true, but I always told you, Miss Myna, that I suspects that Ludie done adds a little something extra that she never told nobody about. Do hope to the Lord that before she passes on she give the secret at least to Eula."

"Well, if there's any secret, I'm sure Ludie will pass it on to Eula, being as Eula works for Mr. Roger. You know how Ludie feels about Roger Byrd and you know how Roger Byrd won't eat nobody's pound cake but Ludie's. Looking back on it, Cora, you got to remember that Ludie and Roger was practically raised together out there at Philpot Plantation, yes, children together."

Myna sat down at the table and watched Thelma attack the butter. "Cora, why don't you pour us all a glass of lemonade. Thelma, you are working up a mighty sweat; a little lemonade would go down nice."

"Would you have ever believed, Cora, that Roger Byrd and Bertha Hayes would end up getting married? I mean, Bertha, an old maid, and Roger going away to college and staying away all those years and then coming back here a widower and with a daughter. Course, Lucille wasn't no baby when they come back, already in high school. Just goes to show, you never know."

She took a healthy gulp of the lemonade that Cora poured for her. "Why, it was Mr. Roger who was responsible for bringing your Uncle Tony here, Thelma. Yup, just went up to the university and brought him back here to be the football coach. Now, look, he's principal of the school, too. And did you know that your Uncle Tony lived right here in this house? Indeed, boarded right here with me and Cora until he married your Aunt Becky and went to live up in your house."

"Yes, ma'am." Thelma kept working. Bet Miss Myna had told her that a thousand times. All old people wanted to do was talk about who was kin and who was doing what and what happened a long time ago. She didn't mind Uncle Tony living at her house, but she could certainly do without that bratty little Alex.

"Cora, look here." Thelma lifted a spoonful of the soft, fluffy butter. "Is this just about right? Can I start putting in the sugar now?"

Cora took the spoon and swished it through the buttery clouds in the bowl. "Yes, indeed, it's exactly right. Can't tell just by looking, Thelma. You got to go by the feel of it, too. Oh, this is going to be a fine cake, I can tell that already. You going to take it home and your mama is surely going to be so proud."

"Likely as not, she won't taste a bite of it." Thelma sighed and brushed the wispy bangs off her sweaty forehead. "I surely do wish that baby would hurry up and get out of her stomach."

Cora and Myna exchanged startled looks. "Law's sake, what in the world are you talking about, child?" Myna demanded. "Where did you ever get such an idea? You know that Doc Smoot will bring that baby in his black doctor bag when the time comes."

Adding a little sugar to the butter, Thelma kept stirring away, keeping her eyes on the mixture in the brown bowl. "Oh, that was just something I heard somewhere. You know, that babies grow in the mama's stomach and then they come out. I was just wondering how they got in there."

"Well, I don't know where you heard any such foolishness as that, Thelma." Myna rose from the chair and stood beside her. "Here, give me that spoon a minute. I'll spell you for a while on beating that sugar in. No, sir, you just take my word for it. Doc Smoot brings babies and I ought to know. After all, he is my own first cousin."

Cora muttered, "Good Lord sakes," and marched over to the pie safe to measure out flour from the bin.

Thelma beat in more sugar. I knew it, she thought triumphantly, I just knew that Vashti and Vangie were making up stories again. Nobody would do nothing so dumb as what they were telling me. I'll never let on to them, though, that I know they were funning me. The joke can just be on those two.

The telephone bell gave three short rings. "Goodness, that's our ring all right," Myna said and she left the kitchen. The rings continued. "Lord, a body would think the house was on fire or something. Lucille don't never ring like that."

"Hello. What on earth is it, Lucille?" She listened intently, glancing back down the hallway into the kitchen. "Well, of course, I'll keep her here. Tell Ruth to have Tony bring her night things and a change of clothes down. And tell her to be sure and put in her new Shirley Temple doll.

No trouble. You'll ring when there's any news, won't you?
All right. Good-bye."

"Thelma," she called down the hall, "guess what?
Right this minute Doc Smoot is on his way to your house
with his black bag. You're going to spend the rest of the
day and night here while he is getting that new baby for
your mama."

"That'll be a lot of fun, Miss Myna." A cloud of flour
dust rose as Thelma beat away at her batter. "Maybe after
Vashti and Vangie come back from their music lesson, they
could come over to play. We could have a tea party and eat
some of my pound cake. I do believe it's going to turn out
just fine, just like Cora said. I do hope that God made us a
girl baby, though. I don't want any more little boys like
Alex running around the house."

Just as Cora and Myna exchanged glances and started
to laugh, Mary William Sheely came bursting through the
front screen door.

"Oh, my Lord, she's loose again." Myna moved
quickly to the kitchen doorway and thrust her bulk at the
windmilling Mary William. "Cora, quick, get over here and
help me catch her."

Mary William propelled her skinny body into the com-
bined bodies of the two women and was enfolded in their
softness. They pushed her into a kitchen chair, and Cora sat
on her while Myna tied her down with the pink polka-
dotted apron that she had rapidly removed.

Thelma climbed down from the wooden stool and carried the brown bowl of creamy rich batter over to the still
threshing Mary William.

"Hey, Mary William, it's just me. It's Thelma," she
crooned several times. Mary William got suddenly quiet
and began to caw softly. "Look here what I got for you.

Look at this good food." Thelma lifted the wooden spoon filled with rich batter to Mary William's mouth.

"Shoot-tee, Miss Myna, she'll be just fine now. Me and Vashti and Vangie are good friends with Mary William. We play with her most every day. We already taught her to almost make hollyhock dolls."

"Good grief," Myna panted, "wonder how she got loose again? I swear that Professor Sheely is just too old to watch after her anymore. Course we all been saying that for ten years now. Not that she'd harm a soul, but she's liable to do some harm to herself. I mean, she just doesn't have nothing upstairs, we all know that."

"Listen, Thelma, you just keep on feeding her that cake batter. I'm going to run over to the church and I surely do hope Reverend Clay is there so he can help us get her back home to her daddy. If he's out doing his calling, well at least I can get Colored Bertha and Sarah to help us. Looks like the four of us could handle it."

Mary William cawed and drooled pound cake batter down her chin.

15

An hour later, Doc Smoot had to send Bubba Taylor off in his old pickup to fetch Sukie Bee back to the house on the hill. Bubba screeched through LeCompte Bottoms, gravel spraying off the tires, and then sped down the dirt road to Sukie's cabin. Wheeling to stop, he honked the horn loud and long and then jumped out of the truck to run and bang on the cabin door.

"Sukie Bee! You in there? Sukie Bee! Drat it, woman, get to the door. This here is an emergency." Bubba shaded his eyes and peered through the screen door.

He jumped when he felt a hand on his shoulder. "You looking for me, Mr. Bubba? What's all this commotion about?"

"Lordy, Sukie, where was you? Nearly caused me to jump out of my skin."

"I was just round back checking my tomato plants. Now, sit down here on the steps and catch your breath and tell me what the trouble is."

Bubba collapsed on the sagging steps and pulled his blue bandanna out of his front overalls pocket. Mopping his face while he caught his breath, he huffed, "It's Alice . . .

she is having that baby . . . not having an easy time of it
. . . anyway, Doc Smoot sent me to come fetch you real
quick. He needs you to come and help midwife Alice."

"You go start up that truck while I go gets my herbs
and things." Sukie moved her girth with amazing speed
into the cabin and back out to the truck, where Bubba was
waiting to help hoist her into the cab.

"I'm getting too old for all this carrying on, Sukie.
Swear to Jesus, never rains but it pours. Anyway, Doc
thinks this baby is a breech; and Alice is so poorly and all.
Anyways, Ruth and Elvira and Becky is running around
like chickens with their heads cut off and Tony took Alex
down to Myna Smoot 'cause Thelma was already staying
there. So now Thelma and Tony and Alex are all staying
with Myna because Alice just keeps screaming to beat the
band. And Bucky is just limping back and forth across the
front porch and I'm trying to calm him down, when
Preacher Clay comes roaring up in his car."

"Dear Lord, have mercy," Sukie moaned, "You mean
Miss Alice so bad that the preacher have to come to pray
over her?" Sukie started a contralto chant, "Death come to
the door, go away death, go away plat man."

"For God's sake, shut up that foolishness, Sukie."
Bubba stopped the truck in front of the house where Bucky
was still pacing the porch. "Randall Clay come to fetch Doc
to take him over to the Sheely house. Seems like something
done happened to the old man, so Doc needs you here so he
can go over there."

Waddling behind Bubba as he raced toward the steps,
Sukie muttered to herself, "Good thing I done packed my
plat man charms in with my things. Plat man trying to get
loose again. Old Sukie can feel it, yes, sir, putting my plat
man charms all around Miss Alice, keep her safe from the
plat eye."

Down the hill, in Professor Sheely's yellow gingerbread house, Myna Smoot sat on the parlor floor. The old professor lay beside her, crumpled in a fragile heap on the threadbare, dusty Turkish carpet that covered the parlor floor. Mary William was collapsed beside him, eyes empty, clawed hands scraping dust balls from the rug. She rocked and softly sang her song. The air in the parlor hung heavy with heat and the smell of closed-up places.

Cora, who knelt on the other side of the prone old man, ponderously rose and began to open the windows in the room. "Wonder how long he been like this, Miss Myna? Seem like he done had a stroke or something like that. Everything in here all closed up and dirty."

"Can't have been too long, Cora." Myna sighed. "Else he still wouldn't be alive and Mary William just got loose a little while ago. I just feel real bad not to have come over here and checked on them more often."

The screen door slammed and Doc Smoot entered the parlor. Kneeling, he felt for a pulse and then took the stethoscope from his black bag, listening as he moved the shiny instrument over Sheely's chest. He rolled back the old man's eyelids, shining a light on each eyeball. "He's had a stroke, all right. Can't tell too much yet except he seems to be partially paralyzed on the left side."

He replaced the instruments in the bag, snapped it shut, and stood up. "I'm going to pick him up and move him onto the sofa there. Cora, you watch over Mary William, keep an eye on her. Myna, you go on back to your house and ring up Lucille and tell her to call the hospital over at Boonetown and have them send an ambulance. And tell her to have the hospital get hold of Doctor Craig over there so he'll be waiting. I can't go. Got to get back to the Taylor house. I'm afraid that Alice is in real trouble with this baby."

Myna started toward the door, then suddenly turned around, dumpling chins quivering, eyes startled with sudden comprehension. "Good Lord, Doc! Whatever are we going to do with Mary William?"

Lucille Byrd had never placed a call farther than Cincinnati, Ohio; however, viewing herself as a professional by now, she had no doubt that she would be able to place a call to Hollywood, California. She sat in front of the switchboard, massive and filled with dignity. The plug was in her right hand and her headphones in her left.

"I can't believe that I'm standing here in Taylor Springs getting ready to talk to a movie star in Hollywood." Sweat popped out on Lizzie LeCompte Clay's forehead and she gave her renowned posterior a little shake. Suddenly, she remembered that she was Mrs. Randall Clay, straightened herself, and assumed a serious and proper look.

"Thank goodness we found those letters in Professor Sheely's desk drawer and found out the telephone number. Of course, Randall and I would never go through anyone's things otherwise, but this was an emergency." She pushed the curls back from her wet forehead and away from her excited eyes.

Lizzie simply could not believe her luck when she found the telephone number. Why, if they'd had to wait for a letter to get to California . . . The day before had really been something with Randall running into the parsonage just after she'd come in the door herself bringing the twins back from their music lesson with Miss Ora and Nora. The three of them were on their way up the wide front stairs, going to change their clothes, when she heard the screen door slam and heard her husband excitedly calling her name. Well, never let it be said that the preacher's wife didn't rise to the occasion. She watched Randall get into the ambulance to take the old man to the hospital, and then got Myna and Cora to help her bring Mary William back to the parsonage.

When they pushed the dazed Mary William, arms tied down again with the pink apron, in the front door, Vashti and Vangie came racing down the hall. "Mama," Vashti hollered, "what is Mary William doing here?"

"Girls, old Professor Sheely had been taken real bad and your daddy has gone with him in the ambulance to take him to the hospital. So we had to bring Mary William here, 'cause there's nobody else to take care of her."

Vashti and Vangie walked slowly toward the rigid Mary William. As they approached, they began to softly chant and rhythmically shake their hands. The rigid Mary William relaxed. By the time they reached her, she had started to drool happily and respond with her own woo-woo.

"Shucks, Mama," Vangie started untying the pink apron, "you don't have to keep her tied up. She'll be just fine with Vashti and me. We can talk to her. You know we visit with her all the time. We'll watch her real good."

Myna gasped, "Well, I never, you two do beat all. Reckon Cora and I better get on back. Goodness, you two don't know it yet, but Thelma is staying over at my house because Doc Smoot is bringing her a little baby brother or sister over at her house. And Alex and Mr. Dagostino are there, too, now."

"Well, Miss Myna, why don't you have Thelma come on over here to play with us and Mary William? Ain't that all right, Mama? Thelma just purely can't stand too much of that Alex."

Lizzie looked with amazement at her two daughters, one on each side of the now passive Mary William, like two bookends holding up a skinny, frayed volume. "All right, Thelma can come over, but the minute Mary William looks like she's going anywhere, you yell for Colored Bertha or Sarah real quick like."

After supper that evening, Lizzie sat on the front porch, trying to catch a little coolness. An angry red sun was on the horizon, the sky smeared with purple and black elongated clouds. The air was sultry with unshed moisture and the sulphur stench of the springs.

She looked at Thelma and the twins as they danced over the yard catching lightning bugs, bringing them back blinking in their cupped hands to show a cawing Mary William. There was no breeze, no coolness in the air. The cotton dress stuck to her body. All it's done is rain, she mused, all of this month. Probably rain again tomorrow. Come August we'll be praying for some of this wetness. Hmm, it'll be August in a few days and then soon it'll be the end of August and time for the Good Time Gospel Boys to come. That's always such a treat. Really the only time that Lucille sings anymore since she moved into the post office, when the Good Time Boys come.

The girls, flushed and sweaty and tired of chasing lightning bugs, sat down on the grass beside Mary William. "You know what I been thinking?" Thelma asked. "I been thinking about getting saved."

"I thought you was going to say you been thinking about how long it's taking Doc Smoot to get that baby out of his doctor bag." Vashti cackled.

"No, Miss Smartie." Thelma crossed her eyes and stuck out her tongue at Vashti. "I been thinking about the revival coming up. I was thinking about answering the call and going up to the altar and everybody looking at this little girl giving her heart to Jesus. Everybody would probably be crying and everything. Once you get saved, why, then you

can join the church and go up to the altar and get to eat
them soda crackers and drink them teensy little glasses of
Nehi grape soda."

The preacher's daughters stared at her in amazement.
"You must have lost your mind, Thelma. Your head must
be as empty as Mary William's."

"No," Thelma continued, lips pursed, "I ain't empty-
headed at all. "If I got saved and got Jesus to come into my
heart, why, I could probably just get the spirit and dance
down the aisle and get right up there and sing with Lucille
Byrd and the Good Time Gospel Boys."

Lizzie, fanning her face with her hand, walked off the
porch and down the walk to the front gate, smiling at the
girls as she passed them. Standing at the gate, she saw Tony
Dagostino crossing over the gravel road.

As he reached the gate, he stopped and looked up and
down at the body outlined by the sweat-dampened dress.
He grinned. "Sure is hot, isn't it, Lizzie?"

"Seems like it's always been hot," Lizzie replied.

"Well, I came to fetch Thelma. Seems like Alice has
delivered a ten-pound boy, healthy, with all his fingers and
toes, and Alice is fine, too. Doc Smoot can't figure it out.
Said once he left to go down to the Sheelys and Sukie Bee
arrived to spell him, why, things just settled down and the
baby wasn't breech after all. Of course, you know Sukie,
she's running around pulling her usual mumbo-jumbo
about how her herbs and charms 'done saved' Alice and the
baby."

"That's good news, Tony. Bucky must be mighty
proud to have a boy."

"Oh, yes, Bucky is strutting, at least as well as he can
on a wooden leg, and Bubba and Ruth are as pleased as they
can be. Now they got two grandsons, but this one is a Taylor."

"We better go tell Thelma." Lizzie started down the walk.

Tony followed her. "Oh, I almost forgot in my joy over announcing the good news. Doc Smoot is going over to the hospital to check on Professor Sheely and says he'll bring Randall back with him."

When they reached the girls and Mary William, Tony leaned over and scooped a squealing Thelma up in his arms.

"Guess what?"

"What? what?" she demanded.

"You, young lady, are the proud sister of a bouncing baby . . ." he paused.

Thelma and the twins started yelling, "What kind of baby?" "A boy or a girl?" "Tell us, tell us."

Tony put Thelma down, put an imaginary trumpet to his lips and blew a fanfare. The little girls jumped up and down, pulling on him and laughing.

"It's a boy," he announced.

"I hate boys." Thelma threw herself backward onto the grass and started to hold her breath so she could turn blue in the face.

Yes indeed, Lizzie thought, between Professor Sheely having a stroke and Alice Taylor having a baby boy, yesterday was one full day. But today was something really special. She hadn't tingled like this for years. She shifted her weight excitedly from foot to foot as she listened to Lucille place the call to Hollywood.

As she inserted the plug, Lucille explained, "I've got to call Nelsonville first. Hello, is this you, Minnie? Yes, this is Lucille Byrd over in Taylor Springs. I need you to patch me into long distance in Louisville. What? Minnie, I don't have time to talk about it now. You can listen in once we make the connection, which I'm sure you'll do anyway. Now, get me Louisville, this is an emergency."

Lucille raised her eyebrows in exasperation. "Hello, is this Louisville long distance? Yes, operator, this is the Taylor Springs operator. I need you to patch me through to Hollywood, California."

Lizzie watched, wide-eyed.

Hunkering her bulk down into the chair, Lucille continued. "Yes, this is a person-to-person call to Eliot Mansfield at Grover 7-6642. The person calling is Mrs. Randall Clay of Taylor Springs."

Lucille turned to Lizzie. "She's ringing St. Louis now to start making the connections. I don't know how the relay goes, maybe to Denver. It'll be a few minutes. Lizzie, would you mind to go get me a Coca-Cola and a Baby Ruth candy bar while we're waiting? And tell Mr. Bob we're ringing through, because he wanted to come in here when we talked to Hollywood. This is a first, you know."

Lizzie walked rapidly into the store. It certainly wouldn't do not to be right by the switchboard when Lucille finally got the number. "Mr. Bob," she called to the cluster of folks gathered around the soft drink cooler in the back of the store. "Lucille has placed the call and they are relaying it clear across the United States right now. She says for you to come on and she wants a Coca-Cola and a Baby Ruth candy bar."

Bob McAfee scooped two wet bottles out of the cooler. "Now listen everybody, you can come down by the door to listen, but you can't all crowd into the room. We don't want Lucille and Lizzie getting all flustered by a bunch of people." He popped the caps off the bottles on the opener that was attached to the side of the cooler, and they fell with a plop onto the oiled wooden floor.

"Now, follow me quiet like." He walked with exaggerated softness to the front of the store, picking up a candy bar from the open box on the front counter.

Approaching Lizzie, he handed her one of the bottles. "You might want to wet your whistle with this, Lizzie." Lizzie gratefully took a swig of the drink. Her mouth was dry and she swallowed nervously. As she and Mr. Bob entered the doorway into the post office, Lucille whispered, "They just rang Los Angeles."

Lucille suddenly shifted her vast weight and pulled herself to an erect sitting position. "They're ringing now." Her jowls quivered with dignity. "Yes, operator, this is Taylor Springs. You have my party now. Thank you. Hello, yes, this is a person-to-person call to Mr. Eliot Mansfield from Mrs. Randall Clay in Taylor Springs. Is this Mr. Mansfield? Please hold the line for Mrs. Clay."

Rising ponderously from the chair, Lucille motioned to Lizzie. Breathing rapidly, Lizzie sat down, and carefully adjusted the operator's headpiece over her brown curls. She breathed deeply and turned to give the crowd in the doorway a dazzling smile.

"Mr. Mansfield," her voice flowed as golden and slow as honey. "Can you hear me? Yes, I can hear you fine, but like from far away. This is Mrs. Randall Clay and I am the wife of the Reverend Randall Clay of the Southern Methodist Episcopal church here in Taylor Springs."

She fixed an appropriately grave expression on her face. "I'm afraid that I have some bad news for you. What? Yes, it's your father. Oh, no, he's still alive. But he's had a stroke, or at least that's what Doc Smoot thinks, and he is in the hospital at Boonetown. No, he's in a coma like. Yes, my husband rode over in the ambulance with him. Well, the doctors haven't said. They can't tell much yet, except he's unconscious and seems like his left side is paralyzed." The crowd in the doorway pushed a little further in, awed by Lizzie's performance. "Mary William is all right. She is staying at the parsonage with us. No, we wouldn't dream of putting her away anywhere, besides there's no place here to put her. No, I don't reckon you have seen her in a long time. I know you never been to Taylor Springs since the Professor and Mary William came here; believe me, we'd all have known if a movie star came to visit."

Nonchalantly she took a sip of Coca-Cola, and looked over at her audience. They smiled their approval. "Well, Mary William is just like she always was. No, we'll be happy to watch after her until you get here, after all, that is our Christian duty. Yes, you can telephone for news. No, there's no number, you just get connected to the operator here, her name's Lucille Byrd, and then she'll just ring the parsonage. Yes, I'll have my husband tell your daddy that you and your wife are on your way, maybe he can hear and it will comfort him. Good-bye now."

Lizzie removed the headpiece, stood regally, and announced, "Eliot Mansfield and his wife will be taking the *Limited* to Chicago and then another train into Louisville where he will have a limousine and chauffeur waiting. He is coming to his daddy's bedside and will make arrangements for the care of his sister."

A sigh of approval came from the crowd, which parted like the Red Sea as Lizzie made her regal way into the store and out the front screen door.

16

Eliot Mansfield and his wife did not arrive in Taylor Springs until the third week in August, two weeks later than expected. When his wife had called Lucille Byrd to explain that Eliot had suddenly taken ill in Chicago with what seemed to be a touch of *la grippe* and the doctor recommended that he stay there in the hotel until he was completely recovered, Lucille conscientously relayed the news to the parsonage, knowing that Myna Smoot and Ruth Taylor, being on the same party line, would listen in and let the rest of the town know what was happening. Besides, Mr. Bob McAfee was standing in the post office door when the call came in and he immediately took the news back to the men standing around the soft drink cooler.

"*La grippe*? What the tarnation is that?" Bubba Taylor asked.

"Don't know. Sounds like a suitcase to me." Airy LeCompte snorted.

Mr. Bob chuckled, "Don't be showing your ignorance now. I think it's something like a cold in the guts."

"Oh, you mean a movie star has got the trots?"

"I surely would trot something if I had me a wife that

looked like that. Seen her once in a picture over in Nelson-ville. Whoo-eee! Talk about a pecker-acher."

"Shush now," Bob cautioned as the bell on the opening screen door jangled. "Might be ladies coming in." The laughing men looked up to see Vashti and Vangie Clay leading Mary William into the store, followed by Thelma Taylor. Serious expressions on their faces, they slowly advanced toward the group clustered around the cooler.

Thelma walked over to Bubba Taylor, pushed the red bangs off her sweating forehead, and put down the covered basket she was carrying. "Howdy, Grandpa. Sure is hot, ain't it? Don't reckon you'd like to buy me and the twins and Mary William a Nehi grape, would you?"

Bubba Taylor looked down at Thelma. "What in the world are the three of you doing up here with Mary William? Vashti, Vangie, you know your mama told you not to take her out of the yard by yourselves after you brought her up to the house to see Thelma's baby brother. You three just went off and started your playing and forgot all about her and then what happened? Now you tell me, what happened?"

The twins bowed their tousled red curls and stared down at their dirt-caked bare toes. Mary William's hands started flying and her arms began windmilling.

"Oh, my Lord," Mr. Bob shouted. "She's off again. Airy, run back and get one of them Moon Pies. Food calms her down. Take hold of her, girls."

Vashti and Vangie began slowly flapping their hands and singing woo-woo to Mary William. One on each side of her, they gently sat her on the floor, her back against the cooler, while Thelma started stuffing the Moon Pie in her mouth.

"Whoo, Grandpa, you know you can't talk rough in front of Mary William. It sets her off every time." Thelma glared. "Besides, it ain't Christian and I've been doing a lot of thinking about being Christian. I wouldn't be the least bit surprised if I don't get saved soon."

The men looked surprised and then chuckled softly. "Well, I never." Airy LeCompte looked over at Bubba. "That granddaughter of yours is sure feisty."

Bubba, in a softer voice, continued, "Now, ladies, what happened that your mama told you not to take Mary William out of your yard by yourselves?"

Mr. Bob popped the caps off three dewed bottles of grape and handed them to the girls, and stuck another Moon Pie in Mary William's clawed fingers.

Thelma took a long swig of grape and wiped her mouth with the back of her grubby hand. "Grandpa, you know as well as we do what happened. We took Alex and Mary William outside and we was making clover chains. Next thing you know, we looked up and Alex and Mary William wasn't there, so we run to find Daddy and Uncle Tony to help us look for them and we finally found them down by the spring, just sitting under a shade tree."

"Well, good, I'm glad you remember, 'cause they both could of drowned since they are both around two years old and don't know nothing. Now, would you like to tell me why you are disobeying your mama and what you all are doing here?"

"That's what it's all about, Mr. Bubba." Vashti picked up the basket and carried it over to the wooden counter. "We are here because we wanted to do some business. Right here in this basket we got something to sell that will protect people and keep any harm from coming to them, like what could of happened to Alex and Mary William."

She whipped the cover off the basket and dumped its contents on the counter. "Looky here, we got genuine plat man charms to sell."

"Well, for God's sake," Bubba Taylor intoned, "where in tarnation did you girls get them things?"

Airy LeCompte blanched. "What are those children doing fooling around with voodoo? That's colored folks' mumbo-jumbo."

Thelma smiled. "Ain't that a good idea? Buy a plat man charm and the plat man can't get to you. It's surefire protection. And they are genuine. Sukie Bee done taught Vashti and Vangie how to make them right. Got to have bones and . . ."

Her grandfather interrupted. "That's enough, missy. You all just stay right there, don't move, and don't say another word." He marched to the front of the store, into the post office doorway. "Lucille, ring up the church and get me Brother Clay right away."

By afternoon everyone in Taylor Springs knew that Professor Sheely's movie star son was laid up in Chicago with some kind of sickness, and that Preacher Clay's daughters and the Taylor girl were mixed up in some kind of darky voodoo charms. It was told that Reverend Clay was praying nonstop in front of the altar at the Southern Methodist Episcopal church, and that a posse led by Bubba and Bucky Taylor was trying to track down Sukie Bee.

Bertha Hayes Byrd pinned the navy blue straw hat on her head, picked up the white gloves and the navy pocketbook, and walked heavily down the winding stairway that led to the wide foyer of the Byrd farmhouse. Eula, a worried frown creasing her forehead, stood waiting for her. "Is Ben ready to drive me, Eula?"

"He's out there waiting, Miss Bertha. He just got back from seeing if Mr. Roger was down with Khaki, but neither one them down at our cabin. I don't like it, Miss Bertha, something strange going on. And to think about a bunch of men out looking for Sukie Bee. No telling what might happen. Sukie Bee ain't harmful."

Bertha patted Eula's thin, tan hand. "Don't fret yourself, Eula, until I find out what is going on. Now remember, if Dr. Byrd shows up tell him where I've gone, first to the parsonage and then to the Philpots. And if he's imbibed a little too much, Eula, make sure he stays right here. I just have a feeling that he and Khaki . . . well, never mind."

Lifting her chin, she sailed out to the waiting Packard, where Ben helped her into the back seat. As he carefully drove down the bumpy dirt lane, she questioned him about looking for Dr. Byrd and his father.

"Miss Bertha, didn't look like they had been down at the cabin. No sign of either one of them. Stopped at the parsonage to ask Sarah and she hadn't seen either of them all day. Can't figure out how Mr. Roger left the farm and us not knowing. I didn't drive him and Mr. Roger never walks anywhere. Anyway, things are sure a mess. Reverend Clay is over praying in the church and won't let nobody talk to him and he ordered Miss Lizzie and Sarah and Colored Bertha not to let the girls or Mary William out of their sight."

"Well, Ben, you just drive me right to the church. Randall Clay will see me whether he wants to or not. I'll get to the bottom of this foolishness."

"I certainly hope so, Miss Bertha. This is mighty bad business about a posse out looking for Sukie Bee. That could turn real ugly. She looked up into the rear-view mirror in time to see Ben's gaze become hard and hateful. It reminded her of how Roger's eyes could look sometimes.

"Wait for me right here, Ben," she instructed as he pulled up in front of the church. She marched up to the wide wooden front doors and pulled on the brass handle. The door swung open and she strode determinedly into the sanctuary. Looking down toward the altar through the haze of trapped heat and the multicolored light streaming in through the stained glass windows, she was startled to see that no one was there. Looking slowly around, she finally saw him, a heap lying prostrate in front of the stained glass window, the memorial to Burton and Ramona Clay, looking up at the crucified Christ and moaning "Mama, Mama."

"For heaven's sake, Randall Clay, quit that caterwauling and get up on your feet." She advanced toward him like an armored tank rolling toward the enemy lines.

Randall rolled over on his back and then sat up, a dazed look in his eyes. "Oh, my God, Aunt Bertha, it's happened again . . . those charms, just like I found before here in the church. My sins, payment for my sins . . . It's Mama, she's up there and she's telling me about my sins of the flesh." Pulling him erect, Bertha slapped his face. "Sins of the flesh indeed. Don't be a total fool, Randall. Ramona is dead; in fact, Ramona lived dead. Too bad she tried to make her only son believe that the feelings of life were a sin. Now you listen good to me. All we got here is three little girls with good imaginations pretending and playing a game. Probably heard Sukie Bee talking about the plat man and charms and just took it from there."

Randall shook his head; his eyes cleared.

"Now, you go get Adam Poe and Brother Jordan and the colored preacher and you four men of God get out there and stop that foolishness of a posse trying to track down poor old Sukie Bee. Bunch of dumb old men always sitting around in the store and gossiping like a bunch of women."

Randall stood before the glass image of the bleeding Christ, his silhouette outlined in the red light streaming through the window. "You're remarkable, Aunt Bertha," he smiled, "and I have a feeling you're right. Someday we're going to have to sit down and talk about all this. It just seems as if these spells come over me and my mind is fevered, just not clear."

Bertha smiled and straightened her blue straw hat. "All right, let's go now. You get on over to the parsonage and let Lizzie and the girls know what's going on. I've got to get on out to see Miss Ora and Miss Nora."

Nora Philpot saw on the veranda, waiting. In one hand she held a thin black cigar, a feathery plume of smoke rising straight up in the sultry, still air. Her other hand lay ready on the shotgun that rested on her lap. Through the open windows of the front parlor, she could hear Ora's sharp, crisp voice, Ludie's mumblings, Sukie Bee's keenings, and the slurred, deeper rumblings of Roger Byrd and Khaki.

By God, she reveled, life is still exciting. Eighty years old now, Ora and me, and things are still happening. Of course, we never talk about them, but we sure do orchestrate them. Besides, people of quality do not discuss certain things. It is a courtesy we extend to one another in order to live in a civilized manner.

Just listen to Sister in there, telling Sukie Bee that of course there is no plat man and that Sukie Bee never made a charm or did voodoo in her life. That all this is just the vivid imagination of children. And Ludie agreeing with her. And Roger and Khaki telling Sukie Bee that that's right, and that's why they brought her out here to hide her until somebody can talk some sense into that group of old farts that are supposed to be looking for her.

Wonder what that group of ignorant old men are thinking? Just because Vashti and Vangie and Thelma dump some chicken feathers and bones down on the counter of McAfee's store, they think there's really voodoo going on in Taylor Springs. Doesn't matter if there is or not. We aren't going to admit it, so it isn't true.

Hearing a car's engine, Nora raised her head and the shotgun at the same time, then lowered it as she saw the Packard touring car come sweeping up the lane. Ben and Bertha, she mused. Well, looks like we're all here, now.

"Hello, Bertha, Ben. Go on in the front parlor, everybody's there. I'm doing guard duty. Always was good at that, right, Bertha?"

Inside, facing her husband, Bertha exclaimed, "Really, Roger, you and Khaki just caused us a lot of grief disappearing like that. Eula and Ben and I were really worried." She plumped herself down on the sofa and removed her gloves. "How ever did you get Sukie and get her out here?"

Dr. Roger Byrd nervously cleared his throat. "Well, when Lucille heard the men in the store talking about getting up a posse to get Sukie Bee . . ."

Sukie Bee gave a mighty moan and a trembling started throughout her mountainous body.

"Well, Lucille phoned me at the farm, my dear. I had her send Bob McAfee down to get Khaki and Sukie Bee in his pickup truck. I sneaked out and walked down to the highway, where they picked me up and then we drove out here, knowing that Sukie Bee would be safe with Miss Ora and Nora."

"Plat man loose again," Sukie Bee intoned. "No use you tell me, Miss Ora, that there ain't no plat man, ain't no voodoo. You know better, you an old woman now, you know ever' time plat man been loose here."

Ora walked slowly to the window that opened onto the veranda. Turning, she addressed Ludie. "See if you can't talk some sense into Sukie Bee. You know how things are,

Ludie, surely she'll calm down and listen to you so that we can present a rational, united front and persuade this ridiculous posse to disband. I'm going to fetch some lemonade. This heat is unbearable."

Great guffaws of laughter broke from Sukie's mouth, her jowls trembling as she threw her head back.

"No call to run to the kitchen, Miss Ora. Can't run from the plat man this time. I done kept him in check all my life, doing things my mama taught me. Ever' one sitting here knows that's so. . . . Can't cover it up forever . . . bound to bust loose. I was trying, though. Even training that Vashti for to take my place, 'pears like she had the gift even if she be a white child. But them children done dumped them charms, done made everybody see them, now they ain't going to work no more. Peoples can suspicion, but they ain't allowed to know. 'Cause once they know, then we got to say the truth, rather than what we been pretending on was the truth."

Khaki looked long and hard at Sukie Bee, willing her to shut up.

"Ora Philpot," Sukie Bee boomed sonorously, "I do voodoo. I learned it from my mama who learned it from her mama who learned from her mama. I can do spells and make charms and I can look into the waters of the springs and see backward and forward in time. I know the plat man rode in on them buffalo trails with them first men what come here. I've seen it in the springs. And I know that everybody sitting here has been touched by the plat man, but my voodoo been able to control him up to now."

"Stop this foolishness, you ignorant old nigger woman," Khaki cautioned her. "You talking nonsense."

"I ain't and you know it, Khaki Hayes. Everybody know how that first Massa Philpot done mixed up his white and colored children and how his oldest boy, the one so

white, ran away and come back here as a white man and a
doctor. And then how his children done married back into
the Philpot family. And how the other light-skinned boy
run away and become a Taylor. Just 'cause it ain't never
been said aloud don't make it not so. And Sukie Bee knows
that Mr. Roger Byrd is a Philpot."

Roger paled. "For God's sake, Sukie Bee, have you
completely lost your mind? Do you realize that you are insulting Miss Ora and Miss Nora, two maiden ladies, if I
must remind you."

Sukie grinned, "Ain't insulting nobody, Mr. Roger.
Just saying that if it hadn't been for my voodoo the whole
world be saying that one of the Philpot sisters was your
mama and Mr. Charlie Byrd your real daddy. My plat man
charm kept it from getting out."

"And my plat man charm never let nobody come right
out and say that Khaki Hayes was your boy and that Ben
sitting over there is your grandson. And that Miss Bertha,
your wife, knows about being bedded down by Philpots,
too. And what I seen in the waters about you up north in
that school—a little girl and then death and then more little
girls, even your own. Old Sukie Bee kept that all under
control, kept that old plat man from busting loose. Just like
keeping old plat eye from doing too much harm when
Lizzie LeCompte raising Old Nick with everything in pants
around here, even the preacher man and the schoolteacher
man."

Sukie leaned back with a satisfied sigh. "Leastways
kept plat man away long enough to get them twins born.
They got the gifts, but they surely did mischief this time.
I'm telling you, he loose now and nobody going to be able
to control him."

Nora advanced through the door with the shotgun
aimed at Sukie Bee's head. "Sukie Bee, if you do not shut

up this lunacy, I shall be obliged to blow your head off. We are all going to ignore what you just said. It is obvious that your mind is not clear; however, I do believe you are rational enough to understand that you are never to repeat what you have said here to another living soul. It is not true, do you understand, it is not true. Now, if you understand what I just said, then nod your head yes. If you do not nod your head yes, then I shall blow it off your shoulders."

Eyes rolling back in her head, Sukie managed to nod. As Nora lowered the shotgun, soft puffs of held breath were released from everyone, except Ben, who laughed.

They all remained frozen until the ring of the telephone released them to turn and watch Miss Ora Philpot glide regally into the hall.

"That was Lucille," she announced as she reentered the parlor. "She rang up to say that Randall, Brother Poe, Brother Jordan, and the darky preacher all went out to look for the posse. They found them down by the springs and have convinced them that this whole affair was nothing but some chicken feathers and an imaginative story made up by some little girls. I think you may all go home now. Things are back to normal."

17

The day after Thelma Taylor and the Clay twins had answered the altar call and given their souls to Jesus, Eliot Mansfield and Claire LaRue finally arrived in Taylor Springs.

The week-long revival meeting, hosted by the Reverend Randall Clay and the Southern Methodist Espiscopal church, had been one of the best in the town's memory. The visiting evangelist, Brother Roy Smothers out of Atlanta, Georgia, was so hellfire and brimstone that the mourner's bench was full every night and the altar packed with backsliders renouncing their wicked ways and testifying for the Lord.

And when, on the last night of the meeting, the preacher gave the invitation and the choir moaned "Just as I am, without one plea, but that thy blood was shed for me . . . O Lamb of God, I come, I come," the congregation gave a great, collective sigh as the three little red-headed girls started up the aisle to the altar, holding hands, fat tears rolling down their cheeks.

After they had knelt down at the altar, been prayed over, confessed their sins, and been pronounced saved by the blood of the lamb, Brother Smothers raised the girls from their knees and turned them to face the congregation.

"Suffer the little children to come unto me. Tonight these three young girls have given their hearts and lives to Jesus. Such rejoicing there must be in heaven right now, just as there must be rejoicing in the hearts of their mamas and daddies. Reverend Clay, Mrs. Clay, come down here and stand by your daughters as they are entering into the company of the saved. Oh, your hearts must be bursting, yes, fairly bursting with joy."

The choir continued softly in the background, "I am washed in the blood of the lamb," as Brother Smothers intoned, "And Mr. and Mrs. Taylor, come and be with little Thelma. Yes, bring the baby, the whole family, we should all rejoice together that the lost have been found, have been saved."

So Randall and Lizzie LeCompte Clay stood on one side of the three girls, and Bucky and Alice Taylor, holding Thelma's new baby brother, stood on the other side. The little girls smiled tremulously, the baby started yelling, and Mary William, who had been left sitting in the back with Colored Bertha, came windmilling and woo-wooing up the aisle.

"I can't help but say it," Vashti announced the next morning, "but we did the whole thing pretty good." She sat with Mary William in the big wooden swing hanging on the parsonage front porch, pumping it back and forth. "The only way it could have been better was if we had gotten saved up at Mawmaw LeCompte's church. Them Holy Rollers do it so good. Why, we could have rolled in front of the altar and had the Devil cast out and everything."

Thelma, sitting on the front steps by Vangie, looked up

and rolled her eyes. "You know I was planning on getting saved anyway, Vashti Clay. I told you all that a long time ago and I don't think we needed to go rolling around, what with having our white party dresses on and everything. The only thing that ruined the whole sacred experience was Mama had to bring up that dumb baby and he started screaming."

Vangie started giggling and punched Thelma with her elbow. "Shoot, that baby brother of yours is here to stay, Thelma. Besides, he didn't cause no more commotion than Mary William did when she come down to the altar."

"Don't care," Thelma announced, "Mary William is just like that. Everybody knows her. I surely do wish there was some way to get rid of that dumb baby."

"Well, you done tried holding your breath until you turned blue and the baby is still here." Vashti pumped the swing harder. "Besides, if you can put up with Alex, you can put up with your baby brother. Anyway, I was well satisfied with the whole thing."

Getting saved certainly did get the girls out of the trouble they'd caused trying to sell the plat man charms. By asking and receiving forgiveness for their sins, they regained the freedom to leave their yards and wander the town again. The only sad thing remaining from their attempt to make a little money was that nobody in colored town wanted them to come and visit anymore. Elvira told Thelma that she was getting too grown-up to go traipsing around in colored town and Colored Bertha told the twins that if they set one foot down there she would personally wear out their hind ends.

Suddenly, Thelma prissed up from the steps and started turning cartwheels over the dried-up grass.

"I see London, I see France, I see Thelma's underpants," Vangie started yelling. Vashti joined in and Mary

William started bouncing up and down in the swing. Thelma collapsed on the lawn, laughing.

"It is so hot. I got an idea. Let's go over to Miss Myna's and see if Cora will fix us some lemonade. They don't care that we got to drag Mary William with us." Vangie opened the screen door and hollered in, "Colored Bertha, Thelma and Vashti and Mary William and me are going to walk up and pay a visit to Miss Myna."

Colored Bertha's voice echoed from the kitchen, "You all just wait there one little minute." She appeared at the door, wiping her hands on her apron. "Come on over here to the door where I can see you. You not going anywhere if you're looking like trash. Reckon you all right, but wipe off Mary William's face. Lord, I'm beginning to wonder if that brother of hers is ever coming to claim that poor soul. Now you be back here by dinner and don't you go nowhere else, you hear me? Your mama and daddy'll be back from Boonetown by dinnertime and you better be here, and Thelma supposed to be back up on the hill for dinner." Waving good-bye to Bertha and taking Mary William in tow, the girls scampered up the walk, out the gate, and onto the dusty road.

Myna Smoot, sitting out on her front porch, was trying to catch a breath of air. Fanning her flushed face with her apron, she scrunched her nose as she caught a whiff of the springs. It smells like this every August, she thought. Just purely stinks, but I guess we all are used to it and just live with it. Well, looks like the Clay twins coming down the road with Thelma and Mary William. She thought back to last night when the girls answered the altar call. That certainly was a sweet sight. Three little red-headed girls in white dresses going right up in front of the church to get saved. And then seeing them stand up there with Lizzie and Randall and Bucky and Alice. Just goes to show that things usually work out in the end. Yes, sir, just trust in the Lord and keep your mouth shut, that's the way things work out. All that nonsense with Sukie Bee and plat man charms—all forgotten as well it should be. Look at that, do believe they're coming over here.

"Howdy, girls," Myna hailed. "What are you up to this morning? Why don't you come up on the porch and visit with me a spell? I bet Cora could fix us up some refreshments real quick." As the girls started up the walk, Myna rose and walked over to the porch railing.

"Well, will you look at that coming down the road. Look, girls. I never seen such a fancy car in all my born days, not even Roger Byrd's Packard touring car."

Claire LaRue did not share Miss Myna Smoot's exalted opinion of the Cord convertible that Eliot Mansfield had arranged to have waiting for them at the L & N Depot in Louisville. The hot air had blown her carefully coiffed platinum blond curls to hell and gone, and Eliot, dismissing the chauffeur, had driven the winding roads like a drunken maniac. Of course, Eliot had been carefully sustaining a delicately balanced state of drunkeness for several years. When they got off the train in Chicago this time, however, Eliot was roaring drunk.

By the time the studio's representatives had gotten them checked into the Palmer House, Eliot collapsed, comatose, into a drunken stupor, which led to delirium tremens. It took the ministrations of a discreet doctor and two burly bodyguards, hired by the studio, to dry him out during the ten-day period that they were secluded in the hotel suite. Claire paced the rooms, screwed the bodyguards, and cursed the day she got involved with Eliot Mansfield.

Talking pictures had brought him from Broadway to the movies. Hollywood needed actors with voices, and Eliot had a voice that he played like a magnificent instrument. However, from the moment he stepped foot off the Los Angeles *Limited,* he began his plaint: he had sold his soul for a mess of pottage, had bastardized his talent for a huge pot of gold. Immediately, he became a box office success and a member of the group of swashbucklers who boozed and fornicated their way into instant legend, all the while lamenting the prostitution of their artistic talents in motion pictures.

In his third picture, *The Little Corporal,* a sweeping saga of the Napoleonic era, he played Napoleon, which caused a few Hollywood snickers as Eliot was a very short man and in closeup scenes had to stand on a box in order to be at eye level with the other actors. Claire LaRue was cast as Josephine and, of course, received top billing.

The platinum blond bombshell was the major star of the studio and had had no trouble at all when sound arrived in Hollywood. She was a quick learner, and from the moment she arrived in town with D.W. Griffith, she began carefully imitating those people whom she intuitively gathered had the proper speech, the proper dress, the proper manners, and the proper life-style. She had no intention of ever giving up her wealthy and glamorous existence, and shuddered with distaste when she remembered the life of Brunhilda Loudenbeck, who had escaped from Tennessee with the Good Time Gospel Boys Quartet.

Not that anyone in Hollywood knew who she really was or where she had come from. D.W., that genius, had created a totally new person when he stepped off the train with her in Los Angeles. She was Claire LaRue, orphan, from a distinguished Mississippi family, distant cousin to D.W. himself. But even D.W. didn't know where she really came from. She would never tell him her real last name or how she came to be with the Good Time Boys the night he discovered her in the tent at Camp Crestview. Poor D.W., a has-been now, while Claire LaRue was still on top.

She had carefully built her reputation as a cool patrician lady who allowed none of the usual Hollywood prying into her private life. She remained aloof from the vulgarities of the movie world and gratified her sensual needs privately, discreetly, and always outside of town. Thus, the whole of Hollywood was rocked when Claire LaRue began an open, tempestuous, torrid love affair with Eliot Mansfield during the filming of *The Little Corporal*. When they eloped to Reno and were married before the film was completed, the event made headlines all over the world.

The studio insisted on the marriage. Claire didn't want to marry him and Eliot didn't want to marry anyone. Claire often thought how if she hadn't gotten so hot over the son of a bitch and lost her carefully maintained control, she wouldn't be tied to this drunk. But the minute he first touched her on the set, it was as if every nerve in her body screamed. She would have screwed him right in front of the camera, right then, if he hadn't whispered, "Later, when the scene is finished, I'll come to your trailer."

Their heat was so blatant, their caresses so public, that the studio, fearing the scandal and the Hayes Office, arranged the elopement. After all, what was a little wedding when careers, reputations, and big money were in jeopardy? As soon as their relationship was legalized, their love affair ended.

Eliot resumed his wanderings with his cronies, swigging booze, sniffing snow, smoking tea, and screwing anything that moved. Claire resumed her indiscretions outside the movie community. Divorce was out of the question; the studio forbade the split of the much publicized perfect marriage of their two biggest box office draws.

Oh well, Claire thought, putting her chiffon handkerchief over her nose in order to block out some of the
dust and the sulphur smell, I suppose it could be worse. At
least he isn't dead drunk, just been sipping enough for the
past three days to keep a glow on. And we'll certainly get
enough press about how two of Hollywood's brightest stars
have come to the bedside of Eliot's desperately ill father, a
retired professor of divinity. God knows that the studio will
never let it get out about having to arrange care for an idiot
sister. Now that girl is something I can hardly wait to see.
Imagine Eliot having a lunatic in his family, bound to be
bad blood somewhere. This funny little town that we just
drove through, it reminds me of Tennessee. All these people, and it's as if they have no idea of what's going on in the
rest of the world. Their world begins and ends in this little
valley.

Eliot braked the Cord to a rapid halt when he saw the
crowd of females standing on Myna Smoot's front porch.
He looked searchingly at the faces, and when he recognized
the vacant eyes and drooling mouth of his sister, he whispered, "Oh, my God, there she is, Claire, that's Mary William."

Claire turned her head and gazed at the stick figure
who was surrounded by three little red-headed girls. The
stick figure was covered by a shapeless, flower-printed cotton dress. She wore white cotton cuffed socks and untied
brown oxfords on her splayed-out feet and a huge red ribbon perched on on her lanky, scraggly, straight-cut hair.
Her clawlike hands began to curl and uncurl as she began
keening a weird noise.

Claire returned her gaze to her husband, that dashing
denizen of Hollywood fame and acclaim, that man she hated
but was tied to out of mutual greed, and began laughing
loudly, "For Jesus' sake, what the fuck are you going to do

with her, Eliot?" She continued laughing, tears rolling down her cheeks leaving small mascara tracks, until she gasped, "Well, for God's sake, let's get out of the car and go up there. If I don't get to a bathroom soon, I'm going to wet my pants, I've laughed so hard."

Eliot opened the car door and helped the gorgeous, glamorous Claire LaRue descend, muttering, "My dear, I suspect you'll have to make do with an outhouse, which, for you, seems somewhat apropos."

Bowing toward an awestruck, rigid Myna, Eliot said, "How do you do, madam. My name is Eliot Mansfield and this is my wife, Claire LaRue. I do hope we're not imposing, but I do believe that this is my sister, Mary William Sheely."

"Heavens to Betsy, we wondered when you were going to get here. My name is Myna Smoot and yes, this sure is your sister. Your daddy is still over at the hospital at Boonetown. Why, you must have driven right past it and not even known he was still there. Why, the twins' mama and daddy are over there right now visiting him. That's the Reverend and Mrs. Clay, they're the ones been taking care of Mary William. And that's the twins right there—just like two peas in a pod—anyway, they're the only ones that can do anything at all with Mary William, so, naturally, she's had to stay at the parsonage. They're just over here visiting me for a spell. And this other little girl is Thelma Taylor."

Myna stopped suddenly, drew a deep breath, and fanned her flushed face with her apron. "You know, I never seen real movie stars in the flesh and blood before. What will you think of my manners? Now, you just come on in out of this terrible heat and I'll get Cora to get you some refreshments. Some lemonade would go down right nice, I'm sure."

Vashti and Vangie anchored Mary William on either

side by firmly holding on to her agitated hands. Vashti looked up at the two gorgeous creatures. "Don't you worry none about Mary William. She'll be just fine as soon's she gets used to you. We'll teach you how to calm her down."

Eliot and Claire looked at each other and then back at Mary William and the three girls. Thelma stepped out and made a sweeping curtsy. "Since my name is Taylor, I reckon it's my place to welcome you to Taylor Springs. I surely do think we ought to take Miss Myna up on that offer of lemonade. Why don't we just go into the parlor and I'll tell you all about how the twins and me got saved last night. Yes, sir, we gave our hearts and souls to Jesus."

18

They sat outside the cabin hoping for a breeze, but the dusky air was still and hot and dry. Sukie Bee's gargantuan rolls of flesh undulated over the edges of one of the kitchen chairs that Khaki had politely carried out to the yard for the company. Ludie, spare and dignified, sat regally on her chair as if it were her throne, while Colored Bertha and Elvira occupied the other two seats of honor. Eula and Sarah perched on the steps watching Khaki and Ben take turns cranking the ice cream freezer.

"Need more ice here, Ben boy," Khaki pronounced. Ben walked to the side of the porch and unwrapped the gunny sack from the cake of ice. Taking the ice pick, he began chunking away, big slivers falling on the spread-out sack.

"Shoot, it so hot this ice gonna be melted before that ice cream gets froze."

"Ben," Ludie pointed to the slivers, "you chunking that ice too big. Proper way to do it is in teensy little pieces. Put them big chunks around that churn make the ice cream turn out grainy ever time. Got to do things proper or no use doing them."

Ben picked up one of the large slivers of ice and began attacking it again with the ice pick. "Lord, Grandma, the way you carry on about proper you'd think you was white and a Philpot."

A streak of heat lightning laced the air above the hills. Sukie Bee shuddered. "Enough of that talk, Ben. No need to keep carrying on. Say the truth and old Sukie here almost gets her head blowed off."

Khaki interrupted, "Shut up that nonsense right now, Sukie. You too, Ben. I don't care if you think your grand-daddy the king of England. The fact is you is colored and that's all you ever gonna be and all you ever gonna have is what you earns by the sweat of your brow." He cranked the churn handle with even more vigor.

"Amen," Ludie mumbled. "Now, Bertha, Sarah, go on and tell us all about the movie stars and the rest of what happened."

Colored Bertha sat up importantly, shifting her weight on the rickety chair.

"Well, like I already told you, Mr. Randall and Miss Lizzie done gone over to Boonetown to visit Professor Sheely at the hospital. Reckon they figure it their Christian duty, because Doc Smoot done told us that he still be in a coma or something, he don't talk or move or nothing. So's Vashti and Vangie and Thelma and Mary William was out on the parsonage front porch, and they yelled to me they was going up to visit Miss Myna. I figured that would be all right, 'cause Miss Lizzie done told me they was free to roam a little bit since they got saved the other night, done repented their sins and all. Course she said they can't do no visiting down here in colored town."

"Well, thank the Lord for that," Elvira interrupted. "Done told Thelma and them twins myself they ain't to come down here no more. The commotion they caused.

They getting too big to be down here anyway, only lead to trouble."

"Anyway," Colored Bertha continued, "I went out to the back to help Sarah here hang up the wash. Course, Miss Lizzie done told me that my work now is to watch over them girls, but I still got time to give Sarah a hand with the housework and the cooking. Sarah," she glanced over toward the steps, "she catching on real quick like. Course it take time to learn how to do things like my fried chicken or my sponge cake."

Sarah grinned and discreetly punched Eula with her elbow. "For heaven's sake, Bertha," Eula laughed, "will you get on with it about the movie stars?"

Colored Bertha started again and told it just the way it happened.

The twins and Thelma, dragging Mary William behind them, burst through the front door of the parsonage calling for Bertha and Sarah. They raced through the empty hall and kitchen, out onto the back porch, and down into the yard.

"Colored Bertha, Sarah, guess what?" Vangie yelled. Startled, Bertha dropped one of Mr. Randall's best white preaching shirts on the ground and turned to Sarah. "Lord God, what mischief they been up to now?"

"They're here," Vangie's disheveled red curls bobbed up and down as she jumped excitedly. "Mary William's movie star brother is here, and he has a movie star wife. They are the most beautiful people you have ever seen and they came driving up in this car like you never seen in your life before."

Well, glory be, Bertha thought. 'Bout time. Thought we was gonna be stuck with Mary William forever. Time things returned to normal around here.

"Well, where they be, these two movie stars? And how

come Mary William ain't with her brother?'' Bertha stood glaring, hands on her hips.

"Miss Myna done took them over to Professor Sheely's house so's they could settle in and freshen up. Mary William has to stay with us. You know she won't do right for nobody else, Bertha. She took one look at her brother and his wife and started in jerking and yelling.''

"Anyway,'' Vashti interjected, "We did the proper thing and invited them down here for dinner. Told them that Mama and Daddy would be back from Boonetown so's they could hear how Professor Sheely was doing and they could talk things over.''

Thelma turned to go back into the house. "I have to ring up Lucille to get hold of my house so I can let somebody know that I'm staying here for dinner. Vashti and Vangie done invited me, too. I really think them movie stars expect my company. They surely did appreciate my story about how we got saved last night and was welcomed into the congregation of Christ.''

"Sarah, we best get ourselves into that kitchen, girl. Can't be letting the family down, especially when Miss Lizzie ain't even here and don't know all this going on. We knows how to do it proper. Got to get that silver and crystal out. No, sir, we not going to shame our family.'' Bertha gathered the twins and Mary William, beckoned to Sarah, and marshaling her troops, led the way into the parsonage.

Lizzie LeCompte Clay walked into her front parlor only to stop dead and stare in stunned amazement. There stood her daughters, red curls brushed and tied back with blue ribbons, white pinafores ruffled over their baby blue dotted swiss dresses, white patent Mary Jane slippers on their usually bare feet. There stood Thelma Taylor, carroty dutch bob combed, dressed in one of the twin's yellow party dresses, just a tiny bit too big and too long. There in a corner quietly sat Mary William, dressed in Lizzie's own best blue georgette, the one with the ruffled collar, which hung on the skinny body with the skirt hitting midthigh on the shapeless legs that were covered with Lizzie's best silk stockings. And there was Colored Bertha, in her Sunday black dress that was covered with an organdy apron, handing out punch in the silver cups to two of the most glamorous creatures that Lizzie had ever seen outside of the pictures in *Photoplay*.

"Well, hello," Lizzie dimpled, smiling directly at the rakish-looking man sitting on her sofa. He stared as she removed the yellow straw hat, shook her brown curls free, and glided toward the sofa. She ran the tip of her pink tongue over her pouting lips. "I'm Mrs. Randall Clay and you must be Eliot Mansfield, Mary William's brother." Eliot Mansfield jumped to his feet to get a better look at the most luscious piece of ass to ever come out of LeCompte Bottoms.

Vashti and Vangie ran over and gave their mama sweet little hugs and explained to her how Mr. Mansfield and his wife had arrived. Lizzie just as sweetly patted their heads and told the girls just to wait a minute and to mind their manners, why, she hadn't even had a chance to welcome Mrs. Mansfield yet.

"Of course, it does seem hard to think of you as Mrs. Mansfield. To those of us who are your fans, you are Claire LaRue. I do hope that the girls and Colored Bertha have made you comfortable."

Claire opened her bag and extracted cigarettes and a long gold cigarette holder. Her carmen nails flashed as she fitted the cigarette into the holder. "Eliot, my sweet, light me." She drew in the smoke and let it plume out of her nostrils. "Mrs. Clay, I can't begin to tell you what an experience this is."

Colored Bertha sneezed, interrupting her story. The ice cream churn was cranking slower and slower, its slow grinding rhythm counterpointed by the measured blinking of fireflies. Bertha sneezed again.

"Lord, it's got to be this sulphur air from the springs. Ever' year it gets worse and worse. Well, I tell you true, you ain't never seen anything like it. Never seen two white folks act out like that in public. White folks good at covering up. Telling you that Miss Lizzie and that movie star man be like they in rut, the way they look at each other. Ain't I telling it true, Sarah?"

Ludie sighed. "Miss Ora and Nora be scandalized if they heard this."

"Surely, surely." Elvira nodded her head. "Don't like to speak ill, but we all know that Miss Lizzie done used to be a trashy girl. You all know what she done to my Bucky and poor dead Junie and even to Preacher Clay. You know them twins belong to my Bucky. Shame, though, since it seem like once she married up with Mr. Randall, she done learned how to be a proper preacher's wife."

Ben walked over to the ice cream freezer and packed more ice chips and rock salt around the churn. "How come you people think that white folks behave better than colored folks? You don't think they piss and shit and fuck just like us niggers?"

"I'm just going to act like you never said that, Ben." Eula stood up and walked from the steps over to him. "Son, you got to get these crazy ideas out of your head. We are a part of these people. They take care of us 'cause we are their own. You keep carrying on, you going to bring a lot of grief to all of us."

"What Bertha is saying is the true story," Sarah's clear voice rose from the stoop.

"Mr. Randall come into the parlor then and they all sat

down and drank that punch. He started telling Mr. Mansfield all about Professor Sheely and how he was just lying there, seemed to be no hope for him to ever talk or walk or do nothing again. So they all started talking about where they could put Professor Sheely and Mary William away.

"Claire LaRue said, well, surely there are institutions where good care will be taken of your father and sister. Oh, she was something else. She was dressed in pants, she really was. She had on these pink trousers, just like a man's, and a real thin pink blouse. It had these billowy sleeves and I swear she didn't have a stitch on underneath it, no slip or camisole or nothing. You could see everything she had. And she has this hair, well, it's almost white and these black thin eyebrows and painted up all over her eyelids and cheeks and mouth. Just like them posters of her outside the picture show.

"Her being so good looking sure didn't stop that movie star man from ogling Miss Lizzie, though. Tell you, enough heat coming out of those two to start a fire. Mr. Randall didn't seem to notice nothing, even though either one of them barely touched a bite of dinner and I mean Bertha and me fixed up roast chicken and everything, one of them high and mighty meals like Miss Bertha done taught Colored Bertha to cook. Tell you one thing, that Claire LaRue knew exactly what was going on. Just kept looking on and smiling to herself.

"She said, why, I would never have believed that I would find such superb cooking in a place like this, Mrs. Clay. That woman really bitchy and poking fun, but Miss Lizzie so wrapped up in that movie star man she never caught on. Then she said roast chicken and asparagus vinaigrette and broiled tomatoes in a little town like this. What other surprises are awaiting us?

"Miss Lizzie looked up and said, why I really don't

know what Colored Bertha and Sarah fixed for dessert. However, there is something that might surprise you, something that's going to happen tomorrow night. We don't have much entertainment in Taylor Springs, why, we even have to go to Boonetown or Nelsonville to see your movies. But once a year, we have an artistic event that the whole town turns out for, and I'm sure that you and Mr. Mansfield wouldn't want to miss it. In fact, folks would be mighty disappointed, knowing you're here in town, if our two movie star visitors weren't there.

"Then Miss Lizzie told her that the Good Time Gospel Boys were going to be performing up at the Holy Roller church tomorrow night, and Claire LaRue, who was sipping on her iced tea, started a-choking and a-spluttering. Mr. Randall got up and started a-pounding her on the back, and Mary William started waving her arms and jumped up on her chair and then fell right into the middle of the table."

Sukie Bee began chuckling, a little clucking sound that quickly grew to a laugh sounding like two locomotives letting off steam. As the waves of laughter rippled over the jellyroll body, the chair she sat on creaked and wobbled. The flesh rolled, and finally the chair swayed and collapsed, and Sukie Bee landed on the ground with a mighty crash, still roaring.

"Sweet Jesus," Khaki yelled as he and Ben raced from the ice cream freezer over to Sukie. "You all right, woman? Here, Ben, help me pull her up." They grabbed Sukie's arms and hoisted the still shaking girth to a sitting position.

"Lordy, lordy," she laughed, gasping for air. "Surely that would have been a sight. Sarah, fetch me one of my Camel cigarettes. Told you all. Told you nothing but commotion going to happen now."

Sarah put the cigarette in the heaving Sukie's mouth and lit it with a lucifer match. Sukie expertly rolled it to one corner of her mouth and inhaled the smoke. As the smoke streamed out, she said, "Well, go on, girl. What happened next?"

"Why, Mr. Randall and the twins got Mary William off of the table, Vashti and Vangie waving their hands and doing that little dance they do like when they has to calm her down. Claire LaRue stopped a-choking and stared like she never seen such a sight in her life. Miss Lizzie jumped up and said for the girls to take Mary William upstairs and get her cleaned up and that everybody should come into the parlor for coffee. Thelma said she reckoned the twins could clean up Mary William by themselves and she'd just go into the parlor and have coffee, too, being as she was certainly interested in how they was going to solve the problem of what to do with Professor Sheely and Mary William."

"Ice cream's ready." Khaki announced. "Eula, go get the bowls and spoons. Surely is too bad that Vashti and Vangie ain't here. Those two little boogers surely love to lick the ice cream dasher. Surely do miss those two." He spooned the golden frozen cream speckled with fragrant flecks of vanilla into the bowls that Eula handed to him and then passed around.

Colored Bertha dug her spoon into the custardy mound and lifted it to her mouth. "Mmmm, nobody makes cream like you do, Eula. Course, I reckon it was Ludie done taught you how to do it."

Ludie tasted her own ice cream. "Yes, sir, it's right good, Eula. Might need another egg or two, can't never go skimping on the eggs. We might be making some of this cream for tomorrow night's big do. See what Miss Ora and Nora think."

"That surely going to be some to-do." Bertha licked her lips. "All those folks having supper out at the plantation before they go hear the Good Time Boys. Mr. Roger and

Miss Bertha. Why, even Lucille going to leave the switch-board and be there. And all the Taylors, Mr. Bubba and Miss Ruth and Bucky and Alice and the children, and Mr. Alex and Miss Becky and little Alex . . . Preacher Clay and Miss Lizzie and the twins and Mary William . . . Lord, lord . . . and Miss Myna Smoot and Mr. Bob McAfee . . . and them two movie stars and even the Good Time Boys them-selves."

Ludie sighed, "Reminds me of the old days. You don't none of you remember the grand parties we used to have out at Philpot Plantation. Oh, the folks would come from ever'where, and there'd be dancing and collations. All kind of petered out after Miss Ora and Nora come back from being across the water and Mr. Samuel passed over."

"All I know," Eula tossed her head, "is that it going to take all of us to get this party ready by tomorrow night. Miss Bertha sending me out there first thing tomorrow morning, and Colored Bertha and Sarah and Elvira sup-posed to be there toward ten o'clock. Sukie Bee, you sup-posed to come out with Khaki and Ben along about noon. Miss Ora wants you to iron up the tablecloths."

"Don't like it, don't like it none at all." Sukie Bee sat on the dirt, legs spraddled out, the dish of ice cream resting on her big belly. "Philpots and Hayes and McAfees and LeComptes and Taylors and Smoots and Clays all jumbled up together again. And all those spirits, those ha'nts of all those families wandering up on the buffalo trails. They up there with the plat man right now. Sukie Bee can see 'em."

"Just shut your mouth, Sukie Bee," Ludie reprimanded her. "We got appearances to keep up for our white folk. After all, we ain't going to be doing no acting up in front of strangers like movie stars. So you better not be dragging no charms around the plantation tomorrow and you better not be shaming us with no plat man talk. He may be loose, but we not going to talk about it. We quality coloreds because we part of quality white folks. Now you just remember that. We is all bound together."

"Not bringing no plat man charms," Sukie mumbled. "You know it too late for plat man charms to do good, Ludie. Once them twins and Thelma let it out, ever'thing going to come out now, ever'thing. Going to be bad, bad, bad."

"Well, one good thing going to happen," Eula interjected, "Miss Ora done said we could leave the cleaning up 'til the next morning. She surely wouldn't want to deprive us from hearing the Good Time Boys."

Ben hawked and spat. "Now ain't that white of her."

"Don't be worrying about white, Ben," Elvira cackled. "You and Khaki just worry about getting out there and making sure them two big dogs stay penned up. Old man LeCompte don't do too good with them dogs. Course they so old now they sure wouldn't hurt nobody, but it wouldn't never do for them to jump up and pee on two movie stars."

19

Ora and Nora Philphot stood on the veranda, ready to greet their guests. Ora stood erect, her thin body garbed in a long dress of once white lace that had turned a cream color with age. The high neck was fastened with Alvah Taylor Philpot's diamond brooch, and she wore America Tryon Philpot's diamond eardrops. The white hair, still a few traces of red in it, was piled in a regal puff on top of her head.

Nora looked at her twin sister and thought that she looked like the snow queen. Oh, that was Ora all right, always icy cold, collected, untouchable on the surface. She ran her plump little hands down her lilac-printed chiffon skirt and looked down past the handkerchief-pointed hemline to the lilac satin pumps that were killing her feet. Oh well, if they hurt too bad, I'll just kick them off under the table. After all, this dress and these shoes must be twenty years old or more. I bet I just look cute as hell. Wonder why Ora insisted we get all gussied up? Maybe she thinks this is our last hurrah. More and more she dwells in the past, as if Taylor Springs were still what she thinks it once was.

Nora puffed out her short white curls with the hand that sported a huge amethyst ring, the gift of Solomon Philpot to his fiancée, Margaret Hayes. She withdrew the lace handkerchief from her sleeve and dabbed at her forehead.

"Ora, it's so damn hot that if I weren't a Philpot, I'd be sweating. I do hope it cools down a little before we sit down to supper. The dining room is still as hot as hades. If our guests are as overdressed as we are, they'll die from heat prostration before we get through the first course."

"My dear sister, we are dressed as we should be. We are Philpots honoring some renowned thespian visitors by entertaining the first families of Taylor Springs. We must all remember who we are and what we once were."

Nora looked sadly at her and then turned to look where Khaki stood at the curve of the graveled driveway waiting to hand the guests out of their cars. Ben stood beside him, ready to park the cars on the side lawn under the big tree.

Inside the front parlor, which smelled faintly of wood polished with lemon oil and the fragrance of masses of cut flowers, Ludie stood beside the Chippendale table. On it were a huge silver wine cooler and thin crystal champagne flutes. It had taken both Ben and Khaki to carry the massive cooler up from the cellar where it had been stored for years, and it had taken Sarah and Eula hours to shine it to its present sheen.

"Do you realize that this wine cooler was brought into Taylor Springs as part of America Tryon's dowry?" Ora reminisced as the polishing began. "Why, that was back in 1786. Of course, when Papa died and Nora and I were two maiden ladies living alone, we didn't serve much wine, and then, of course, we had Prohibition and one just didn't break the law of the land."

Sukie Bee, standing on the other side of the kitchen by the stove and applying her flat irons vigorously to the damask tablecloth, let out a loud cackle. She knew that the Philpot sisters often had a little nip of her homebrew that Khaki carried off in mason jars. Besides, reckon they didn't count all that blackberry wine that Ludie bottled as breaking the law of the land.

Ora looked sharply in her direction. "Sukie Bee, do be a little more careful with how hot those irons are. That tablecloth is an heirloom. Why it's almost as old as Nora and I."

"You know, Miss Ora," Elvira was beating egg whites with a fury, "you really ought to think about getting you all a kerosene stove. I tell you, it keep the kitchen cool and you don't have to fool with no wood or ashes. Why, me and Miss Ruth done had ours 'most ten years now and I can't tell you what a difference it makes. Cooks good, too."

"Luckily," Ora ignored Elvira, "Papa laid in a good cellar and we have champagne down there. I suppose that champagne will be the most proper wine for our guests. I think I'll go down right now and bring it up. Perhaps we should open one just to make sure that it hasn't gone vinegary."

Ludie smiled proudly as she heard the first car crunch to a halt before the veranda. Them people going to be in for a surprise and a treat, that wine surely was good. Miss Ora done give her a glass to taste. She said Ludie, you the only one here who even remembers what it was like to drink champagne. You remember how it once was. Course that Ben had to up and say, why, Miss Ora, what Preacher Clay and the Gospel Quartet and everybody going to say about drinking going on? That boy—Khaki just going to have to knock some sense in him. But Miss Ora just smile and say why even the Bible says something about having a little wine for the stomach's sake, and don't forget about Jesus turning the water into wine.

The parlor began to fill. The Taylors came first with
their children and grandchildren, Bubba and Bucky looking
bound up and uncomfortable in their shiny blue serge suits,
while Tony Dagostino appeared quite dapper in navy trousers and a white jacket. Ruth Taylor wore a new purple
dress with matching three-quarter-length jacket, which
she'd rushed over to buy that very afternoon at Francine's
Dress Shoppe in Boonetown. Bubba thought it was a bunch
of foolishness, but Ruth knew what was proper for the first
lady of Taylor Springs, and besides, the purple straw hat
trimmed with yellow pansies added just the right touch,
even if it had cost almost seven dollars.

Of course, nobody ever noticed what pale, nondescript
Alice had on, and Becky wore her yellow voile, which set
off her carroty hair, and the children looked adorable, little
Alex in his short white pants and shirt and little red bowtie
and the baby in a white dress and Thelma in white dotted
swiss with a big white bow pinned on top of her head.

Dr. Roger Byrd had the Packard touring car packed full
what with transporting Bertha and Myna Smoot and then
stopping to pick up Lucille and Mr. Bob McAfee at the
store. They all descended solemnly from the car and
mounted the steps to greet their hostesses.

"Miss Ora, Miss Nora, how beautiful you look this
evening." Roger leaned and kissed the sisters' frail, age-
spotted hands. "This reminds me of when I was a young lad
and stood out here to help the ladies out of their buggies
when you used to have your at-homes." He sighed. "Those
were such festive times."

Bertha smiled at the Philpots. "Oh, yes, how I remember those days. Why, as a young girl, I paid my first
formal call right here. I came with Mama and Ramona, and
yes, Roger, you helped me out of the buggy." She looked at
Ora and then Nora. "I'll never forget.

"Lucille," Bertha continued, "you should have seen your daddy then. He was so handsome and so young."

Lucille, her awesome girth outlined by bright red georgette ruffles, stopped her movement toward the front door and turned her black-curled head to look at the small group standing there. The bright red mouth split into a grin. "I remember Daddy when he was young and handsome, Miss Bertha. Believe me, I'll never forget.

"The Good Time Boys," Lucille continued, "got in early this afternoon and asked me to tell you that they'll be along directly. They were getting everything set up and, of course, they had to freshen up a bit." She moved ponderously toward the front door, followed by Mr. Bob, Miss Bertha, and her daddy. A faint, mellow sound like a French horn alternating between the notes of d and g caused the group to stop and turn toward the driveway.

"Why, whatever can that be?" Nora shaded her eyes and squinted toward the road. "I don't see anything, but, Ora, that reminds of the carriage horns in France. Do you remember Versailles and how the coachman used to blow those same notes when the carriage was arriving?"

The notes pulled Sarah, Eula, Sukie Bee, Elvira, and Ludie out of the kitchen door and around front where they stood by Ben and Khaki at the curve of the driveway. The notes got louder and Khaki pointed, "Look there, if that don't beat all!"

The silver Cord convertible roared up the driveway, driven by the raffish Eliot Mansfield. Sitting by his side, swathed in a black feather boa, a tiny cap of black feathers sweeping down over her platinum hair, was the incomparable Claire LaRue. In the back seat, Mary William sat singing her woo-woo song in cadence with the klaxon. She was flanked by Vashti and Vangie, who were waving at the assembled crowd just like they'd seen Princess Elizabeth and

Princess Margaret Rose do it in the newsreels at the picture show.

As Eliot stopped the car, Claire scanned her audience. Two old ladies dressed in costumes that they must have resurrected from attic trunks and dripping with diamonds and amethysts. Two men with weather-stained faces and too-short haircuts, stuffed into shiny serge suits. A gaggle of frumpy women; my God, look at that old broad in that tacky purple. A little boy and a baby and, of course, Thelma—now that little girl was a performer. And who was that whale of a woman floating in an ocean of red ruffles. And the older man, very distinguished looking—must be a Philpot, had the same profile as one of the old ladies. Oh, a sexy-looking man, dark flashing eyes, gleaming white-toothed smile . . . and all the darkies lined up on the driveway.

She turned and grinned at her beloved husband. "Shit, Eliot, it looks just like a scene from *Gone with the Wind*." The minute the car stopped, Thelma Taylor ran down the steps and threw herself in front of them, holding her breath until she turned blue in the face.

Tony Dagostino bounded down the steps, swept up the blue-faced Thelma in one arm, and extended the other to help Claire out of the car. "You'll have to excuse Thelma, she tends to the overdramatic at times, especially when someone else is getting all the attention. She'll be fine in just a minute."

Claire swung her long silk-clad legs out the car door and took Tony's hand, noticing his appreciation of her legs and the rest of her body as she stood up. She looked directly into his eyes and laughed. "Yes, I can understand that, since Thelma regaled us yesterday with the story of how she and the twins had found salvation. She may very well be good material for Hollywood."

Vashti and Vangie climbed out of the back seat dragging Mary William with them. Vashti ran over to Thelma, who hung sacklike over Tony's arm, and began pinching her fiercely on the arms and legs. Thelma began to wiggle and breathe again. "Works every time," Vashti announced. "Thelma was just mad because Vangie and me got to ride in this fancy car with Mr. Eliot and Miss Claire. She is such a baby."

Tony put the wiggling, pouting Thelma down. "By the way, I'm Tony Dagostino. When I'm not being Thelma's uncle, I'm the principal of the Taylor Springs School. By marriage, I'm a part of the Taylor clan that's congregated up there on the porch."

Eliot extended his hand. "A pleasure, sir. Excuse my presumption, but Dagostino is not a name that one expects to find in Taylor Springs."

Vangie piped in, "Oh shucks, everybody knows Mr. Tony come here from Chicago. He was a big football star years and years ago and came here to be the football coach. Why, it was so long ago that he even coached Thelma's daddy. That was before Mr. Bucky got his leg shot off, though. Our mama was there when it happened, too."

The Philpot sisters had descended from the veranda and glided over to meet their honored guests. "Welcome to Philpot Plantation," Ora greeted the two movie stars. "It is such a pleasure to be able to entertain artists again at the plantation. Of course, many years ago, when Taylor Springs was a noted resort and when our papa had the military academy right here, some of the theater's luminaries often visited here, even Miss Sarah Bernhardt."

Nora laughed. "Although I doubt that any of them ever had so much commotion on their arrival. Probably so proper they were bored to death."

"Really, you'll just have to excuse Nora. She was always the mischievous one." Taking Eliot and Claire by the arm, she guided them toward Ludie, Khaki, and the rest of the group waiting by the driveway. "Of course, we do regret the tragic illness that befell Professor Sheely and necessitated your visit." She turned to the twins and Mary William, who were tagging along behind them. "Girls, where are your parents?"

"They'll be along directly, Miss Ora." Vangie bounced up and down, excited with the importance of the occasion. "They went by to pick up the the Good Time Gospel Boys, 'cause, naturally, the boys didn't want to drive their big old bus out here."

Ora introduced the Mansfields to the clump of colored folk who stood tall, proud, and polite, their dignity reflecting the importance of the event.

Ludie, Sarah, Eula, and Elvira bobbed swift little curtsys and murmered, "How do." Khaki and Ben doffed their chauffeur's caps, and then Ben extended his hand to Eliot Mansfield. The colored women drew in sharp little breaths, while both Eliot Mansfield and Ora Philpot remained motionless. When Claire LaRue took Ben's hand and said that she was most happy to meet him and to meet all of them and she was sure that her husband shared her feeling, the frozen tableau thawed and Miss Ora led her guests back up the wide steps, across the veranda, and into the front parlor.

They shifted into small groups, champagne glasses in hand, moving from Eliot to Claire, asking about Hollywood and Clark Gable and Greta Garbo and Errol Flynn and the Barrymores, trying to relate the two-dimensional black and white creatures viewed on the movie screen to real, live people. Ora and Nora moved graciously among the groups, inserting tidbits of information about the his-

tory of Taylor Springs and the family relationships that
bound together the people congregated in the parlor.

Ludie stood by the wine cooler and replenished the
champagne. Ruth Taylor, getting her glass refilled, whispered, "Ludie, you know I never had champagne wine in
my life before and I'm not sure it's the Christian thing to
do, but mercy, Ora and Nora wouldn't be doing it if it ain't
proper. Least that's what I'm telling myself." She giggled.
"It tickles your nose."

Ludie said, "Yes'm, Miss Ruth," and thought about the
three bottles that Khaki had brought up out of the cellar and
stashed in the kitchen. Sure hope them dumb niggers ain't
out there getting tiddly, she smiled to herself.

Out in the kitchen, surrounded by the steam seeping
out of the pots bubbling on the wood cook stove and the
fragrant odors wafting from the big oven, the twins, along
with Thelma and Mary William, stood ceremoniously sipping their champagne from jelly glasses. "I'm not sure this
is Christian of us," Thelma declaimed as she drained the
glass. "Specially since we just got saved, and you know all
three of us done signed up for the Youth Temperance
League, swearing that alcohol would never pass our lips.
Can I have just a little more, Elvira?"

"You are such a dummy and a baby, Thelma," Vashti
looked at her disgustedly. "This ain't alcohol; this is champagne wine just like in the Bible what Jesus drunk himself.
Looky here, Mary William done drunk hers and see how
nice she is being, she ain't woo-wooing at all, so's it must
be good for you."

Sukie Bee raised the bottle to her lips and took a great
gulp, smacking her lips. "Goes down real smooth. Too
smooth. Just like that movie star man out there. Took one
look at him, knew nothing good come from that man. He
full of the plat man. He no good."

"Shut that up right now, Sukie Bee. We ain't allowed to listen to that talk no more. You know we got in trouble with all that stuff you told us. We had to go get ourselves saved and even with that we ain't allowed to come visit down in colored town no more." Vangie shook her head angrily in Sukie's direction.

"You better listen to me, missy, better listen good for the last time." Sukie Bee hiccupped. "Never going to talk about it again, but you going to remember this all your life, you and Vashti. Voodoo is what my mama taught me and her mama before her and it go all the way back in time. You do voodoo, you got responsibilities. You is obliged to adore the Bon Dieu and the loa of your ancestors and you is obliged to take care of the twins among you. Now you is twins and Miss Ora and Miss Nora is twins, and we done our jobs beating back that plat man that came riding in over them buffalo trails with them first white mens and that black nigger slave and that high yeller nigger woman. But you girls done showed the charms and named them out loud, and ain't no way to keep that plat man from getting loose once the truth is said. So be it." She chug-a-lugged the rest of the champagne and quietly sat the empty bottle on the table.

"All right, enough of this carrying-ons," Sarah announced firmly. "You girls get Mary William and go on out in the parlor and behave yourselves. Your mama and daddy be here soon with the Good Time Boys and they'll want to see you out there acting real pretty like. Go on now. You, too, Thelma. And don't be saying nothing about what Sukie Bee was talking about, just a bunch of foolishness." The three girls marched the rather limp Mary William out into the parlor just in time to see the Reverend and Mrs. Randall Clay make a grand entrance with Delmer and Levi

and Reuben and Noble Shuck, the Good Time Gospel Boys
Quartet.

The boys, as always dressed completely in the white
clothing that matched their white hair and eyebrows and
colorless eyes, had remained lean and elegant. The only
signs of the passing ten years since they had first come to
Taylor Springs were the web of wrinkles around their eyes
and a certain softness around their once sharp jaw lines.
Standing in the doorway, they greeted the Misses Philpot
and repeated howdies and good to see you agains to the rest
of the company.

Lizzie, dimpling, sashayed over to where Eliot Mansfield was being bored by Myna Smoot, who had been filling
him in on how her daddy went to Harvard and taught right
here in this house when it was a boys' school. Lizzie put her
hand on Eliot's arm and announced, "Boys, I'm right proud
to introduce you to Mr. Eliot Mansfield, the movie star.
Being as you all are in the entertainment field together, I'm
sure you'll have a lot to talk about." As the men shook
hands, Eliot turned to the corner where Claire sat perched
on the corner of the sofa, the most of the space being occupied by the bulk of Lucille Byrd, and said, "Gentlemen,
my wife, Claire LaRue."

The boys looked at Claire, and Delmer said, "My
God!" Claire rose, smoothed the platinum curls that peeked
out around the black feather cap, and walked over to kiss
each of the boys on the cheek. "Hello, Delmer, Noble, Reuben, Levi. It's been a long time."

The buzz of conversation in the room ceased. Claire
looked around the room and gave them the look of innocent
naughtiness that had graced so many movie screens. "Why,
Eliot, you don't have to introduce me. The boys and I go a
long way back. Why, their parents practically raised me
when I was orphaned so young in life. And they're the ones

who introduced me to D.W. Griffith, which is how I got to Hollywood."

Delmer gulped, "Why, yes indeed, that's the facts of it. But we been out of touch so long and we never thought to walk in here today and find you sitting in the Philpot parlor. Small world, ain't it, Brunhilda?"

Eliot lifted an eyebrow, giving Claire a sardonic look, "Brunhilda?"

She laughed, "A nickname that the boys' parents gave me. They always said with my blond hair and blue eyes that I looked really German."

"That's right," Reuben coughed. "Mama and Daddy was always so crazy about, uh, Claire here. Mama said she was the daughter that she'd never had. Course, Mama and Daddy both done passed over now, but we still kept the house in Prattville, Claire, go back there and rest up ever' now and then."

"Well, what a surprise and what an auspicious reunion. This certainly calls for celebration." Miss Ora motioned to the boys and to Randall and Lizzie. "You must come and have a glass of champagne. Randall, this comes from Papa's cellar; it's been lying down there for years."

"Well, Miss Ora, certainly the church does not hold with the imbibing of strong spirits; however, even the Bible does not speak ill of taking a little wine."

Miss Bertha smiled. "It's right intelligent of you and speaks well of your ability to lead your flock for you to realize that the flesh must nurture the spirit, Randall. I'll join you in another glass and perhaps Roger can propose a toast that honors Taylor Springs and its illustrious visitors."

Glasses were filled and Roger Byrd raised his flute filled with the sparkling liquid high, "To the keepers of our traditions, Miss Ora and Nora . . . to the family that gave our town its name, the Taylors . . . to the rest of us who are all tied together by family and mutual interests . . . to our visitors who are distinguished film stars, Eliot Mansfield and Claire LaRue . . . and to the Good Time Gospel Boys, who will bring us delight tonight as they have for the past ten years."

"I'll drink to that." Lucille Byrd raised her glass and tossed off the champagne in one swallow.

Levi clinked glasses with Claire and murmured low, "Did you bring your snakes, Brunhilda?"

Looking into each other's eyes, Eliot and Lizzie sipped from their glasses. Lizzie ran her pink, pointed tongue around the rim of her glass. Eliot, watching her, thought my God, this is the hottest, most exciting woman I ever laid eyes on. As Ludie announced that supper was ready in the dining room, he took Lizzie by the arm and steered her toward the door. "Listen," he whispered, "I have to see you alone. You know you don't belong here, don't you? God, you're better than any woman in Hollywood. We have to talk about this."

Lizzie looked at him through the thick tangle of her eyelashes. "Meet me tonight behind the church, our church, about one o'clock." She raised her head and proudly looked around. My God, she thought, it's not pretending to be a movie star. I can go to Hollywood and be a real star.

20

Lucille Byrd sang that night, Lord, how she sang. She stood there, a giantess covered with red rippling ruffles, black curls haloed around her moon face; wide red mouth open and pointed straight up to heaven; chocolate-brown eyes ecstatically scrunched closed; and the rich, molasses contralto sounds soared up to the roof and down the aisles and out the open windows. The Good Time Boys, straight white pillars behind her, rocked the beams with "Come, come, come," while Lucille belted "Come to the Church in the Wildwood," and Brother Zack Hayes got the glory and danced out in the aisle speaking in tongues.

Ora and Nora Philpot, dressed in their faded finery and jewels, clapped discreetly to the rhythm along with Roger and Bertha Byrd and Randall and Lizzie Clay, who sat in the pew beside them. Ruth Taylor, surrounded by her clan, clapped and remembered the mountains and her father and the burning oil and could almost feel the whippings he had given her. Myna Smoot sat in the front pew rocking as her dumpling body moved to the beat, shaking Eliot Mansfield, who was mopping the sweat from his face with his silk polka-dotted handkerchief. Sitting on one side of him, the

Clay twins controlled Mary William's frenzy by slowly circling her windmilling hands. Sitting on the other side of
him, Claire LaRue closed her eyes and her face flushed as
she dreamed of snakes. In the back pews, all the coloreds
hummed and swayed and clapped their hands; all except
Sukie Bee, who sat unmoving, glazed eyes fixed on the big
cross that rose behind the singers.

When the last of the piano keys were pounded, the paper fans returned to the pew racks, everybody passed out to
the churchyard to visit for a spell. All the children raced
around to the back of the church to look at the Gospel bus,
the blue bus with "The Good Time Gospel Boys Quartet"
written on the side in bold red and yellow script, the same
bus that had been bringing the Good Time Boys to Taylor
Springs for the past ten years. When Ben LeCompte tried
the door, it was locked as it had always been locked for the
past ten years.

Vashti, pulling Mary William along by the dress tail,
motioned to Vangie and Thelma to follow her over by the
bushes where they could not be overheard. "I've got it,"
she whispered, "I know how we can get a look in the bus
tonight. Thelma, ask your mama if me and Vangie can
spend the night with you. Then we'll beg our mama, tell
her we been so good taking care of Mary William for so
long, that we deserve to and that Colored Bertha can spend
the night in our room and take care of Mary William."

"How's that going to get us in that bus?" Thelma
asked prissily.

"Listen now. If we spend the night with you, we can
sneak out real easy because your window opens out onto
the roof over the front porch. Once we get out there, all we
have to do is climb real quiet like down that side rose trellis.
Nobody'll hear us or ever know we're gone. The only way
we could get out of our house is to go out the doors or the

bottom windows and they'd sure 'nough hear us. Well, what do you think?"

"I think it's just perfect." Vangie danced in circles, her red curls flying as she pirouetted. "I just think it's perfect, too," Thelma said, giggling, and followed Vangie's circles until they bumped and knocked each other to the ground. They rolled around laughing until Mary William excitedly joined them and rolled on top of them.

Too soon their mothers' shrill voices came circling around to the back of the church calling for them. The children came reluctantly back, dragging their feet through puddles of darkness. Thelma, Vashti, and Vangie begged their mamas to let the twins spend the night at the Taylors.

"Mama, Colored Bertha can watch Mary William this once. Please, Mama, we been so good and been watching her so long," Vashti pleaded.

Thelma nodded gravely. "Yes'm, the twins need a little time just to play and not have to always worry about Mary William." She turned to Alice Taylor, who was holding the despised baby brother. "Don't you think so, too, Mama? Besides, I ain't been able to have anybody over to spend the night for the longest time because of you being so poorly with the baby and then having to be quiet after he was born."

Lizzie pursed her lips while her thoughts raced. With the girls gone and Mary William locked in with Colored Bertha, it's going to be easy for me get out of the house. Randall'll be asleep five minutes after I do it to him. "Well, I suppose Colored Bertha could take care of Mary William for tonight. She'd just have to lock the bedroom door to make sure that . . . would it be too much trouble for you, Alice?"

"Course not. With all the people we have up at the house, two more little girls aren't going to make a bit of difference. They can borrow Thelma's nightgowns, won't even have to go home."

Lizzie nodded her head and told the twins to run over to the side yard where the colored folk were congregated and tell Colored Bertha she needed to speak to her. She and Alice chatted about the supper at Philpot Plantation and about what in the world the Mansfields would be able to do about his daddy and Mary William. Alice said Ruth had suggested that maybe Myna Smoot could take both of them in, with Cora to help should be no problem nursing the old man, but Myna said that she simply could not be responsible for looking after Mary William. Myna said well, really, Ruth, you know nobody can do nothing with Mary William except her daddy and now he's nothing but a vegetable and, of course, Vashti and Vangie, but little girls can't have a heavy burden like that full time.

"Well," Lizzie replied, "I never understood how the twins could control her. It's just like they read her mind or something, sounds silly, I know. Oh, here you are, Colored Bertha."

"Vangie already told me what they want to do when she dragging me over here, Miss Lizzie. Reckon I have to say yes since those children do need some playtime. Seems like none of us ever thought about that." She hugged the twins, who had been hers ever since they were born. "Now, we'll just take Mary William with us, Miss Lizzie. You takes one hand and I'll take the other, stroke her hands real gentle like just like the girls do it and ever' thing be just fine."

Vashti and Vangie watched their Mama and Colored Bertha lead a strangely docile Mary William away, and then with a whoop ran with Thelma to pile in the back seat of the Dodge, where Bucky waited behind the wheel. He turned around to look at his three daughters and then thought of how Lizzie had looked at that movie star at the Philpot's tonight, just the same hungry way that she used to look at him ten years ago.

Back at the parsonage, Colored Bertha led the zombielike Mary William into the bedroom. Sure am glad you so tired, Mary William, she thought. Must have been all that party at Miss Ora's and Nora's or maybe that champagne wine. She pulled the nightshirt over the unresisting head and down over the stick body, which was still clad in bloomers that bagged around the knees and the shimmy that flapped over the straight upper torso. Colored Bertha hummed as she took the hairbrush and applied it to the lank hair. Now we going to get you in bed. There we go, pull them covers up. Now just going to slide this bolt on the door. Look at that, she done asleep, glory be. Just going to take this old stocking and tie her ankle here to the bedpost. That way, she try to get up, I'll know it from her thrashing around. Good, ever' thing all fixed up now. Colored Bertha, still fully clothed, laid down on the other side of the bed and was soon snoring louder than Mary William.

In the other bedroom, Randall Clay dropped his shoes and skinned out of his trousers and drawers. Lizzie stood in front of the bureau, clad in a white satin slip, dreamily staring into the mirror as she brushed her curls. He came up behind her, putting his hands on the jutting breasts, pushing his erection against that astounding ass. She placed the brush on the dresser and ran her hands up and down his naked thighs. "My goodness, what do we have here," she purred as she rubbed against him. Randall turned her around and nibbled on her pouting mouth. She slowly skimmed the slip over her head and stood naked before him. He tongued her erect, pink nipples and licked the smooth path down her chest to her navel. She moved away from him and spread-eagled herself on the bed. He covered her body with his and said, "Sweet Jesus, Lizzie, you just love to do it."

A half-hour later he lay beside her, breathing deeply, sleeping soundly. She stretched her body and looked at the clock on the bedside table. An hour until she met Eliot Mansfield. Thank you, God, she earnestly prayed, for finally giving me the chance to do it with a movie star, and thank you because I know he's going to take me with him to Hollywood. She could already see her picture in *Photoplay*.

Claire LaRue threw the sheet off her sweating body and smiled as she heard Eliot trying to move quietly in the adjoining bedroom. Floorboards faintly creaked as he tiptoed down the hall; the plaintive squeak of the screen door reached her ears. Good night, sweet prince, she thought, good-bye, dear husband.

Vashti, Vangie, and Thelma, hands linked together, raced down the hill. Caroline Smoot Taylor's big stone house loomed behind them, outlined by the light of the full moon that hung in the heavy, hot darkness. Out of breath, they stopped halfway down and looked down on the town.

"It's really scary out here," Thelma panted. "I think I'd just as soon go on back home."

"Don't be such a baby, Thelma. Ain't nothing out here but us." Vashti poked her. "Look down there. Sure looks different in the dark, don't it? See, there's our house and the church and Miss Myna's and the Sheelys. And way over there is the springs where all those dark trees are. Just think, they are all there sleeping in their beds and not a one of them knows we are out here."

Vangie shivered. "Good thing that we done found out there ain't no plat man. Remember when Sukie Bee told us he really liked to get loose when the moon was full?"

Vashti pulled on Thelma and Vangie. "Come on, now.

We'll get on the path that goes behind all the houses up to the main road and the Holy Roller church. That way we'll be sure nobody sees us, if somebody should just happen to be awake. And no need to be scared of no plat man. Just in case that Sukie Bee is right, I've got my charm right here in my pocket and I also got my gold cross that Aunt Bertha gave me right around my neck. We are as safe as we can be."

Sukie Bee stood by the springs, a cloth bundle clasped tightly in her hands. She looked at the full moon as it rode high over the hills crossed with the old buffalo trails. She waited stolidly for the first glimpse of the gleaming yellow eyes that she knew would soon be seen floating down from the ridge.

Ora Philpot sat in the bentwood rocker and looked out her bedroom window. She thought of Mama and Papa and what life used to be in Taylor Springs. Funny, she and Nora being eighty years old. She didn't feel eighty years old; inside she was still young in her memories. She could still feel Bud Byrd moving inside her hot, young body. She could still feel that same body tear as she gave birth to Roger, alone and frightened in that Paris clinic. She could still taste the succulent sweetness of young Bertha Hayes. She chuckled aloud softly. All the time, all our lives, everyone thought Nora was the wild one, her being so feisty and all. Everyone thinks that I am the proper one who has kept it all under control. And that I have. There are appearances to keep up and I have made certain that this town, the Philpot birthright, has maintained the veneer of civilized behavior that makes our survival possible.

Tossing in her bed, Nora wondered what she was going to do about Ora. I swear she gets crazier every day. All my life I have had to watch her, take care of her. This idea that just because she is who she is allows her to do as she pleases and that so long as something is not named that it is not true. My God, I had to threaten to blow off poor old Sukie Bee's head just to protect Ora. Funny how she always appeared so cool outside, but God, so hot inside. Seducing Bud Byrd, and he wasn't the first, either man or woman. Roger Byrd, Ora's son, and poor Lucille, her grandchild. And Khaki, Khaki is her other grandchild. Oh, she knew well enough what Roger was up to with Ludie. But through all the years, when I'd call her to task, she'd just smile at me and ignore me. Ben worries me the most, though; he's surly and says things. Ben, Ora's great-grand-son. Good Lord. Maybe she thinks it's all right because all this mixup has been going on ever since a Philpot, a Taylor, and a McAfee rode over those hills and found the springs. I don't know, but I've got to do something with her. I've just got a feeling something is just going to explode, and Ora couldn't take that since she's the last of the Philpots. All these years, Ora's been the only person I've had to love, except, of course, Burton Clay, and I had him such a short time it hardly counts. Every time I see Randall Clay up in the pulpit, I think of Burton. They look so much alike. Burton would never have come to me, though, if Ramona had done him right. He was a lusty man and I did need someone to treat my migraine headaches. He died in my bed and in my arms and hasn't Ora just thrown that up to me all these years.

The same moonlight streamed through the open window into the wild, rolling eyes of Mary William Sheely. Her fingers scurried crablike up and down her body until the wetness flowed between her legs, easing the hurt in her abdomen. She did not like the sloshy feeling of lying in the wetness and sat up abruptly to leave it. One stick leg thumped to the floor; the other was constrained. In patient frustration, she moved the leg until, at last, the stocking with which Colored Bertha had tied the ankle to the bed-post unknotted itself enough so that Mary William could pull her foot through.

She stood and remained very still, sniffing for the familiar odor of the twins. It was not there and the tendrils of thought with which they transmitted the images to her mind were missing. Rocking back and forth, she rested beside the bed, hearing Colored Bertha snore. Quietly flapping her arms, she moved toward the bedroom door, slid back the bolt, flew down the stairs, and out the front door. She did not begin her woo-woo song until she was windmilling down the road that led to the springs.

Colored Bertha rolled over into the puddle left by Mary William. Awakened by the wetness, she lay puzzled and then extended her arm to find only empty space. She rolled from the bed, her eyes searching the moonlit room, only to find the loosely knotted stocking still on the bedpost and the drawn bolt on the bedroom door. She ran into the hall yelling, "Mr. Randall, Miss Lizzie! It's Mary William. She's done escaped. I can't find her." Mr. Randall answered her, but they couldn't find Miss Lizzie either.

Roger Byrd impatiently cranked the telephone. For God's sake, why wasn't Lucille answering? He turned and turned the handle, hearing only the unanswered buzz on the other end of the line and Bertha's faint moans that came floating down the stairwell. In frustration, he ran up the steps, his sweat-soaked nightshirt stuck to his body. Shucking it off, rapidly throwing on his clothes, he told Bertha just to rest as calmly as she could and that since he couldn't rouse Lucille he was going to drive into town to fetch Doc Smoot himself. Probably it was just indigestion because of the champagne, but better have Doc come right out to make sure.

The moonlight reflected the three red heads as Vashti,

Vangie, and Thelma stealthily crept around to the back of the Holy Roller church. Crouching low, they hugged the bushes and then fell to the hard ground to crawl around the front of the Good Time Gospel bus. They looked up to see the folding door was wide open. "Would you looky there?" Vangie hissed. "First time ever we seen that bus door open."

When the crowd had left the churchyard that night and the Shuck boys had unlocked the bus doors, the air inside was hotter than the fires of hell, as Delbert put it. Levi said for Jesus' sake, leave the door open and get all them windows open. If it don't cool down in here, it'll be too hot to hump Lucille. Lord knows that that's hot enough work to begin with. As they waited for Lucille to leave her room at McAfee's General Store and sneak back across the road, they passed the bottle of bourbon back and forth and exclaimed their surprise at seeing Brunhilda right here in this podunk town and about how she was just as cool as a cucumber in covering up that she'd ever been a part of the act. Reuben reminisced about how that girl could fuck and they laughed about her damn snakes. By the time they pulled Lucille's bulk through the bus door, they were right worked up, and, of course, Lucille was ready. She'd been waiting for a whole year.

Vashti, Vangie, and Thelma lay on the ground staring at the open door of the forbidden bus. Through the open windows and the open door, sounds wafted out, moans and slurps and groans and slick slappings. Putting her finger to her lips, Vashti rose to a crouch and moved toward the door, motioning for the other two to stay where they were. She cautiously crawled up the bus steps and stood in the driver's area, which was partitioned off from the living quarters. Moving quietly to the opening in the partition, she stared into the moonlit interior.

Wide-eyed, Vashti viewed the massive mounds of Lucille Byrd's naked flesh. Lucille rested on her knees and elbows, her mountainous buttocks raised high in the air. One Good Time Boy stood behind her, moving rapidly back and forth. Two others lay on either side of her, sucking and kneading the heavy, globular breasts. The other Good Time Boy kneeled in front of her. Lucille moaned and moaned and then screamed as her tent of flesh collapsed on the floor.

Vashti backed slowly out of the bus, down the steps, and pulled the other two girls silently back to the front of the church. Her face white with shock, she stood trying to breathe and stop the frantic pounding in her chest. "They're hurting her," Vashti whispered. "The Good Time Boys are trying to kill Miss Lucille. We got to go for help."

Thelma started to whimper. "Shh," Vashti warned, "they'll hear us and then they'll try to kill us, too. Where we going for help? Nobody around here. Miss Lucille's the only one who lives around here and she's in the bus, stark naked, being killed."

Vashti plomped on the ground and hugged her knees. "We got to split up. I'll run home and get Daddy. Vangie, you and Thelma run to her house and get Mr. Bucky and Mr. Bubba. You'll have to go with Thelma 'cause she's too scared to go alone." The other two nodded and then the girls ran fast through the night so they could stop the killing of Lucille Byrd. The plat man charm lay on the ground by the bus door where it had fallen out of Vashti's pocket.

Halfway up the hill to the Taylor house, Thelma started screaming from pure terror and Vangie began yelling, "Help, help, somebody help." By the time they reached the Taylor front porch, Bubba and Tony Dagostino were bursting out the front door.

"For God's sake, it's Thelma and Vangie," Bubba gasped. "What in the tarnation is going on around here?

What you girls doing out of the house? Where you been? Where's Vashti?"

The two little girls collapsed on the top step, sobbing. Tony put his arms around them, "There now, calm down, shhh, it's all right." The screen door banged as Bucky limped out, followed by Ruth and Becky and Alice.

"No, it ain't all right," Vangie sobbed. Thelma screamed and ran into her mama's arms while Vangie told the grown-ups all about what was happening down in the Good Time bus and how they had to go save Lucille Byrd from getting killed and how Vashti had run the other way to get help from their daddy.

"I just can't believe what I'm hearing," Ruth exclaimed. "Lucille Byrd in the Good Time Gospel bus this time of night. You girls making this up? This some kind of story to cover up that you sneaked out of the house? Screaming and noises going on inside the bus? Now you get in that house while the menfolk go to find Vashti."

The next morning a hot sun rose in the heavy sulfur air that pressed down on Taylor Springs. The first rays climbed the ridges, illuminated the buffalo trails, and crept down into the valley.

The diffused light sank down on the surface of the murky springs water and seeped back into the heavy plant growth on the banks. Sukie Bee, wide haunches spread on the ground, sat leaned back against the still. Beside her, arms and legs tied together, Mary William Sheely lay quietly keening her woo-woo song. A plat man charm rested on her bony, bloody chest.

In the grove back of the Southern Methodist Episcopal church, the light rays struggled through the limp, hanging leaves of the trees to outline the nude body that lay face down in the heavy dried bush. The blade of a butchering knife was buried to its hilt in the body's back, and the protruding, bloody handle was covered by the same swarm of green flies that crawled over the body and the bloody plat man charm clutched in its right hand.

The light spread across the graveled road, oozing in the open parsonage door to reveal only empty space. It bounced off the stained glass windows of the church, moved on to lighten the bedroom where Claire LaRue slept alone with a smile on her face, shone down on a closed and empty McAfee's General Store, and then broke through to reveal the vacant space behind the Holy Roller church. The Good Time Gospel bus was gone; the only thing left was the plat man charm lying on the ground.

The same beams struggled to pierce the dusty windows of the Holy Roller church and light the murky, dusky interior where a body, split open from the groin to the neck and tied upside down on the big cross behind the pulpit, drained blood on the circle of plat man charms piled beneath its head.

21

It was only logical and expedient for the sheriff to decide that it was Mary William who had done the killings. After all, she did escape from the parsonage and was found the next morning tied up down by the springs. Sukie Bee testified that she'd come upon Mary William, bloody and screaming, and had tied her up to keep her in place. It only made sense that poor Mary William was the one who had done it. Lord knows, Mary William didn't have any brains or any sense of right or wrong, and Lord knows when she was in one of her spells she was strong as the devil. She just got loose and went berserk. Some folks had been expecting something like this out of her for years and weren't the least bit surprised. And what with Professor Sheely being paralyzed and nobody left that could really take care of her, Mary William was going to have to be put away anyhow, so best to do it right now and get this whole mess cleaned up.

Of course, this solution didn't stop everybody from talking about Lucille Byrd and what had been going on in the Good Time bus while Mary William was out loose killing people with a knife. Once Thelma and Vangie ran crying and hollering to the Taylor house, the story was all over town by the next morning. Trying to absorb the news of the two killings and the laying of Lucille was almost more than folks could follow. And then trying to piece together if the events could possibly have any connection was enough to make heads spin.

Once Bob McAfee got the store opened up, trying to run the switchboard and tend to clerking at the same time, most of the town gathered there to discuss the goings-on. The men clumped around the soft drink cooler and the women circled around the dry goods counter to discuss, in appropriately hushed tones, the gory killings and Lucille's shenanigans. Most of them were just waiting in hopes of being interviewed by the reporter from the Louisville *Clarion* who was supposedly over at the Holy Roller church talking with Brother Jim Jordan. When the word got out that the people from Fox Movietone News were in town, down at the Sheely house with Claire LaRue, the crowd moved like a swarm of lemmings from the store to stand, silent and gaping, outside the house. They were waiting to see what would happen and just maybe get their picture taken by the movie camera.

To make it even better, the newspaper reporter joined the crowd outside the Sheely house and walked right up to talk to Myna Smoot. She told him that as far as she could tell Claire LaRue was bearing up real well. Poor woman surely was bound to be prostrate with grief, considering that her husband was found all naked and bloody, stone dead with a knife sticking in his back. To think that something like that could happen to such a distinguished movie star was just beyond belief. And to think that it was his own, poor demented sister that had done him in. And to think that the only reason he'd come to Taylor Springs was to arrange for his sister's care and that same sister killed him. Of course, poor Mary William probably sensed some way that he was going to put her away and that is probably why she did it. No, Myna could not even guess why Eliot Mansfield was found naked, his clothes thrown in a heap on the ground. Of course, with Mary William anything could happen, you never knew.

A lot of people talked with the reporter about the plat man charms. Airy LeCompte told him all about how the little Clay and Taylor girls tried to sell them voodoo charms in McAfee's store and how the blame was placed on a colored woman named Sukie Bee. Brother Jim Jordan of the Holy Roller church told him that voodoo was practiced among the coloreds and only the saving grace of Jesus could drive such heathen practices out. For a fact, Brother Jordan was certain that Mary William had been possessed by voodoo gods when she had done this horrible thing. When the reporter went down to colored town, all the cabins were shut and nobody answered the door. When he went to the Philpot plantation, Ludie respectfully informed him that the three ladies were not receiving and, mercy no, she didn't know nothing about no silly voodoo charms.

Bertha Hayes Byrd was in seclusion at the Philpot Plantation and refused to see anyone, much less reporters. Why and how Mary William also killed Roger Byrd, and hung him upside down on the cross in the Holy Roller church, was left to the imaginations and speculations of the townsfolk. The only fact known was that on that night, Roger Byrd had left the farm to go fetch the doctor because Bertha was bad sick. He'd tried to use the telephone, but the switchboard never answered his ring. Of course, the reason for that was because his daughter, Lucille, wasn't at the store, but was over in the Good Time bus doing you-know-what. Everybody found this out because Ruth Taylor had been out to the Philpots to see if she could help Bertha in

any way. Nora had told her that Bertha was in no condition
to see anyone and about how Roger was out that night
going to fetch the doctor. Nora said that she and Ora were
as distraught as Bertha, since Roger had been like a son to
them. Of course, Nora didn't say anything about Lucille,
but then you wouldn't expect her to, would you?

It was rumored that Lizzie LeCompte Clay had taken
to her bed, unable to cope with what had happened to the
twins. At least nobody had seen her around town. The Reverend Randall Clay was seen visiting Claire LaRue, helping
her through her sorrowful time and helping make arrangements for shipping her husband's body back to Hollywood.
At least that's what Bob McAfee reported that Randall had
told him. Randall also visited the Philpots often, which was
only natural considering that his Aunt Bertha was there,
suffering from shock and grief.

Colored Bertha told Elvira, who later told Ruth Taylor, that Miss Lizzie was resting in bed just blaming herself
for not being in the house when Mary William got loose
and for letting the twins spend the night away from home.
Colored Bertha had explained that, no, sir, Miss Lizzie was
just not herself. Why, when Colored Bertha and Mr. Randall found Miss Lizzie that night, there she was just sitting
in the back pew inside the church. Said she just felt the need
to pray and be in God's house. Imagine how she felt when
she found out later what Mary William was doing and what
was happening to the girls while she was sitting there praying.

And it was Miss Lizzie herself that found poor little
Vashti early the next morning hiding in the privy, all curled
up in a little ball on the floor. And that poor child, her face
was all bruised and marks were on her throat and big
scratches covered her poor little arms and legs. Vashti ain't
spoke a word since and just lies all curled up on her bed, big

brown eyes staring off into nowhere. And Vangie just wanders the house and has these terrible dreams at night, and screams and screams. Mr. Randall, he was trying his best to take care of all of them and trying to help that movie star woman and Miss Bertha. And he was being bothered all the time by that newspaper man. Mr. Randall just told him that plat man charms was just a bunch of foolishness and probably Mary William done found some of those silly things that Thelma and the twins put together trying to sell them. Just some chicken feathers and chicken bones put together by some little girls with a lot of imagination.

Nobody in town saw Lucille Byrd until the day of her daddy's funeral. Eula told Colored Bertha who told Cora who told Myna Smoot that the morning after the killings when she went to work the Byrd house seemed empty. Usually, she could hear sounds of life, well, like Mr. Roger coughing and hacking up in the bedroom, but that morning she didn't hear a sound.

"I called out several times for Miss Bertha, but never got no answer. Too quiet in that house, could feel something was bad wrong. I went looking through all the downstairs rooms; nobody there, nobody answering me. Went upstairs and saw Miss Bertha's bed all messed up, but nobody there. When I cracked open the door to Lucille's old room, I tell you I didn't believe my eyes. There was Lucille lying directly on the pink counterpane, looking up at the ceiling and just smiling away. She looked at me and said, 'Morning, Eula. I'm going to be staying here for awhile. The Good Time Boys pulled out last night, had other places to go.' So she's there and Miss Bertha is at the Philpots and Mr. Roger is stone dead. And all Lucille does is eat and smile and eat and smile. Sure do beat all."

Ora Philpot made the decision that Roger Byrd's funeral would be held at the Southern Methodist Episcopal

church, just as it would have been if he had not been split
wide open and hung upside down on the cross in the Holy
Roller church. His widow had wanted to have Roger rest in
the Philpot parlor and then have her nephew, Randall, conduct a private service with just Ora, Nora, and herself present, and of course, the family coloreds.

"Bertha, you always were a silly fool." Ora's gaze
rolled heavenward. "The way the entire town of Taylor
Springs is carrying on about Lucille and the murders. You
know I had to castigate that newspaper reporter myself for
the nonsense he has been printing about us. Roger Byrd
must have a proper funeral that befits his position in this
town."

Bertha wiped at her red-rimmed eyes with a linen
handkerchief.

"Now listen to me, Bertha, and stop that self-pitying
whining. We don't know who killed Roger. And, no one in
their right mind would believe it was Mary William. What
with Lucille's trashy behavior being found out and Roger's
rather sensational demise, it behooves us to conduct his funeral in the manner befitting our station."

Nora Philpot looked at her sister and shook her head.
"Ora's right, you know, Bertha. We're just going to have
to carry it off. It doesn't help any that little Vashti Clay was
found in such a condition and Vangie doesn't seem to be
faring too well, either. Thelma Taylor seems to be the only
little redhead who is thriving. Ludie told me that she even
got in the Fox Movietone News."

Bertha looked at both of them in disbelief. "I swear,
you're both crazy as bedticks. All this going on and you're
still only concerned with doing the proper thing. And what
about Lucille? Ludie tells us that she's out at the farm, but
she won't come to the telephone or even come out here to

talk to us. You think she'll come to her own daddy's funeral?"

Ora stood, poised like the figurehead on an old wooden sailing vessel. "My dear, I sincerely hope not." This conversation was relayed by Ludie to Eula who told Khaki who told Elvira who told Ruth Taylor. Ruth Taylor, in breathy, shocked tones, told the rest of Taylor Springs.

Of course, the whole town turned out for the funeral. The Southern Methodist Episcopal church was so packed that there was hardly room for the ornate mahogany casket that housed the remains of Dr. Roger Byrd. Before the ceremony began, the mourners filed by the open casket and commented on how natural Roger looked and what a fine job McAfee's Funeral Home over in Nelsonville had done. The mourners then marched by the front pew to stop and pay their condolences to the black-garbed, veiled widow, who was flanked on either side by the Philpot sisters. No one commented on the fact that the deceased's only child, Lucille, was not in attendance.

The service began with the choir twanging "Nearer My God to Thee" and the Reverend Randall Clay had just begun a prayer entreating God to welcome their dear, departed brother into the pearly gates with open arms when the magnificent bulk of Lucille Byrd filled the open church doors and majestically moved up the aisle. As she advanced toward the casket that held the waxen remains of her daddy, her red mouth opened wide and the rich, molasses contralto voice soared throughout the church. "Amazing grace, how sweet the sound, that saved a wretch like me. . . . I once was lost, but now am found, was blind but now I see." Standing before the casket, chocolate-brown eyes scrunched ecstatically closed, she finished her song, smiled at the congregation, and left the church. Nobody except Ben Hayes ever saw her again.

The day after Dr. Roger Byrd was buried in the family plot at Philpot Plantation, Lucille Byrd sent word by Eula that Ben was to come out to the farm the next morning as she needed to talk to him. He went and found her waiting on the front porch, big body spilling over the rocking chair, moon face split with a smile.

"Sit down," she gestured. "I got something to tell you because it's fit that you should know, and because you and I have some arrangements to make. I'm doing this because come afternoon, I'm going to Nelsonville to take the L & N down to Montgomery, Alabama. The rest of my life is going to be spent down there in Prattville, going to be keeping house for the Good Time Gospel Boys." She held up her hand to stop his question before it could be asked.

"No fear, they'll welcome me. They got no choice, and at last I'm free to go. You see, when I killed him, although that wasn't my reason, I freed myself."

She went on to tell how it happened. There she was in the bus with the Good Time Gospel Quartet enjoying herself just as she did every year when they came to Taylor Springs. She looked at him with a little half-smile and said that she reckoned that annual visit was the only thing that kept her going all these years. Anyway, the five of them had just wiped the sweat off their slippery bodies and put on their clothes, when from outside the bus they heard scuffling noises. They froze as the sounds of grunts and moans and finally the beginning of a squeaky, thready scream, halted in midpitch, poured in the open windows of the bus. Lucille was the first to move, lumbering through the bus, out the door, followed by the boys.

"It was Daddy. I saw Daddy struggling on top of little Vashti, his hands around her throat, her red hair flying as she turned her head trying to free herself. I knocked him off of her, flat on his back, and then sat down on top of him.

He didn't say a word, just looked up at me with empty eyes. Levi picked up Vashti and cradled her in his arms, crooning and comforting her. But she was rigid as a board and did not utter one word, not even a cry.

"I told Levi to bring the child over next to me. He knelt down and I put my face next to hers and told her to listen to me and to listen good. I told her that everything was all right now, that nobody was going to hurt her anymore, and that Levi was going to put her down and she was to run, run home very fast. Levi stood her on the ground and she just stayed there. I whispered, 'Run, Vashti, run like the wind,' and all of a turn, she streaked off like a red blur in the moonlight."

She'd forced Roger Byrd to tell her what happened by closing her hands around his throat and tightening them until he whispered hoarsely that he'd talk.

He told her how he was driving to Doc Smoot's when all of a sudden, just before he got to the church, one of the little Clay twins jumped right in front of the Packard's headlights. He stopped the car and got out and listened as she breathlessly told him all about what was happening to his daughter in the Good Time bus and please come with her to save Lucille before she was killed.

He didn't really believe the little girl, but followed her around back anyway, and, motioning for her to wait, he quietly climbed in the bus and watched Lucille Byrd getting laid by the Gospel Boys. He quietly left the bus, unbuttoned his fly, and walked over to the waiting little girl, clamping a hand over her mouth and throwing her to the ground. She wiggled and fought and bit his hand, and then started to scream. That's when he started to choke her.

Lucille listened, and remembered and remembered. She tightened those hamlike hands around her daddy's throat and pressed until his eyes bulged and his tongue fell swollen out of his mouth. The Good Time Boys helped her rise from the dead body of Roger Byrd and she told them to get in the bus and leave. She could take care of everything; she was obliged to take care of her own.

"After the boys pulled out, I walked across to the store and got one of Mr. Bob's meat cleavers and the basket of plat man charms that the girls had tried to sell at the store that day. I went back and carried Daddy into the church, split him wide open, tied him upside down on the cross, and put the pile of charms under his head. I was in the church when Bucky and Mr. Bubba and Tony and Randall went around to the back hollering for Vashti. Once they saw that the bus was gone, they left. Anyway, splitting Daddy open and hanging him up on the cross was just what he deserved. Daddy was evil and that was my way of letting the world know it."

Sukie Bee had already told Ben Hayes who had killed Eliot Mansfield. On the night of the killings, she was wandering around with her bundle of plat man charms. The moon was full and she'd seen the plat man eyes glowing as they floated down from the ridge. She knew the twins were in danger, and even though Sukie knew it was no use, she felt obligated to wander and watch and spread the charms around.

"I tell you true, I knew it was too late. During the time the Good Time Gospel Boys and Miss Lucille was a-singing, I looked up at that cross and I saw it, I saw it just as plain as day. I saw Mr. Roger upside down on that cross, split open from his tail to his gullet, dead as a door nail. Yes, I got the vision and I knew it was coming true. But I thought maybe if I spread the charms around at least it might chase the plat man back over the ridge after he done his mischief.

"I'd come up from the springs and crossed back into

that grove of trees behind the church. Figured I'd go up and stand watch up at the Holy Roller church, but I wanted to go the back way so's nobody would see me. Don't never want no more posses after me, no, sir. All of a sudden, I just stopped dead because right in a little clearing, not fifteen feet from me, I saw Miss Lizzie and that movie star man standing, and they was both buck naked. Could see them plain as day, full moon shining on them. They just stood there, facing each other, Miss Lizzie running her hands all up and down her body, and a-doing other things I ain't about to name. The movie star man was just standing there looking at her and a-growling low in his throat.

"I thought to myself, O sweet Jesus, move out of here, Sukie Bee. But before my feet could go, that man just moved on Miss Lizzie and they kind of collapsed on the ground. He was on top of her and them two didn't know nobody else was in this world. Next thing I knew the movie star man's wife come through the trees, up behind them. The moonshine was just lighting up that white hair of hers and dancing off this big butcher knife she was a-holding straight out in front of her.

"All of sudden like, she sprung and buried that knife clean up to the hilt in that man's pumping back. Then she laughed. Miss Lizzie was lying under that bloody, dying man, like she couldn't even begin to understand what just happened. That Claire LaRue just kept on laughing.

"She said something like 'you better push that garbage off you and get up, my dear.' And that Miss Lizzy better get up quick 'fore she got blood all over her. Then she tells her she best get her clothes on and get out of there. That she wouldn't tell nothing if Miss Lizzie wouldn't tell and she suspicioned that the preacher's wife wouldn't want the whole town to know how she was fucking Eliot Mansfield behind her husband's church. Swear to the sweet Jesus them's the words she used, Ben.

"Then Miss Lizzie, her eyes wide open and kind of staring, rolled herself out from under the man and began putting on her clothes. And the movie star man's wife began telling her how she knew all along that Miss Lizzie and her husband were hot for each other and she'd just been waiting for them to meet. She knew it would happen and she'd followed him when he sneaked out of the Sheely house that night.

"Then that Claire LaRue says she really don't know how to thank Miss Lizzie because her meeting up with her husband finally gives her the opportunity to get rid of him. No one ever going to suspect what really happened there and no one ever going to suspect her. Then she throws back her head and laughs some more, saying she's finally free of that pitiful excuse of a man.

"That movie star woman stood and watched Miss Lizzie run fast out of the trees and alongside the church. When Miss Lizzie passed out of sight, she walked over and knelt down beside the movie star man, a-feeling his pulse. She stood up and smiled down on him. Then she said something like 'Good night, sweet prince,' and walked away just as cool as a cucumber.

"I was still a-trying to get my feet to move, didn't want to be found around no white man's corpse, when I felt something hit me full in the back and then move on past me. Looked up, and Lord God, it was Mary William, spinning like a top, arms a-flapping and cawing like a crazy crow. Jumping right on top of that body, course she ain't got sense enough to know it her brother, she straddled over it and started smearing her hands in the blood and wiping it all over herself.

"Well, I finally got my feet a-moving and I run right into her and knocked her flying. Reckon I done knocked the breath out of her or something; I ain't a skinny woman by any sight. Anyway, she was lying there still with her eyes all rolled back so I quick tied her up real good. I put one of my charms in the movie star man's hand thinking it just might keep the plat man evil inside that dead man, and then I just picked up Mary William and carried her back to the springs.

"So, you see what I tell the sheriff is true. I did find Mary William wandering around all bloody and I did tie her up to keep her in place. Put the charm on her chest, just in case the plat man try to do her more harm, too. When the sheriff say that Mary William must of done the killings, I figure it best that way. Besides, old Sukie ain't about to tell no white sheriff that Miss Claire LaRue done killed her husband while he humping the preacher's wife. Who you think believe that coming from an old nigger woman who already been in trouble with voodoo?

"Reason I'm telling you all this is that somebody besides me need to know the truth. The truth got to be guarded. I ain't going to be on this earth forever and nobody know yet who really split open Mr. Roger. Couldn't of been that Claire LaRue; she ain't got no reason. Now you young yet, and you laugh at Sukie Bee and the plat man. But you see now how he got loose and what has done happened here. You think about what I done told you, Ben Hayes. After I'm gone, somebody got to watch for the plat eye, somebody among us got to be responsible for the twins.

PART FOUR

1960

22

They're almost all dead now, of course, dead for many years, little pockets of dust neatly tucked inside the ring of hills marked with the great buffalo roads that lead down into Taylor Springs.

There's nothing much left of the town, either. A gas station with a single pump, a small store that stocks mostly milk, cigarettes, soft drinks and bread, a few houses, and the Holy Roller church. Everything else either fell down or was razed or burned. The few children left on the surrounding farms go to the consolidated county school over in Boonetown, just as the few folks remaining go to the Boonetown Mini-Mall to do their shopping.

Philpot Plantation still stands, though, its Georgian rose-bricked grandeur restored to what it was when Asa Philpot first built it back in 1785. The house is listed on the Historical Register and has been featured in many publications citing its beauty and its history. Its present owner, a movie star from Hollywood, evinces a visible pride that Philpot Plantation is once again what it was.

As Nora Philpot lay dying back in December of 1940 she called for Ben Hayes to come to her bedside and told him that

Philpot Plantation was to be his, that it was his proper inheritance. Lucille Byrd had written her, she said, and told her of their conversation before Lucille left for Alabama.

"I know that Lucille deeded you Byrd Farm. Right now Bertha is living there and has the right to remain there so long as she lives, but even though no one around here knows it, the farm belongs to you. Lucille writes that she wants no part of Philpot Plantation even though she is named in my will, and has written me to say that she will sign it over to you after my death. She and I have made the arrangements."

The old lady's fierce eyes bored straight into his. "You should have it, Ben. I've thought long and hard about this ever since Ora died two months ago. You are the last male in the Philpot line, you know that. You know that Ora was Roger Byrd's mother and that Roger was your grandfather. And you know it goes even further back than that. Why, Asa Philpot's first half-breed son rode right into this valley in the arms of Asa's colored wench, who was about as light colored as Asa hiself. That baby was Esau Hayes. He got the Hayes name because when old Asa finally went back to Virginia and brought America Tryon back as his wife, she made the colored girl jump over the broom with the black slave who was called Hayes. Then America made the colored girl and Esau move out of the big house and into the slave quarters, right into Hayes' cabin. The boy ran away, must have been around fifteen years old then. Old Asa posted a bounty for him, but who was ever going to recognize a nigger slave who was fair complexioned and had blue eyes. Esau came back to the springs years later as a white Hayes, as a doctor, in fact.

She chuckled weakly and commenced coughing. "Lord, I'm beginning to ramble on like Ora used to do. The point is that you are the last of the Philpots. But, Ben, the time isn't right, yet. Now, here's what you have to do."

She told Ben that after her death, Ludie, Khaki, Eula,

and Sarah were to move to the plantation and run it as if
Lucille had arranged it that way. There was money, and she
had arranged with Lucille to send it monthly, so everything
would look proper. When Bertha Hayes died—which
wouldn't be long because poor Bertha had never been the
same since Roger's murder and with what happened to her
great-nieces, the Clay twins—he was to sell the Byrd Farm,
which Lucille would also arrange. The sale would bring
more than enough to keep the plantation in operation.

"Ben, there's a war on and more than likely you'll be
going soon. You won't be coming back from the war, boy."

He looked at her in amazement. She raised her eyebrows at him and laughed. "Ben, you're going to die in the
war. Ben Hayes will be no more. You'll come back later,
back to Taylor Springs to live on Philpot Plantation, but
you'll come back like Esau Hayes came back, a white man.
If he could do it, we can do it."

So Ben Hayes went to war, serving as an Army cook. It
was the same war that killed Tony Dagostino on the island of
Guadalcanal. Being his age and having a family, he didn't
have to go, but he enlisted. It was his only escape from the
broken dream of owning a part of Taylor Springs; the town
only tolerated those that didn't come from its own soil.

After Tony's death, Becky Taylor Dagostino left the
big stone Taylor house and took little Alex to Louisville,
where she got a job teaching school. She met a young captain who was stationed at Ft. Knox, married him, and
moved to Buffalo, New York.

Bucky Taylor took Alice and Thelma and the baby up
to Detroit, to do his part by working in a war industry
plant, being as he couldn't serve in the armed forces what
with having only one leg. Probably, it was the best way to
get away from Taylor Springs and the ghosts that haunted
him and his family.

It was Ben's wife, Sarah, who wrote him about the Clays. Sarah continued to work at the parsonage and help watch the twins. She said she felt an obligation since poor little Vashti continued to remain vacant-eyed and speechless, although she did move around now and did eat her meals. Vangie was doing better and rarely had her bad dreams, but she insisted on taking Vashti wherever she went. "It puts me in mind," she wrote, "of how the both of them used to lead Mary William around."

Ben got the wire from the Red Cross telling him that Sarah was dead from pneumonia. Then a letter came from Eula lamenting how Sarah had taken a bad chest cold after spending several hours out looking for the twins on a raw January day. She finally found them just sitting on the ground by Sukie Bee's abandoned still. The cold went into pneumonia and Sarah never pulled out of it. Six months later, Ben's parents, Eula and Khaki, got the wire that regretted that their son Ben had died in the service of his country. Of course, he sent the wire himself.

Until 1960, the only contact the supposedly dead Ben Hayes had with Taylor Springs was through Lucille Byrd. She wrote him when Byrd Farm was sold, she wrote him when his parents died, and she wrote him when the luscious Lizzie LeCompte Clay was axed to death by her husband, the Reverend Randall Clay. The body of Lizzie, the axe stuck in her cleaved skull, was found in the basement of the Southern Methodist Episcopal church in one of the Sunday school rooms. Randall Clay was seated on the floor in one corner of the room, his arms hugging his knees, which were drawn up to his chin, repeating over and over that the Lord should forgive him for his sins because he had finally killed Lilith, the witch, the wicked one.

Lucille wrote him when Vangie, who had graduated from Transylvania the year before and was working on a

master's degree at Emory, returned to the springs to see her
father placed in the same mental institution that housed
Mary William Sheely and to take care of Vashti, who still
remained speechless. Vangie and Vashti moved in with Ruth
and Bubba Taylor. Ruth felt it was her Christian duty to
take them in. After all, she could look over Vashti while
Vangie went to teach in the high school at Boonetown
every day, and besides, all Ruth's children and grandchildren had scattered to the far corners of the earth, and
Vashti and Vangie were just like her own anyway.

When Ben was mustered out of the Army in the spring of
1946, the first place he went was to Prattville to see Lucille.
She welcomed him with a kiss. After all, she told him, you are
kin. That was the second shock. The first shock was that when
she greeted him, Ben did not recognize her. He saw a very tall,
very thin, elegant woman whose black hair was drawn back in
a chignon, and whose large, brown eyes swam in a Garbo
face. It was only when she spoke in that molasses voice that he
knew it was Lucille. He told her where he was going, what his
intentions were, and that he'd be in touch. Lucille laughed.

The second place Ben went was to Hollywood, California, where he contacted Claire LaRue. After they had a talk,
not only did she arrange for his first screen test and subsequent
roles in the movies, she also made sure he had adequate funds
and the necessary introductions from her to pursue a career.

And that's how Ben Hayes became a success, a movie
star. He never doubted that he would. After all, he had always been a handsome man, dark complexioned, with his
hawklike nose and brilliant blue eyes. And he knew he
could act; he'd been doing that all his life. After all, he was a
child of Taylor Springs.

But it was not until 1960 that he was ready to follow
Nora Philpot's plan and return to Taylor Springs as the new
owner of Philpot Plantation. He came back as the famous star

of the silver screen, Travis Tryon. His first caller was Ruth Taylor, who still aspired to be the first lady of a place that was no more. She made no connection between Travis Tryon and the young colored boy she had known as Ben Hayes. She invited him to supper, up to the Taylor house on the hill. "Nothing formal," she tittered, "there's just me now. My husband passed over several years ago and my children are scattered. Of course, the Clay twins are with me."

And so Ben went. Vashti, the impish child of his memory, was a thin, speechless wraith, her spirit trapped somewhere behind her vacant eyes. Vangie stood a ripe redheaded woman, whose life had been devoted to caring for her twin.

He married Vangie that year and moved her and Vashti to the plantation. The next year Vangie bore twin sons who had red hair and hazel eyes. When Vangie and Ben brought the babies home to Philpot Plantation, the sleeping twins were carried to the nursery and placed in the same wicker bassinets the babies Ora and Nora had occupied so many years ago. The twins lay still, and Ben and Vangie quietly left the nursery to go down into the parlor, where they stood under the portrait of Asa Philpot to drink a toast to the health of the twins. As they touched glasses, they heard laughter and looked up to see Vashti entering the room cradling a baby in each arm.

"Vangie, Vangie," she called from the door, "look what I found! Why, I declare that they are almost the spitting image of us. These two rapscallions are going to take a lot of looking after." She laughed again and then looked directly at them, her eyes clear and seeing. She smiled and said, "Why hello there, Ben."

And on nights when there is a full moon, Ben Hayes stands guard outside Philpot Plantation, straining to see if there are any lights floating down the ridges on the old buffalo trails. After all, Sukie Bee had passed on to him the guardianship of the truth and the obligation for the twins among them.